Insurrection

A WHITE COUNCIL NOVEL

Brandon Hargraves

Copyright 2023 by Brandon Hargraves

All rights reserved. No part of this book may be reproduced in any manner whatsoever without written permission except int he case of brief quotations embodied in critical articles and reviews.

First printing, 2023

Contents

Prologue ix

I	Harpies and Hacksaws	1
II	Before the Storm	14
III	The Winner Is...	38
IV	A New Enemy	61
V	Instead of Permission	76
VI	The Rusted Hammer	86
VII	The Butcher of Midtown	104
VIII	Reunion	114
IX	Taken	125
X	Clash of Ideals	138
XI	Siege of Oasis	153
XII	Isolation	164
XIII	In the Shadows	176
XIV	Fallen City	185

XV	Beneath the Citadel	195
XVI	Sting	211
XVII	Trial	222
XVIII	Keeping the Peace	231
XIX	The Other	247
XX	The Red Moon	255
XXI	Running Blind	265
XXII	The Night is Darkest	277

End of Part 2	283
Praise for the Author	285
The White Council	287

For India
Without you, I don't know where I would be

INSURRECTION

Prologue

Zen surveyed the dark Citadel square for any indications of peacekeepers. All he could discern was the statue of the Eternal Dragon towering over the core of the Midtown District. That was one good aspect about the Outriders terrorizing the city; the Sacred Order had shifted primarily to the Temple District to watch over the White Council. Only peacekeepers remained to oppose his operations.

"The cases of Elfdust are hidden in that building," Zen's nephew, Kaden, pointed to a raggedy looking stone building with boards over its windows. "Not another soul in there."

"Ridiculous," Zen grunted, shaking his head and chuckling under his breath. Kaden cocked his head. "Wait... You're serious? Come on, Kaden. Put yourself into the mind of a peacekeeper. What is the first building you would search if you were looking for dealers in the city?"

Kaden looked down towards his feet. "Probably the one that looked abandoned, right?"

Zen nodded. "Set up the rest of our guys as archers in the windows of each building in the square. In the abandoned building too. And move the Elfdust into a trash container in that alley."

Kaden saluted and jogged back into the abandoned building. It wasn't the boy's fault. He just didn't know better. That was Zen's job, as he had promised himself. Not to teach him the rules of his trade or the ins and outs of the Citadel Underground. You couldn't prepare a person for every possibility in Zen's chosen lifestyle. It was his job to teach Kaden how to think.

Another man exited one of the other surrounding structures, sliding a sword back into its sheath. Zen's right-hand man, Deklin, had come to Midtown a few hours earlier to vacate some rooms for their operation. Zen could see the sleep still in the corners of the man's eyes. The blout had passed out.

"Everythin's good on my end, Z," Deklin barked. For Fos' sake, his voice was loud.

"Quiet!" Zen shouted in a whispered tone. "You do realize what we are doing, right?"

"'Course I do," Deklin bellowed, plopping onto the dragon statue's giant foot. "I am covering for you. Glad to be of assistance. I don't know what you would do without me."

Zen scowled at the man, but turned away, trying to ignore him.

Deklin cleared his throat.

Zen groaned. "You will get your payment once the job is finished, Deklin. Not a minute sooner. If I don't have success, then neither will you."

"Ah," Deklin said. "We've known each other a long time,

Zen. I know you're good for the money. I just feel like you should cut your losses tonight. These guys are dangerous."

"We have to do this," Zen said. "We've been bumbling around the underworld for too long. Our product is great and it's time the world knows it."

"This has nothing to do with the Elfdust," Deklin said. "Do you even know why they want it? What's their plan? Why are they willing to pay so much? I feel like you rushed into this, Z." Four of Zen's lackeys entered the dimly lit square with bows engraved with a carving of a snake gripped tightly in their hands. They murmured softly about the red moon illuminating the city. "Your men think this whole night is a bad omen."

"Silly superstitions," Zen scoffed. "They also believe fog allows goblins to teleport into their closets. Should we halt our plans because of some bad weather?"

"If the weather's bad enough."

The archers established themselves in the windows, leaving Zen by the statue with Deklin and Kaden. So many varied cultures had made their mark on the Citadel in his time there. Zen didn't know much of what the historians taught, but the White Council had managed to grow the Citadel into a melting pot that united all four of the White Islands. It was a remarkable accomplishment.

Whistles echoed through the peaceful city; bizarre sounds disguised as a bird's call. Deklin drew his sword, sending a quiver through Zen's spine. Three masked men passed into the city square donning midnight black coats. Their masks covered their entire face. Zen couldn't even deduce the color of their skin.

"Which one of you is Zen Stonrend?" The man in the center asked in an intense, hushed tone. Zen stepped forward, not recognizing the man's voice. His initial contact had been a woman.

"Good," the man continued. "You three can grab the product and follow us to the meeting place."

"This is the agreed upon meeting place," Zen said, waving a comforting hand at Deklin, urging him to sheath his sword.

"You think we would do business here in the street with your goons watching over us?" The man said, gesturing up at the surrounding windows. "You must earn your trust with us, or you can walk away without payment."

Deklin shot Zen a knowing glance. Zen closed his eyes, then nodded. "Kaden, grab the Elfdust."

"Smart man," the buyer said. "Tell your watchers to stay back. If I believe they are following us, things will not go well for you tonight."

Zen nodded, lobbing a fist up in the air. Kaden departed the alley with two cases in his hands and the masked buyer led the three of them away from the Eternal Dragon. They walked until Zen was convinced his henchmen wouldn't even be able to hear them scream, and then they walked more. The red moon reflected off the silky black coats of the buyers. Outriders, his contact had called them. Zen didn't exactly agree with their philosophy, but this was an opportunity he couldn't pass up. He would do whatever was required in order to do business on this level.

The masked men led Zen and his crew into a substantial brick building at the edge of the Midtown District. It was a large warehouse that used to operate as a clothing distributor for the Citadel. Now, apparently, it was a front for the criminal underworld. On the inside, the storehouse was abandoned. Thank the maker it didn't look abandoned from the outside. Kaden would never have let Zen hear the end of it.

The farther they proceeded into the building, the more people materialized in the shadows. Every one of them wore the same masks as the men who had brought them there. Just a blank slate, a circle with a line through it stamped on the cheek. The mask wasn't what drew Zen's attention, though. These people didn't wear the same silky black coats, but instead donned chainmail with beautiful steel swords. The more Zen inspected the hallways of the building, the more people he spotted, some of them lurking deep in the shadows with short bows, ready to make quick work of their meeting.

Their escorts led them through a pair of wide oak doors into a giant room at the center of the facility. A narrow balcony lined the edges of the room, an archer positioned every few feet with arrows already nocked.

Someone stood in the center of the room encircled by soldiers wielding spears. Zen glanced over to Deklin, who peered back and forth between the two doors at either side of the room. Zen noted the crates stacked along each wall. His product might end up in one of those crates soon.

"Hmph," the person in the center grunted. Abruptly, they snapped their fingers and the spearmen dashed around Zen's crew, surrounding them on each side. Deklin was the first to draw his blade, but Zen quickly followed suit.

The boss laughed in a feminine voice. *This* voice Zen

recognized. She quickly regained her composure. "I would like to see the product I'm purchasing."

"I think we're entitled to some answers, first," Zen said, fixing his eyes on the spearmen. "We had agreed on a meeting location. I feel like I am on the back foot, and I don't like that."

"You feel like you're on the back foot," the woman snickered, "because you *are* on the back foot. In a new relationship like ours, one can never be too careful. We only do business with organizations we trust, and you have yet to prove yourself. Now, please don't make me ask again."

Zen and Deklin looked at each other before Zen motioned to Kaden. The boy stepped forward and laid the cases of Elfdust at the woman's feet. She shooed him away and opened the cases, revealing the explosive powder Zen had invented. A single spark and the bright green dust would level the entire building.

The woman howled a burst of laughter, slamming the cases closed. "And this stuff is as powerful as you say?"

Zen nodded. "With enough of that stuff, you could take down the entire Citadel."

The woman stepped forward and extended out a hand to Zen. "We are going to go far, you and I. Tarik will be pleased. I believe this is the beginning of a new age. Our plans can final..."

As Zen squeezed the woman's hand, a splatter of blood sprayed out of her mouth onto his cheek. Zen gawked as she tried to cough, but he could only hear a gurgle as she choked on the blood. Her hand slipped from his grip as she crashed to the floor, an arrow piercing through her neck.

Zen's heart dropped, bile threatening his throat. He turned to call out to Deklin, but the soldier already fended off the surrounding spearmen with his blade. Zen scrambled to Kaden as one of the soldiers moved toward him with rage in his eyes, but another arrow flew into the soldier's back and he collapsed lifelessly onto Zen's young nephew. He snatched Kaden by the collar and yanked him behind a stack of crates as the archers from above rained down a barrage of arrows at his crew.

"What is happening?" Kaden sobbed, jerking his head down to his chest.

"This isn't how this was supposed to go!" Zen shouted, pressed up tight against the crate. An arrow erupted through the wood an inch from his head. Wood splintered out and stung at his neck. He peered over the crate, where all of the spearmen had been cut down by Deklin. Curses, this guy was incredible. Not a day of formal training in combat, but he still outclassed any soldier Zen had ever seen. Deklin had grabbed the case of Elfdust and used it to deflect arrows away from his body.

"Deklin!" Zen yelled. "Let's go!" He grabbed Kaden by the shirt and yanked him to his feet, tossing him toward the door they came in through. Deklin followed close behind, blocking arrows as they fired at them. Zen looked as Deklin closed the oak doors to see one of the archers falling from the balcony and smashing to the ground below, a masked swordsman staring at them from amid the carnage.

"Nobody ever listens to Deklin," Deklin said, fiddling with

the Elfdust leaking from the beat up case he had used as a shield. Zen opened his mouth to respond, but the smell of blood promptly silenced him. He turned around to see the dismembered bodies of their buyer's henchmen slaughtered throughout the hallway. Kaden released the contents of his stomach on the closest wall. Zen couldn't blame the boy.

"Peacekeepers?" Deklin asked as he crept farther into the clearing.

"No," Zen said. "Peacekeepers are protectors of peace. Not butchers."

Without another word, Zen's crew sprinted back through the facility. Red moonlight glared off the crimson puddles pooling on the floor. Zen could hear his footsteps squish under each step, tracking the remains of the deceased across the storehouse. He ran at the back of the pack so he could keep his eyes on Kaden. The boy deserved more. Deserved better. After watching his parents die from the Great Sickness, he deserved to live a long life. He didn't deserve to die here in this forsaken place.

Zen ran into Deklin as the man stopped in his tracks. Just ahead, a masked man stood in the way with a sword in his hand, drops of red dripping from the tip of the blade. Just a single man? How could he cause this much trouble?

"Let us through," Deklin commanded. "And you will live."

The swordsman didn't answer.

"We won't mention this to anyone. No one will seek retribution for what has happened here today."

The swordsman reached behind his back and unclipped a bow from his person, tossing it to Zen's feet. Carvings of snakes slithered up the shaft between splatters of blood.

"If bloodshed is what you wish," Deklin said, tossing the case of Elfdust to the side. "Then I will oblige."

Deklin charged forward, gripping his sword in both hands. Kaden screamed, charging in after him. Zen reached out to pull him back, but he was too late.

Deklin swung his blade downwards at the swordsman's shoulder, but he quickly ducked beneath the steel, slashing at Kaden, who was close behind. Kaden reacted slowly, barely able to get his weapon up to deflect the attack.

Zen leapt forward in an attempt to overwhelm the swordsman. A whirlwind of steel blew through the hallway as the swordsman bounced between the three fighters. He moved precisely, never exerting more energy than needed. Their blades grazed within inches of his thinly covered skin. The man had done all this wearing nothing but a cloth shirt and trousers.

Swiftly, the swordsman blocked an attack from Deklin while kicking Zen away, Zen's sword flying out of his hands. Like a flash of lightning, he ducked beneath Kaden's blade and plunged his own into the boy's stomach. One strong jerk, and the swordsman was squared off with Deklin alone.

Deklin slashed at the stranger in a barrage of heavy strikes. He screamed as steel smashed against steel, sparks flying off of their weapons with each blow. Zen gnashed his teeth, climbing back to his feet and clawing for his blade across the hall. Once he finally grasped the handle, he turned to see the swordsman charge forward, slamming his shoulder into Deklin's body. He turned hastily and sliced through Deklin's hand, following up with a strike through his chest.

Zen fell to his knees. His best friend and his nephew lay

in their own blood on the floor in front of him. He led them into this. He didn't listen to Deklin. He infected Kaden with this life. This was his fault.

"Why?" Zen looked up at the swordsman with tears in his eyes as he approached. "Why?"

The swordsman rested his blade against Zen's neck. "I protect the one I love."

Zen sobbed uncontrollably. Not for his own life. No, his own life wasn't worth the tears. He cried for the lives of everyone he knew. He killed them all.

The blade fell against Zen's neck.

I

Harpies and Hacksaws

The first light of the day kissed the lush green Cirrane heathland. Bunnies disappeared into their burrows as the gray moonlight melted into purple and orange sunlight. Rolling hills with trees dispersed throughout extended miles in each direction. No signs of any human civilization.

Dawn trudged carefully, her blessed bow clutched tight in her left hand and the matching magical glove fit snug on her right. Every few seconds she peeked toward Cain who crept across the fields alongside her, waiting for his signal. He hadn't even drawn his blade yet, though Dawn knew that he probably wouldn't. He often didn't need his sword.

Their energy merged with that of nature, the trees an extension of their own arms and legs, each hill a beautiful blemish on the wonderful canvas of their bodies. Each puff of the wind behaved like breath in their own lungs. As the leaves rustled and blew through the air their own breathing calmed.

A chirp echoed in the distance. Cain threw a closed fist in the air, halting them both in their tracks. Silence emanated throughout the plains as they kept their eyes on the horizon. Dawn glanced back and forth across the sky, unblinking. Shivers shot down her back and cold sweat threatened her eyes from her brow line. She ran her hand through her long brown hair, shaking away any excess sweat that lingered where it wasn't welcome.

When Dawn looked to her mentor, she noticed that his gaze was not on the skies, but instead on the grass beneath him. He knelt down to rub the individual blades between his fingers. A sticky, purple residue attached itself to his fingers, but he wiped it against his trousers. Dawn could see his face in contemplation. Processing. Thinking.

Quickly and silently Cain stood and pointed to the east and the two reavers scurried toward the rising sun. They came across an insignificant stream cutting between two vast ridges impeding their vision. Rushing water masked the sound of nature around them, roaring through the ravine.

The beast rocketed over the top of the easternmost peak and down toward the companions with a sharp coo. Like lightning, it drove into Dawn with giant claws, knocking her backward into the grass.

The monster perched itself atop a mossy rock downstream. It was birdlike in appearance, with many humanlike features as well. Two massive eyes examined its surroundings from within their wide sockets. The combination created an abomination. It raised its foot up to its mouth, licking blood from its enormous talons with a long, snake-like tongue. Its wings retreated into its body as it cleaned itself, crying out with a blaringly high pitched screech.

Dawn pushed herself back to her feet, grass rustling beneath her. Just the whistle of the pasture perked the fiend's huge ears. Dawn jerked back on the illusory bowstring, an arrow of light materializing between the shaft and her fingers. Too late. The beast spread its wings and with a screech, launched itself toward her again.

Dawn discharged her arrow wildly and lunged out of the way, this time splashing into the stream that flowed beside them. She leapt back to her feet, now soaked from the fresh Cirranian water.

"Slow yourself!" Cain shouted at her. "You aren't faster than a harpy. Don't try to be!"

Dawn glared at the beast as it flipped back around to charge her again. This time she didn't attempt to shoot it. She just watched. It approached hastily and without hesitation. Once it got near, Dawn lunged out of the way and pulled back on her bow one more time, aiming toward the harpy, who had already begun to flip back around again. Forcing out a breath, she released her shot into the aberration, striking it on its right wing.

With a sharp cry, the beast tumbled down into the stream, tainting the once crystal clear water with its crimson blood. Dawn pulled back on her bow again, waiting for the monster to emerge from the water to land one last blow.

Just then, an intense pain stabbed into her shoulders. Claws clutched her and jolted her into the air, flinging her bow behind to the ground. She ascended higher and higher until finally the claws released her. Her heart leapt into her throat, unable to even release a scream. Her voice left her. Her thoughts left her. She watched the ground come closer and closer, readying itself for its ultimate strike.

Suddenly, a gust of air stalled her and laid her down on the soft grass. *I could have done that,* Dawn berated herself. She glanced up and glimpsed Cain shooting a blast of frosty lightning into the sky, silencing the coos of the harpy that had ambushed her. The beast that had fallen into the river clambered to its feet, so she drew her sword and swung for its neck.

Cain approached behind Dawn with her bow in his hand, offering it to her. "So, what did we learn?"

"That I might be afraid of heights," Dawn laughed, catching her breath.

"Dawn," Cain snapped, retracting the bow from Dawn's reach. "This isn't a joke. You could have died, and I won't always be around to save you."

"I know, Cain!" She frowned. "I need to learn how to take care of myself. I get that." "So what did you learn?"

"You'll never see the arrow that takes you down," Dawn recalled her father's lesson, shoving her sword back into its sheath.

"And!" Cain interjected. "The call of a harpy is terribly annoying." He laughed, handing over Dawn's bow once again. "Best to kill them quickly. For the sake of your sanity."

Dawn snorted as they started their journey back to civilization. "You said that harpies are some of the weaker Fallen out there; weaker even than the charun. Barely even a threat for someone like you. If I can't even take on one of them, how would I ever take on some of the more dangerous ones?"

"You forget that you did take on one," Cain smiled. "It was the fact that there were two that was too much for you."

"You know what I mean."

"You're still learning, D," Cain's voice was soft. Cool, like the frosty magic he so often used. "Have grace for the season you're in. Never underestimate the power of small beginnings."

"I've been at this for a year, Cain," Dawn stated. "I should be farther along by now."

"You should have seen Ragnar when he was just one year into his career," Cain laughed. "He definitely wasn't the 'Ragnar the Wrecker' that you know now. You're young. Allow yourself to learn."

Dawn didn't respond. If she couldn't even protect herself, how could she protect the people she loved? She needed to be stronger than this. She needed to be better. And she needed to learn fast.

The sun sped across the sky as the reavers passed silent green shoulders of hills until they looked out over a small village hugging the edge of the water. A dinky wooden sign, tattered and falling apart, stood near the road. "Korio," it read, though the letters were smudged and hardly legible. Along the road, which had diverged into more of a dirt path than an actual road, hundreds of little shrubs packed together to hold back the dust of travelers from the gardens beyond. Tall pine trees scattered around the town with stumps of their deceased ancestors dispersed nearby.

Dawn and Cain walked into the town, passing stacks of

logs piled and tied with twine into groups of ten. They looked out over the looming body of water to see another vast island a ways out. Korio was the southernmost city of Cirrane, overlooking the island of Napora.

Along the water's edge, a large mechanical hacksaw swung back and forth, powered by a huge wheel charging the machine with hydropower from a river that flowed into the sea. Six men hauled logs onto the machine as two others carried the smaller chunks into piles nearby.

"Things like that used to be done with magic and faith," Cain's countenance soured. "I swear, the more technology advances, the more primitive we become."

"Oh, come on Cain!" Dawn nudged him with an elbow. "It isn't that bad!"

Children ran through the streets toward the well at the center of town. Dust and smoke kicked up underneath their feet as they laughed together. They tossed a rubber ball back and forth to each other, wailing and mocking whenever someone would drop it.

Krom appeared from behind one of the rundown wooden houses alongside Kaela. "Look who's back!" He shouted, running towards Dawn with open arms. As he approached, he slowed his pace until he came to a stop in front of her, his face twisting in disgust. He pointed his nose to the sky, sniffing the air around them. "Oh my gosh..." he pinched his nose shut. "You smell awful!"

Dawn shoved him backward. "You try hunting a demon through the night, pretty boy!"

"Hey, I offered," Krom responded. "And *you* turned me

away. You said that reavers just *HAVE* to use magic. And that, my friend, is against my religion!"

Kaela smacked her hand into her forehead. "You don't have a religion, Krom. You're an Atheist."

"Exactly!" He snapped his fingers and pointed at her.

Kaela led them through the town toward a larger lodge near the water. Fishing boats came and went from the docks along the coast. Kaela had explained to Dawn when they arrived about the two major trades coming out of Korio; lumber and fish. The small town was a nice change of pace from the bustle of the Citadel. A gentle reminder of what Dawn's life used to be back in Quarrine.

"Once you two get washed up a bit," Kaela said. "My family would love to have us all for dinner before we head back to the Citadel. They plan to serve beaver."

"Beaver?" Krom scowled. "How could you eat a beaver? They're so cute!"

"Cows are cute too," Dawn laughed. "I actually really like cows. But you know what I like even more than cows?"

Krom raised an eyebrow.

"Steak."

Krom glared back at Dawn with a grin. "I guess I can try it. That doesn't mean I approve of their murder though."

They walked back to Kaela's family home, one of the larger buildings in the town. The structure reminded Dawn of the homes in her old village. Splintered wood and faded paint throughout the house masked by the brilliant smell of freshwater streaming just outside the many windows. Kaela directed Dawn to the washroom on the bottom floor. "My father already filled the bath with water," she gestured. "I am sure you could heat it with your own magic?"

"Of course," Dawn smiled, closing the door. She removed the sweaty, wet hunting tunic that clung to her grimy skin and stepped into the water, waving her hand and whispering a few words under her breath. A soft red light illuminated from her fingertips and soon the water warmed, steam filling the room.

The bath wrapped around her like a cocoon, hugging every inch of her pale skin ever so gently. She extended her arm out to grab a cloth from a cabinet nearby and scrubbed away the oils and residue from the hunt. The steam entered her nostrils and calmed her. All the cares of the world around her evaporated into the air.

Finally, she emerged from the water and whispered another prayer under her breath, instantly drying her moist skin. As she dressed in more comfortable clothes, she glanced into a bronze mirror hanging on the wall. Her fingers traced the scar running across her cheek. The person she saw was different. A new being. A stranger. If someone had told her two years ago that this is where she would be on this day, she would have laughed. It would have had to be Cammie who said it, with his overly active imagination. Just the thoughts of a mere child.

As she pulled a low cut cotton shirt over her head, her hand reached toward her bare neck, grasping at the empty space. The outline of her amulet almost materialized in her mind. A gift from her father to remind her of her family. She clenched her eyes shut and exhaled a forceful breath, opening the door to the washroom to find herself back in the house. The aroma of seared meat wafted through the halls.

Dawn entered the living area where Krom and Kaela had settled with Kaela's younger sister, Alyina. They had been staying with Kaela's family for nearly a week while she and Cain investigated the harpies reported in the area. Not everyone believed in monsters and demons, but they were still quick to call for reavers when something seemed out of place.

"So the Council priest turns to the lady peacekeeper," Krom said. "And he says, 'Are you staring at me?'"

Kaela held up a hand. "Is this a dirty joke?"

"Excuse me, ma'am. I am a gentleman. Do you think I would tell a dirty joke with your little sister in the room?"

Dawn and Kaela locked eyes. "Yes."

"It's not a dirty joke," Krom groaned.

Dawn found a seat next to Kaela, running her fingers through her hair to keep it from tangling. Kaela poured her a cup of mulled cider, clanking her own cup against it.

"Anyways," Krom continued. "The lady peacekeeper says to the priest, 'I recognize you. I think we met once at the temple of Fos.'"

"This is a dirty joke," Dawn laughed.

"It's not a dirty joke! So, the priest says, 'There are a lot of priests in the temple, and even more in the Citadel. Most of them are wearing robes that look just like mine. How can you be so confident that the person you met was me?

"And the peacekeeper says..." Krom's face fell. "This is a dirty joke."

Kaela smacked him on the leg and ripped the mug from his hand. "I think you may have had enough there, funny guy."

Krom smiled as the company laughed together. It felt nice to not have any stress after a long hunt. Dawn and Cain didn't generally have that luxury. Most towns just paid them and sent them on their way once they finished the job.

"Kaela says you finally caught the monsters!" Alyina shouted in a high pitched squeak. "Does that mean that we're safe again?"

"Safe from the harpies," Dawn smiled, glancing around the room. "Hopefully we will be out of your hair soon."

"That's right," Kaela responded. "We'll have to be going back to the Citadel soon."

Alyina's face fell. "But you just got here," she whimpered, gazing up at Kaela with big green eyes. "Can't you spend some more time with us?"

"We've already been here a week, kiddo," Kaela said. "We all have responsibilities back in the city, and it's going to be another week's journey to get back. Krom and Dawn have Hilios practice, and I have to go back to peacekeeping. We are all important people in the Citadel."

"I still can't believe my sissy is friends with Hilios superstars!" Alyina cried. "I read about the Wings of Radiance every week when the news reaches Korio."

"They're the best in the world," Kaela smiled, squeezing Krom's hand.

"Not yet," Dawn waved a finger.

"Yeah," Krom smiled. "Still need to show that Phoenicia Rodes who's boss. The whole world will soon know that the

Quarrinians flying for the Wings of Radiance are the greatest in the world."

"That's why we need to go, hon," Kaela redirected her words to her sister. "They have to get ready for the Hilios finals, and I have to go back to protecting the city."

"Hopefully you can come visit again within the year this time," Kaela's mother, Tess, rounded the corner with a plate of small fried bites of bread. She placed the plate on the table in front of them, instantly piquing Krom's attention. "We miss seeing you around here, Kae."

"I can't be around all the time, Mom," Kaela retorted. "I have a job, and a life in the Citadel."

Dawn glanced up at the fireplace in the corner of the room. An urn dressed in brilliant gems and shining an elegant blue and silver color sat atop the mantelpiece. Engraved on the front was the name of its inhabitant: Ephras, followed by the thirty-six year span of his life. Almost a year had passed since that tragic night, and not a day went by that Dawn didn't relive it.

Suddenly, as Dawn gazed toward the fire, the face of Ephras' murderer flickered in the smoldering flames. Moldolor. He stared menacingly at Dawn with his gleaming blue eyes. Finally, she pressed her eyes shut, turning her face from the evil sorcerer.

"Will you at least be back to commemorate the anniversary of your brother's death?" Tess continued interrogating Kaela. "I am sure he would like his family to be together in a time like that."

"I will try my hardest, Mother," Kaela sighed, reaching

for a bread bite. Silence filled the room, accompanied by the crackling of the wood inside the fire pit.

Dawn reopened her eyes, spotting Cain entering the room dressed in fresh clothes. He wasn't the type to wear something comfortable unless sleeping in his own home, so he still fashioned himself in leather and hide as if ready to go on another hunt. If Dawn knew anything, it was that trouble could come when it was least expected. A lesson she had to learn the hard way.

"I thought I heard something about beaver," Cain chuckled as he sat in a chair near the fire. "I'm interested to see Krom's face once he tries it."

Krom's head shot up, mouth full of bread from his most recent snack. Crumbs littered the minor amount of facial hair growing in on his chin. "Why me?" He spat.

"You're fun to watch!" Alyina laughed as the Quarrinian sprayed food with his words. Krom finished chewing and swallowed with a loud gulp before smiling back toward the girl.

Kaela squirmed in her chair, her muscles tense. "Shouldn't we call Dad in from the mill?" She asked. "I'm sure he'll want to eat with us."

"Your father is working hard so we can have heat this winter," Tess snapped. "The supply of the Citadel doesn't reach all the way down here, and we have to fend for ourselves. You know that. Or have you forgotten your time in the south?"

"This may be our last meal together before we leave," Kaela pouted. "He doesn't want to see us off?"

"He has work to do!" Tess repeated. "*YOU* of all people should understand that!"

Without another word, Kaela jerked out of her seat and bolted out the front door, slamming it behind her. The house shook from the force of the door, rattling the silverware and ceramics set on the nearby dining room table.

"I... think it may be best if we got going," Cain calmly stood to his feet, gesturing to Dawn and Krom to stand with him. "Thank you so much for your hospitality during our hunt, and I am sorry we won't be able to stay for dinner." Tess shook her head, darting back to the kitchen.

As Krom stood, Alyina grabbed a hold of his sleeve, whimpering. "Do you have to go?"

Krom knelt down to lock eyes with the young girl. "I promise, I will do whatever I can to make sure we come back in the fortnight for your brother's anniversary." He rested his hand on her cheek. "That means Kaela too." Alyina smiled, wiping a tear from her bright green eyes as her guests walked out the front door.

II

Before the Storm

"I told you, I don't want to talk about it!" Kaela snapped as they entered the Gate District of the Citadel. "I swear, Krom. You don't know when to back off."

Her shouts drowned in the noise of the Gate District. Important people like peacekeepers and reavers didn't usually have to traverse through the deteriorating district when they left the city, instead having a special entryway that led directly to Northtown. Dawn appreciated being able to see how other people in the city lived their lives. The Market District was a great buffer between the wealthy and the working class.

"You have been silent the whole journey home," Krom inquired. "You have to open up eventually, Kae."

Kaela turned to Krom and snatched him by the collar, shoving her finger in his face. "You don't get to call me that. Only Ephras got to call me that." Without another word, she stormed off toward the Gate District's peacekeeper barracks.

"I told you to leave her be, Krom," Cain said. "She needs time and company. What she doesn't need is to feel attacked by those who are closest to her."

"I just..." Krom pouted. "I just don't know how to help her unless she opens up."

"She doesn't need your answers," Cain chuckled. "She needs a friend. Can you do that for her?"

Krom's face fell, silent before the two reavers. After a thought, he nodded.

"Good," Cain continued. "For now give her some space and she will calm down. Don't you two have Hilios practice soon anyways?"

Dawn smirked. She had a competitive soul. Even when she still hunted kline outside her village with Maron, she had to compete with him. Of course, Maron never quite grasped the concept of hunting, but it was a contest nonetheless. She was born to be the best she could be.

Cain waved down a carriage, tossing a coin to the coachman to take them all to the Hilios practice fields in the Market District. Dawn had been living in the Citadel for nearly a year, and the enormity of the Market District still astounded her. It was just one district, yet still it was larger than any single city in Quarrine and somehow it still felt cramped. That was city life.

They eventually pulled up to the fields and piled out of the carriage, offering thanks and a tip to the kind coachman. Dawn sometimes liked to go between districts by foot to really experience the enormity of the city, but the coaches were a wonderful convenience when they were in a hurry. Sometimes, the trek from the Gate District to the Temple

District would take hours on foot, where the carriage got them there in a fraction of the time.

"Look out," Krom warned. Just ahead, Phoenicia Rodes exited her own practice field with her team, the Citadel Angels. Five fair skinned ladies, none of them exceeding thirty years old. Rodes brushed out tangles in her long blonde hair as she approached the returning party.

"You have time to play monster hunter with our championship coming up?" Rodes sneered. "Good thing the Wings of Radiance have some actual fliers on their team. Otherwise our match may not be any fun at all."

"We don't need as much practice as you do, Rodes," Krom retorted.

Rodes spat at his feet. "How dare you speak to me, char skin."

Krom reached for the blade on his hip, but Cain jumped between them. "Get lost, Rodes!" He commanded. "Settle it on the field."

Rodes gave a vile grin, then turned to Dawn and blew her a kiss before leading her posse away. Krom released his grip on his blade.

"I am so sorry, Krom," Dawn placed her hand on his shoulder. "They're vile little cockroaches."

"Entitled Cirranians," Krom mumbled. "About as humble as a hippo on a rainy day."

"Hey!" Cain corrected. "Don't put me on the same level as... wait. What does that even mean?"

Krom chuckled. "It sounded good in my head. And hey... In my experience, you are the outlier. If it weren't for your hospitality, this city would have chewed me up and spit me back to Quarrine in a heartbeat."

As Dawn and Krom continued to their designated field, Silas had already started practicing with their two other teammates. Mae, a girl only a few years older than Dawn with shoulder length red hair and freckled skin, rode atop a jet black pegasus. The most beautiful pegasus Dawn had seen in her time as a Hilios contender. Most pegasus were white, or some shade of off white, but Mae's beast was the deepest black, its coat glistening in the sun's rays.

"It's about time you showed up!" The other rider shouted down from the back of his pegasus. "I don't like to be kept waiting."

Dawn scoffed under her breath, but before she could speak, Silas interrupted. "You know they were on important Council business, Titus. Defending our world from demons is much more important than being on time to practice."

"Monster hunters or not," Titus responded. "It is rude to keep *The Best* waiting."

"That's funny," Mae chuckled. "Because *The Best* just got here."

Titus had only replaced a team member a couple weeks prior due to an injury, yet still he believed that he was the reason their team was undefeated. Dawn and Krom grasped their blessed bows and pulled the magical gloves over their hands, hopping on their own pegasus. During a Hilios match, players would wear sanctioned gloves that sent electricity through their targets, incapacitating them. Dawn had a different glove for hunting the Fallen; one that formed deadly light arrows with any blessed bow.

"You think these two are better at flying than three Council Fliers?" Titus forced an obnoxious laugh.

"Two?" Krom asked. "Definitely not. If we are just talking about Dawn... then absolutely."

Titus released an arrow toward Dawn, who caught it in her glove, quickly pulling back on the invisible bowstring and shooting toward Mae. Even with Titus on the team, they had all become such a great unit. They had learned to breathe, move, and think as one. Silas' skill as a commander definitely translated on the playing field. They loved one another and their bond was magic. Without speaking, they quickly flew up and down the field, shooting their arrows toward each other with confidence. Not confidence in their own shot, but confidence that their teammate would be there on the receiving end to continue the play.

* * *

Cain watched the magnificent display of skill from the ground as the team glided through the sky. Their speed was incredible, and he believed that if he had been less trained he wouldn't have been able to keep track of the ball of light at all. They faked shots to each other that could have confused the most talented Hilios players. He smirked as Dawn fired the scoring shot into the smallest hoop on the opposing side one after another.

Silas, who had established himself as the goaltender, guarded the opposing goal for the sake of practice. He was regarded as one of the best goalies the sport had ever seen, but still Dawn shot past him with ease, leaving a smile on Cain's face.

After hours of flying, the team landed their pegasus and began their cooldown process. As they closed their practice, a slow clap resonated from across the field. "Bravo!" The voice shouted as he approached the players. It was Councilman Taran, accompanied by two bodyguards from the Sacred Order. He never went anywhere without them. "Such an incredible display of talent. It's no wonder you are still undefeated so far into the season."

"Councilman!" Silas shouted, bowing low in honor of the city's leader. As he bowed, Mae and Titus followed suit, but Dawn and Krom continued to pack their things.

"No need for that, Commander Silas," Taran feigned courtesy. "I am simply here to wish the Wings of Radiance luck in the finals. It is only a few days away, and I believe you can win it all. I don't think in the history of Hilios have we seen a team of newcomers accomplish so much in a single season, besides Phoenicia Rodes. Truly a sight to behold."

Dawn never looked up to the councilman. As he spoke, she just continued to pack up the equipment from practice. The practice light ball returned to a small glass bottle and she removed her pegasus' equipment to lay in a chest sitting against the wall. Krom did the same.

Cain grit his teeth.

***

"My dear, reaver," Taran directed at Dawn. "I believe you and your mentor have just returned from a hunt in the south?

I would love to have you and your companions at the temple tonight for supper so we can chat."

The invitation sounded like a question, but Dawn knew better. She glanced up at Taran, feigning a smile. "It would be our honor, Councilman." Then she turned away again to return to her work.

Taran frowned. "Cain!" he averted his gaze to the reaver standing at the edge of the stadium. "Please dress appropriately. This will be a formal dinner. Not some picnic in the woods like we're a bunch of squirrels."

Cain bowed to the councilman, nodding in agreement.

Taran clapped his hands together. "It's settled then! I shall see the three of you at sundown. And bring your peacekeeper friend as well." Without another word, Taran exited the practice field, led by his bodyguards.

Cain stormed over to Dawn, who had almost finished putting away her practice equipment. "What was that, D!"

"What do you mean?" Dawn sighed.

"You are a leader of the people in this city," Cain stated. "As a reaver, *AND* as a celebrity, people look to you for guidance on how they should live their own lives. What does it communicate when you treat our leadership the way you just did?"

Dawn glared up at Cain. "I gave that man the respect he deserves. I would much rather dine with Annias than him."

"Your preference doesn't matter!" Cain said. "That man, like him or not, is our authority. Fos, himself, ordained him to lead the people of the White Islands. Sometimes we need to set aside our own preferences for the sake of the bigger picture."

Dawn frowned, nodding in agreement. "I don't think I'll ever like him."

"You don't have to," Cain assured her. "But you do have to respect him."

The team all split up to go toward their own homes for the night. As Council Fliers, Mae, Titus, and Silas made their way toward the Northtown District where the Council had barracks for them to lay their heads down and find rest. Krom had been living with Cain at his place in the Northtown District as well, so Dawn parted ways, walking alone back towards Midtown.

* * *

Kaela hesitated on the steps of the Gate District Peacekeeper Precinct. Not her usual jurisdiction, but it made it easy to check in after her extended leave in the south. People bustled on the sidewalks of the city streets with their heads down. Others loitered nearby, leaning against buildings, smoking out of pipes and covering their eyes with peaked hats.

It was the middle of the day and the Gate District was beginning to overflow with people who lined the streets instead of working. The White Council would never allow homelessness in the Citadel, so these people could all afford accommodation somehow.

The Gate District is a slimy place, Kaela thought. From the outside, all the precincts in the Citadel looked peaceful. They were clean. Put together. Clay and marble details made up most of the building's structure, though the Gate District added a layer of dirt and grime to the thick walls. It was difficult to see through the large, curtained windows from the outside, but once inside, the truth revealed itself. Instead of men and women at desks filing away paperwork, it was officers rushing back and forth into rooms, tossing halfway finished reports on their chief's desk. The diminishing number of peacekeepers in the city made for long nights and overworked staff.

Two officers slammed through the oak doors behind Kaela, throwing a large, tied up man into a nearby chair. "Another dust pusher," one officer said. "That vigilante is starting to push all the Midtown crime out into the Gate District. I wonder if the Market is experiencing the rise like we are."

Kaela sat at a desk to fill out some paperwork close by, listening in on the conversation. They addressed a cleric sitting at a desk near the front doors, who gave them some papers to fill out before they could escort the man to a cell. The other precincts had separate entrances to the holding cells, but the Gate District didn't have the finances to expand their facility like that.

"This is our fourth arrest today," the other officer boasted. "Grenak and I are on fire!"

Kaela rolled her eyes. "You said this man was selling Elfdust?" She asked, commanding the room.

The two officers glanced at her, almost startled that she had been listening. "Yeah. He is the third duster we've caught this week. Lotta demand for the stuff."

"And your precinct has been informed about the properties of Elfdust?" Kaela inquired, already knowing the answer. Commander Belvin had sent this information out to each precinct weeks ago, after they found remnants of the substance at the Midtown Slaughter.

"Yeah," the one called Grenak laughed. "It blows up. Little bit of fire makes the powder combust, or somethin' like that."

Well, at least they aren't total imbeciles.

"And who was this man selling to?" Kaela asked, pointing her quill to the prisoner.

The officers glanced at each other. "We're uh... Not exactly sure..." Grenak admitted.

"And I don't see you coming back with any evidence of the deal. Had he already made the sale?"

The officers nodded.

"So you're telling me there is someone out there, with who knows how much of this stuff, ready to attack the city at the drop of a coin. And you're celebrating for bringing in a single seller?"

Their faces fell.

"Make yourselves useful and get back out there!" Kaela demanded. "You may have just taken one of our leads off the streets. Those terrorists will still utilize this product to wreak havoc on our city. But congratulations on the petty criminal you've reprimanded." Without waiting for a response, she grabbed her paperwork and slammed it on the clerics desk before turning toward the exit.

As she walked out, a poster hanging on the doors caught her eye: a visage of a masked man and a bounty over his head. The Butcher of Midtown, the poster called him. Kaela knew him as the Masked Vigilante. She shook her head and pushed through the doors into the Citadel streets.

***

Whenever Dawn was left alone, she felt uneasy. It had been a year since the night in the prison, but she still felt like she was being watched. Even in the afternoon sunlight she thought she saw shadows moving in between the alleyways of the city. Unkind eyes watching her, waiting for the perfect moment to strike.

Never did anything come of it, though. She always kept her head on a swivel, seeking out those who would attempt to harm her, but she never actually saw anyone. Just the bustling inhabitants of the city, people of every race, working their fingers to the bone and rushing their way through life.

She entered her home to get ready for dinner with Councilman Taran. It was still hard for her to call it her home. It had once been her Aunt Eva's. Dawn still saw images of her body lying in the living area every now and again. Her lifeless, drained body. A visage that would haunt her for the rest of her life.

She readied a bath and prepared a nice, appropriate outfit to wear to a temple dinner; a long red skirt and a white and gold corset top. Before coming to the city, she would have never seen herself wearing something so outrageous. But as she grew more and more famous from her works as a reaver and her glory as an undefeated Hilios champion, she had been invited to more and more fancy dinners where her comfortable leather skins lacked the adequate elegance.

With the sun beginning to descend and shining into the windows of her home, Dawn left and hired a carriage to take her to the Temple District, where Cain, Krom, and Kaela were all waiting for her.

"I'm not saying I hate cats," Krom laughed toward Kaela. "I am just saying that when it comes to the superior species, dogs are objectively better."

"You're nuts!" Kaela shouted. "Dogs love everyone. As long as I have a chunk of meat in my hands, any dog... Any breed at all... is going to love me. Cats are truly loyal. It doesn't matter if I have a snack or if I just want to sleep. Cats can be trusted."

"Trusted to murder me," Krom said. "I've seen the look in your cat's eyes. If she could, Mrs. Whiskers would kidnap me, take me somewhere outside the city, and cut off my fingers to send to my family as a ransom. And when she was done with me she would hide my body."

Dawn approached with a grin on her face. "Glad to see you two made up."

"She can't stay mad at me," Krom said. "Not with a face like this!" He pushed his hands against his cheeks and gave a goofy smile.

"Maybe I should let Mrs. Whiskers have you," Kaela laughed, pushing Krom on the arm.

Cain rolled his eyes. "They have been arguing about cats and dogs for fifteen minutes."

"Hey!" Krom shouted. "This is an important subject, worthy of strenuous debate."

Cain exhaled a sigh. "Shall we go inside?"

The four strode toward the Temple of Fos. Even though only one temple had been active for many years, Dawn couldn't help but to eye Seor's temple every time she visited the district. The same dread filled her heart when looking at the temple as when she watched Ephras' life slip from his body.

They continued into the temple where they were met by a member of the Sacred Order. The Order was different in the Temple District. Normally, a guard wore colorless plate; the natural silver of steel reflecting in the sunlight. Inside the Temple of Fos, their plate was a dark obsidian, blacker than the midnight sky on a starless night.

The guard led the companions up multiple sets of stairs, passing levels and levels of different rooms. Some levels were dedicated to teaching and learning, stacking books and transcripts up to the ceiling. Others were dedicated to experiments and discovery, where there were words of caution written all over the walls. The temple had an entire floor dedicated to forging weapons, and another for blessing the Hilios equipment that Dawn had become so accustomed to.

Finally, after walking up what seemed like a never ending staircase, the guard disembarked the stair and led them down a hallway into a grand banquet hall. A long rectangular table had been set for what seemed like fifteen or twenty guests, with fine dishes and silverware lined up perfectly along the exquisite linens.

"Woah!" Dawn exclaimed, running over to the windows lining the western side of the room. The glass overlooked the entire city, from the Temple District all the way to the Gate District. "I feel like I can see everything from here!"

"We like to think so," Taran said, walking in from a door across the room. "It helps us councilmen feel better, thinking we are actually keeping an eye on the entire city."

Dawn attempted to look straight down into the Temple District and her stomach turned. "How high up is this?"

"The Temple of Fos has ninety-eight floors," Kaela stated. "And this isn't even the top." Dawn slowly backed away from the window, noticing that Krom had already pressed his back up against the table away from the glass.

"Please," Taran started. "Have a seat. The waiters will bring our food right out."

Dawn scanned the room, unsure where she should sit. Taran made his way to the head of the table, which was to be expected. She watched as Cain and Kaela took a seat nearer to the councilman and followed suit.

A sharply dressed man walked into the room with a bottle, pouring into each person's glass one at a time. The ruby red wine sparkled with hints of silver. Dawn could smell the spices infused with the concoction: like cinnamon, wildflowers and candied apples fused into one beverage. Dawn watched as her mentor took a single sip, then placed the glass back on the table, not to touch it again. Dawn had never been much of a wine drinker, but even she understood that this beverage was above average. She couldn't even begin to guess how expensive the bottle would have been if it was sold in the Market District.

"Cain," Taran directed his attention. "Any news from the south? I believe your most recent hunt was in Korio, was it not?"

"Yes, Councilman..."

"Please!" Taran interrupted. "Your courtesies are too kind, but call me Taran. After all, it is just us."

"Of course," Cain agreed. "We removed a harpy infestation near the village."

Taran's eyes gleamed. "Any signs of sorcery?"

"No more than usual for a hunt like this," Cain responded calmly. "Any dealings with the Fallen will be somewhat... otherworldly. It's just the nature of the job. But I believe you are referring to Moldolor?"

"Of course," Taran said. "It's been nearly a year since you and your associates claim to have seen him, yet we haven't seen or heard anything since. I am beginning to wonder if something else happened down there."

Dawn squirmed in her seat.

"Is that why you called this dinner?" Cain inquired.

"Of course not!" Taran said. "I just want to know what is happening in my country. I hardly get the opportunity to venture out to the Citadel's neighboring towns and villages. I don't even get to go to Barlo anymore. The Outrider attacks keep the White Council pretty busy within the city walls."

As the councilman spoke, the waiter brought out their dinner plates. Upon each plate was an intensely flavored and juicy lamb shank, partnered with chopped and steamed potatoes and crispy grilled asparagus. Once Taran gave the nod to begin eating, Dawn cut into the lamb and bit down on that juicy first bite. It must have been roasting for hours within the spices, because she could pinpoint each bite of rosemary and sage. Even compared to Cain's exquisite cooking, this was a dish to behold.

"You know," Taran continued the conversation in between bites. "The Outrider rebellion is growing more tenacious than it ever has. They've begun targeting high class members of society who have any relationship with magic. I suggest all of you keep your heads down."

"But Krom doesn't even use magic," Dawn inquired.

"That doesn't matter," Kaela said. "He's assisting in magical business. Between Hilios and befriending reavers and peace-keepers, the Outriders don't really see a difference."

"That sucks!" Krom said with a mouth full of potatoes. Cain elbowed him on the arm and he finished swallowing his food. "I can't agree with them and their views against magic and still be friends with the people who utilize it?"

"Thus is the way of a radical," Taran said. "If you aren't with them, then you're against them."

"Radical is one word for it," Kaela mumbled. "I prefer to call them what they really are. Terrorists." She looked at Dawn, waving a fork in the air. "Did you know that they created a substance that explodes when it is put to fire. It's making citizens afraid to even reside in the city."

"Yes," Taran agreed. "And it almost seems as if their attacks are random. One day there will be an explosion in the Gate District. The next, a riot in Northtown. There is no order to their mayhem."

"No order, besides that they seem to be keeping out of Midtown," Kaela corrected. "It seems that the vigilante has reached their ears and is forcing them to stay away."

"Vigilante?" Dawn asked. "There's a vigilante in Midtown?"

"A scourge if you ask me," Taran spat, pointing his fork toward Dawn. "The people call him the Butcher of Midtown. A man who thinks he is above the law can only do harm.

I can't wait for the peacekeepers to finally apprehend the menace."

"But isn't he helping?" Krom asked, wiping his lips with a napkin. "If he is keeping the criminals out of his district, isn't he doing a good thing?"

"There is a reason we have peacekeepers, Krom," Kaela stated. "If one man gets to enforce his own version of the law, what's to stop another? Where do we draw the line?"

Dawn's breathing grew heavy as she noticed her Reflection standing in the corner of the room. Watching.

"We draw the line at the people doing harm," Krom said. "He's helping you, and he's keeping the city safe."

"Safe?" Kaela scoffed. "The people he killed certainly weren't being kept safe."

"Bad people," Krom said. "People that were doing harm to the innocent people of this city. Shouldn't you be thankful for the work he is doing?"

"This is not up for debate, son," Taran stated. "He's breaking the law, so he must face the consequences."

"This is ridiculous!" Dawn snapped, pushing away from the table and standing to her feet. "I swear, you people are all twisted! You call good evil, and you call evil good! It's like you can't even tell the difference!"

"Sit down, Dawn!" Cain demanded.

"No!" Dawn shouted, pointing to Taran who watched his guest with a smirk. "You are doing the same thing with Maron! He has been a prisoner for a year because you think he's evil. You believe he's partnered with Ulumbra, and with Moldolor. But he's not! He's a good person. Even the best people make mistakes!"

Taran chuckled calmly. "I agree with you, Dawn."

Dawn raised an eyebrow.

"The best do make mistakes," Taran said. "Does this excuse their actions? Should consequences differ from one person to another because of class, or status, or reputation? Or should we be consistent in how we deal out punishment to all who break the law?"

Dawn growled, storming toward the door. The Sacred Order guarding the door slammed his spear into the floor, tilting it to block Dawn's exit. "Let her go," Taran sighed, waving his hand. "I've had my fill of her anyways. Escort her out of my temple."

The guard retracted his spear and opened the door for Dawn. She rushed down the staircase toward the entrance of the grand temple, pushing her way out the front doors.

Dawn raced through the district to the outer walls. Her heart raced in her chest, replaying the conversation over and over in her head.

"Well, that was dramatic," a voice boomed in her head. She glanced around to see her Reflection walking directly behind her. "Do you feel better now?"

"Go away!" Dawn screamed. "I can't deal with you right now."

"You still don't get it," her Reflection responded. "You can't get rid of me, Dawn. I am a part of you. I am the part of you that you don't want to deal with. I am the part of you that you don't really understand yet."

"I understand just fine," Dawn said. "I understand that it was really you that blew up in there. Yet here I am, reaping the consequences of your actions."

"I won't manipulate you," her Reflection said. "I only get involved when you want me to. You can't blame a sword for cutting a man down. You can't blame an arrow for shooting from a bow and piercing into a person's heart. You swung the sword. You shot the arrow. You're the one in control."

Dawn opened her mouth to speak, but there were no words. It was true. She really did mean what she said, but a year ago she wouldn't have had the courage to say it. Was she losing control of herself? Or was she gaining the courage to speak what was on her mind? Dawn knew there was a line, and she had to walk it carefully.

Her Reflection stayed silent as she walked back to her home. The streets were fairly quiet for this time of night. Dawn had quickly gotten used to life in the city, where it didn't often matter what time of day or night it was, there was always something happening on the streets. Especially in the Market District, where people would go to spend their free time.

This night was different. Only a few people walked the streets with her. No clamor from radical protests. No squalor from some big event. Just peace and quiet.

Without the distraction of the busy street, Dawn could examine the posters that clung to the walls more closely. As she read, her heart sank. Many of the posters were advertisements for the Hilios Finale, but almost all of them had been vandalized. Sloppy red x's splattered over the professionally drawn portraits of Dawn's team. Threats toward their lives read clearly and boldly across the pictures. "Death to the religious elite." Dawn quickly averted her eyes and raced home in the quiet darkness.

***

After the dinner in the temple, Kaela had a shift on night patrol. She had volunteered, since most of the other peacekeepers hated it. Something about being away from their families and their homes during the evening hours. She didn't mind, though. The Citadel was a beautiful place when its inhabitants had gone to sleep. Once the hustle and bustle finally slowed, the city could actually be peaceful.

"Do you think Jackson's shop is open this late?" Dulin asked. The young city-boy wanted to get some experience on the night shift, so he volunteered as well. Kaela was excited to see how the kid acted on a patrol. He had only been a peacekeeper for a few months and was already one of the best officers in the city, next to Commander Belvin and Captain Anvar.

"Curses, Dulin," Kaela laughed. "You're seriously thinking about meat pies right now?"

"What can I say?" Dulin smiled, slapping his hands on his belly. "I'm a growing boy, and staying up late gives me an appetite. Why else would you volunteer for the night shift in the Market District except to take advantage of the market when there are no lines? We can have whatever food we want!"

Kaela shook her head. "If you really want to, we can head towards Jackson's. This isn't a break, though. Keep your eyes open."

Dulin smiled. He was handsome for a city kid, with his short black hair and cleanly shaved face, though city guys weren't really Kaela's type. Spending most of her young life growing up in Korio had given her certain tastes for people. That may have been why she had opened up so much to Krom and Dawn. They had a country aura about them from living in Quarrine.

She often found herself thinking about them. Ever since she had moved to the city, she hadn't really made any real friends. Her brother, Ephras, and sister, Kourtney, were the only ones she really wanted to spend time with. That was before she got herself caught up with the Loans Federation.

Kaela pressed her eyes shut and shook her head. It would do her no good to ruminate on those days. She was a different person now. She had a new life. No looking back. She had made the decision a long time ago to let the past pass.

"How do you do it?" Dulin asked as they passed the statue of the First King of the White Islands. The first monarch to unite the four nations into a single coalition. Most referred to him as Darach the Terrible, but in peacekeeper circles, he was highly revered.

"Do what?" Kaela asked.

"This," Dulin gestured to the streets around him. "Long hours. Never seeing your family. Since I've been a peacekeeper, I think I have seen my sister a total of four times."

"I guess it's something you get used to," Kaela said. "My family doesn't live in the city, so it's a little easier for me to compartmentalize."

"How often do you see them?" Dulin asked

"I just saw them a few days ago," Kaela smiled.

"And before that?"

Kaela's smile disappeared. She hadn't been down to Korio

to see her family since Ephras died. It was just too easy to get sucked into her work.

"This line of work isn't for everyone, Dulin," Kaela said. "It takes a lot of time and energy. Even with your time away from the precinct, your mind finds ways to work overtime. If it isn't for you, then only you can make that decision."

"I don't know," Dulin said. "When you're blessed with a certain set of skills, it feels like you have to use them. Or at least you should. But being the best peacekeeper I can be makes me a worse friend, and a worse brother to my sister. How can I be good in every aspect of my life? I know I am called to this, but I know I am called to her as well."

Kaela had only met Dulin's sister once. Both their parents had been afflicted by the Great Sickness, and those who survived the disease had their pregnancies affected. Dulin was born in full health, but his sister wasn't so lucky. He never told Kaela the name of her affliction, but Kaela knew that nobody suffering like her could forge their way through this world on their own.

"I guess I am lucky enough to only be burdened with one of the two," Kaela sighed. Dulin shook his head.

"I hope that one day you're lucky enough to know the burden I face, Lady Kaela."

As the peacekeepers traversed through the Market District, they would flare the lamps and torches that kept the streets lit up. Better to have more light to see any criminals than to have to rely on their own sight in the dark. In Kaela's experience, the sudden flare up would startle anyone that was unsuspecting too. That was a nice perk.

"Ah, curses," Dulin said as they reached Jackson's Pastry House. "Closed."

"Every store has to close up shop at some point, Dulin."

"I guess. Could have stayed open for a little while long…"

A crash resounded from a nearby street. Kaela and Dulin stopped, ears perked to the sky. Indistinct voices spoke in hushed tones followed by the patter of rushing footsteps. Kaela waved her hand and led Dulin down the street towards the clamor.

They turned the corner just in time to see one of the ruffians escaping into an alleyway. Broken glass scattered across the cobblestone road, coated with a light green dust. Kaela cursed under her breath. Elfdust.

"Follow them!" Kaela commanded, whispering a prayer under her breath. Suddenly, a gust of air expelled from underneath her and launched her to the roof of a nearby building. A quick glance over the surrounding streets and she spotted the terrorists. She pulled her spear from her back and took off across the city rooftops, leaping from platform to platform to close the gap between them.

Dulin followed close behind, racing through the streets. He ducked in and out of alleyways, masterfully finding ways to keep up with Kaela as she hopped onward toward the Hilios practice fields. That must have been where they were going. They were only a block away. It was only a matter of time before they caught up with…

The sky lit up in a flash of green and red, the force behind the explosion blasting Kaela from the rooftop and onto her back. Her head spun, Dulin quickly finding his way to her and helping her back to her feet. One of the Hilios practice fields illuminated the city with green flamelight.

Kaela cursed. She pressed her eyes shut and her Sight flared to life. The fires dimmed so she could see the auras of the people of the city. Relief washed over her when she realized that there were no auras radiating from the destroyed field. No victims of this heinous crime. Captain Belvin still wouldn't be happy...

"I lost them," Dulin said, emotions flooding his voice. "I am so sorry, Commander."

III

The Winner Is...

"I'm just visiting," Dawn said to the guard positioned between her and the heavy oaken door. "Lady Kaela should have left word to allow me in?"

The guard shoved his hands in his pockets and drew out a crumpled note, slowly unraveling it in his hands. Dawn peered over the parchment, attempting to read what was written. It wasn't at all legible, especially considering the wrinkles from being mismanaged in his pocket.

"Ahh," the guard said, looking up at Dawn. "I remember now. Mistress Dawn. Please, right this way." He removed a key from a satchel on his hip and pressed it into the lock, shoving the door open. He guided Dawn into a narrow passage, locking the heavy door behind them. "When you are ready to return, just let me know, and I will let you out."

Dawn gave a nod and continued through the passageway. On both sides of the hall, iron bars held back criminals waiting in their cells. Several sat slumped against the walls of their diminutive chambers while others pressed up against the iron, taunting Dawn as she passed. She tuned them out, hardly even noticing that she was being spoken to. She was good at that, often receding into her own thoughts and meditating on memories of her family and friends before she met Cain. When she did, the outside world seemed to blur, like she was in her own box that separated her from what was going on around her.

Cain often warned against this. "You must stay aware at all times," he would say. "Life is happening around you. Don't miss it by dwelling on the past."

She rounded a corner and proceeded down a set of stairs. Farther and farther she ventured into the prison. Gangsters, thugs, and terrorists watched her progress. Soon the torches lighting the halls grew more and more seldom, until the flamelight hardly lit the corridor at all. She snapped her fingers and summoned a small ball of light to illuminate the dark prison until she found the cell she was looking for.

"Maron," Dawn whispered, a grin encasing her lips. "Sorry it's been so long since I've visited. A hunt took me out of the city for a while."

His cell was damp and barren. Nothing but a cot along one wall and a waste bucket in the corner. He had a plate sitting near the bars bearing remnants of his latest meal. He didn't get up from his bed when Dawn arrived, hardly even turning his head to look at her.

Maron forced a broken smile from within his cell. "You don't need to apologize, Dawn," he said. "You don't owe me anything."

"You know, tonight is the Hilios Finals," Dawn said with a little extra cheer. Maron feigned a smile, but his eyes betrayed him. "It will be the last match of the season. I hope you'll be able to watch us play next year, once the Council comes to their senses."

Maron sighed.

"What?" Dawn asked. "I really am happy for you, Dawn," Maron said. "I just don't know if that will ever happen."

"What do you mean?"

"It's been a year of investigation, and I am no closer to seeing daylight," Maron responded. "The Council has made their decision, whether they've made it public or not."

"Don't talk like that, Maron," Dawn said. "We'll get you out of here eventually. You just have to keep your head up. At some point, Taran has to listen to reason."

"Not unless he's forced to," Maron mumbled under his breath. Dawn sat silently, knowing she couldn't change his mind. "You should go," Maron continued. "I don't want to put a damper on the day of your championship."

Dawn drew her lips to a line and nodded. Before departing, she pulled a folded up paper from her coat pocket. "Take this," she said. "It's the flyer for the championship. One that wasn't vandalized. Thought it might liven up your living spaces."

Maron grinned, grasping the paper from between the bars. "Thank you, Dawn." She studied his face. His smile was real. Genuine. Unforced. She hadn't seen a real smile from him in more than a year.

"I'll see you soon," she promised, turning toward the prison entrance and back into the sunlight.

The streets buzzed with the excitement of the finals. Vendors lined the roads selling snacks and souvenirs, fueling the cacophony. A cluster of katze children rushed Dawn as she passed by, requesting autographs from the famed Quarrinian Hilios Flier.

Tents went up in every courtyard in the city, lanterns lighting up the spaces with bright and fun colors. This was more than just a sporting event. This was a vast variety of entertainment rolled into one single day. Carts rolled through the city carrying itinerant games. People crowded each other, paying to have their own turn to win all sorts of different prizes.

Dawn found herself lingering at a corner where a traveling dark elf bard had set up shop. He played something like a lute, but it was much bigger. Its tone was absolutely vibrant, echoing through a hole cut into its hollowed out body. Some of the people around called it a guitar, though Dawn had never heard of the strange instrument.

He sang a song Dawn had never heard before. This happened often over the last year, as the songs people sang in Quarrine were generally different from the ones people sang in the Citadel. This one, in particular, caught her attention:

> Locked in a prison with no escape
> Keeping track of long lost days
> Where will my weary soul reside
> When there is nothing but darkness inside
>
> Who will want this painful soul
> Whose actions made of me a fool
> Can I ever live with myself
> Where the internal darkness dwells
>
> Can the light of truth free me
> Or all alone will I be
> The fate of my life is gone
> For I have done too much wrong

The elf's silky voice and upbeat melody masked the true tone of the song's lyrics, the crowd cheering to the joyous chords as he sang. Dawn, however, could not cheer. The song cut deep into her soul.

"You have done so much wrong." Dawn nearly jumped out of her skin, her Reflection appearing next to her. "You are the reason so many people are dead. You are the reason so much bad has happened."

She snapped back to reality and moved on from the bard. His voice throbbed in her mind long after she was out of earshot. Only the fireworks exploding in the sky over the Market District, where the Championship Field was located, could shake her from the thoughts racing through her head.

Just outside the Championship Field she noticed a squad of Sacred Order guards circling a small throng. As she approached, the guards opened their ranks to reveal Taran addressing the two championship teams. "Good!" He exclaimed. "Mistress Dawn is here. We can begin."

Dawn leaned over to Krom, who was already completely outfitted in his Hilios uniform. "What's going on?" She whispered.

"Something happened last night," Krom whispered back.

Silas elbowed him, redirecting his attention toward the councilman. "As some of you may have heard," Taran started, "there was an Outrider attack here in the Market District last night. An explosion at one of the Hilios practice fields. The field was empty, so one was critically injured, but we must discuss the effect this has on today's game."

Rodes scoffed. "Why would it affect our game?"

"We have to think about more than just ourselves and our schedule," Krom shot back.

Rodes rolled her eyes. "You would cancel our match? You're that terrified of losing to your superior?"

"Is it safe?" Silas interrupted, addressing the councilman. "If we were to continue with the match as planned, could we guarantee the safety of the people in attendance, as well as the safety of our teams?"

"How could we?" Krom asked. "With how active the Outriders have been, even with everybody on alert? They're still succeeding in pulling off attacks almost daily."

"Would they dare attack such a high profile target?" Mae asked. "With the amount of security at an event like this, there is no way they would risk such a bold move, right?"

"They've been building up to something," Taran stated. "It seems like each subsequent attack grows larger in scale."

"We can't let these terrorists dictate our lives!" Rodes stated. "Hilios is important to the people of our city. It's the one place where we can all come together, the faithful and the atheist alike. I remember being a little girl and going to a Hilios match to escape from the turmoil in the world. To root for my team and leave everything behind. Nothing else mattered. Our people need that right now, and we can give it to them."

"I can't believe I'm saying this," Dawn said. "But I agree with Phoenicia. Just seeing the excitement in the children's eyes as I autographed some toys on the way here. The people need this tonight."

Taran raised an eyebrow, scratching at his chin. "I guess that settles it," he said. "I will have the peacekeepers search the stadium for any signs of danger, and we will have them stationed at every corner, inside and out. We will do what we can to ensure that any attack on this event is a death wish." The teams nodded in agreement and all headed off to their respective locker rooms to prepare for the match. "Dawn!" Taran shouted. "A word please!"

Dawn exhaled a sigh of exhaustion, turning to see the councilman. "Yes sir?"

"It's reached my ears that you visited your friend in prison today," Taran said.

Shock flashed across Dawn's face.

"That's just fine!" The councilman assured her. "I won't dictate how you spend your down time. I just want to make sure that you and I are on good terms."

Dawn choked down the words that initially exploded into her mind, forcefully slowing her thoughts. "Of course, Councilman."

"Good," Taran grinned. "We can disagree on many things, yet still work together for the good of the people. The expression of a differing idea or viewpoint can actually be an act of generosity." He extended out his hand; an offer of peace.

Dawn took a deep breath and squeezed his hand as a sign of reconciliation. She moved the muscles in her face to force a smile. They shook hands for an unbearable moment before he finally released her.

"Good luck today, Dawn," his words rolled off his tongue like poison. It was labeled as genuine, but that made it all the more dangerous.

* * *

Kaela pulled her peacekeeper uniform over her head, ordaining herself with some extra armor and protection for the coming ordeal. Her neck ached from the fall off the rooftop the night before. She could hear the other officers cheering in the rooms outside, arguing amongst themselves about which Hilios team was better. Of course, Kaela had her own preferences towards the Wings of Radiance, but not every peacekeeper held her sentiment.

"Attention!" Captain Belvin's voice rumbled through the wall. Curses, the man had a commanding tone. Kaela quickly adorned the rest of her uniform and pushed out into the mess hall.

"After the attacks last night on the Hilios practice field, the White Council has decided to increase security for today's match. The newly appointed Commander Dulin will take the Gate District Precinct to watch over the exterior of the fields. This means the streets, the vendors, the works. Commander Anvar will take the Northtown District Precinct to man the hallways and corridors inside the facility, and Commander Kaela will take the Market Precinct and the Midtown Precinct to watch over the crowds and the seats. You will get your specific orders upon arrival. Move out within the hour." He waved a hand toward the three commanders to follow him into his office and shut the door behind them.

"You really think Dulin can handle the entirety of the exterior?" Anvar joked, elbowing the young peacekeeper. "Kid's basically still an intern."

Belvin didn't laugh. He didn't even smile. The statement was technically true, but Dulin had proven himself time and time again. "I chose you three because you are the best," he said. "Personally, I think this whole situation is utter foolishness. It'd be better to postpone the match until we can get the situation under control, but Councilman Taran seems to disagree. If something happens out there, I want us to be ready for it." He looked at Kaela. "Once you get your officers in place, I want you to search the facility for any signs of that blasted Elfdust. That's one catastrophe that I would rather not have on our hands."

"You really think the Outriders would try and kill that many people?" Dulin asked. Even his tone made him sound young. "That seems drastic, even for them. It isn't just the faithful that enjoy Hilios."

"I won't risk the lives of our people just because we think

the chances of attack are slim," Belvin said. "Better to be prepared for something, even if it never happens. Now go."

* * *

Dawn rushed to the locker room where her team had already prepared themselves in uniform for the upcoming game. Dawn hastily found her personal changing room and slipped into her tunic. Nerves slithered through her muscles, overwhelming her mind. She found herself trying to pull her gloves over her feet as socks. Why was she so nervous? She had gone through this process a hundred times since she started playing the game.

This match felt... different.

As day became night, the ruckus outside the arena grew. Even from within the locker room, Dawn could hear the shouts of the crowds, chanting either for the 'Angels' or the 'Wings of Radiance'. The energy that filled her was equal parts excitement and pure fear. She had trained and prepared for this moment, yet still it conquered her.

"So much drama before the match," Mae said, shooting her blessed bow at a target on the wall. The luminescent arrow found the bullseye before fading into the wind.

"You know what they say," Krom responded. "If you don't want the drama, then you should live with the vegetarian wood elves in Napora."

Mae cocked her head, a quizzical look in her eye.

"No beef."

Mae groaned, turning and aiming her magical bow at Krom. He yelped, leaping behind a nearby equipment crate. Dawn couldn't help but chuckle a little.

A young girl clad in chainmail entered the room. She scanned the space until she found Mae, who yelped and threw her bow to the ground before rushing over to embrace the newcomer.

"Remy!" Silas shouted. "Came to see Mae off, huh?"

"Just finished my training at the Oceanview barracks to the east," Remy said. "Just in time to watch my sister crush Phoenicia Rodes!"

"Thank you for coming, Rem," Mae smiled. "It means a lot."

"Eh hem!" Krom cleared his throat from nearby.

"Of course!" Mae said. "Remy, this is Krom. He likes to think he's the funny guy, but don't let him fool you."

"Hey!" Krom frowned.

"And that over there is Dawn," Mae waved Dawn over. "She's the real reason we're undefeated." Dawn shook Remy's hand. The girl had the same burgundy hair as Mae, but a much more immature face. It might have been from age, but Dawn suspected it was actually just experience. Mae carried every combat encounter she'd ever had in her face. You could tell she was hardened just by looking at her.

"I expected you to be older," Remy smiled. "I guess you're some sort of prodigy?"

"I just get lucky," Dawn laughed.

"Lucky?" Mae scoffed. "Lucky is winning one game because of you. What you have isn't luck, babe."

The chanting from the arena grew louder. It was almost deafening, even in the locker room. Dawn shivered, feeling a weight fall on her shoulders.

"It's just another game," Silas attempted to encourage her as they mounted their pegasus. "Just like all the ones before."

"You didn't say that during our last match," Dawn said.

Silas cocked his head.

"You didn't say that before any of our other games. That means this game isn't like the ones before, otherwise you wouldn't need to say that."

Silas sighed. "If we play like we have been all year, then we'll come out on top."

Dawn watched as Remy left the room, noticing her Reflection in the corner. The silhouette listened to Silas, eyeing Dawn's team. She stood in silence, half a grin forming on her face.

Stay out of this, Dawn shared her thoughts with the extension of herself. *I'm not ready for the world to know about you.*

The Reflection nodded with a menacing smile. "Good luck," she laughed, then vanished in a wisp of vapor.

The atmosphere in the locker room was that of both tension and excitement. The city had shut down by midday so that everyone who wished to attend had ample time to find their way to the Champion's Stadium. The Wings of Radiance sat atop their pegasus, staring at a giant closed oak door. On the other side of the door dwelled every shouting fan and angry rival.

Dawn's face flushed, breathing heavy. Krom caught sight of her panic. "Are you alright, Dawn?" He asked. "You aren't looking so hot."

"Thanks," Dawn sneered.

'You know what I mean."

"I'm fine," Dawn mumbled. Every game before this she had kept a level head, but suddenly her mind raced. The screaming of the crowd crept into her thoughts, blurring her senses.

An amplified voice reverberated across the threshold of the door. "Welcome to this year's Hilios World Championship!" The voice was Taran's. Dawn could recognize it anywhere. "Please help me welcome to the field, the Wings of Radiance!"

Just then, a horn blared and the door creaked open. Silas led the charge out onto the field, followed by Mae, Titus, Krom, and finally Dawn. The energy rose to a crescendo inside her as her pegasus lifted off from the ground and she flew through the air around the stadium. The magical light set in the ceiling of the stadium shone brighter than any of the previous games of the season. It almost kept Dawn from noticing the sheer amount of people packed into the seats. Almost.

"And now," Taran continued, announcing with his magically amplified voice. Dawn noticed him standing at the top of the stadium in one of his executive booths, protected from anything in the stadium. "Welcome to the field our defending champions, the Citadel Angels!"

Another horn sounded and a gate on the opposing side of the field opened. Phoenicia Rodes led her team out of the lockers. Following her was Althena, Belle, Lyra, and Rosella. They all looked like they were created from the same blonde-haired, blue-eyed mold. They flew in sync toward their own goals, across from the Wings of Radiance.

"Tonight, the White Council's very own Councilman

Annias will be announcing the match. Let this be a match for the ages!"

A whistle blew and a rider clad in black flew into the stadium, positioning himself in the center of the field. Both teams quickly enclosed on his location.

"Seeing that this is the championship match," the referee stated, "you should all know the rules by now. But here we go anyway!" He pulled out a shimmering vial from his breast pocket. "This is the light ball! Only this beam can score a point. Any other shots made with your bows are strictly for incapacitation of the other team. Each player is allowed three arrows they can utilize to incapacitate. After three, penalties will be called for excessive force."

He pointed toward the hoops floating on one side of the field. "The small middle hoop is worth three points. The right hoop is two, and the largest hoop on the left is one. There will be no charging, roughhousing, and no falling to your deaths. Let's make sure we all leave this place alive." Rodes shot Dawn a glare from across the circle of riders. "To your places!"

As he shouted, the fliers alternated between teams and flew in a circle around the rider in black. They sped to extreme speeds until finally a horn blew and the referee released the ball of light, shooting high into the air.

Councilman Annias' voice sounded deep in the stadium. "The match has begun!"

Rodes blazed through the air and grasped the ball of light in her gloved hand. The rest of the fliers exploded in every direction. Rodes pulled back on the invisible bowstring and the ball materialized into a glowing arrow, blasting through the sky into the hand of another Angel. Back and forth, they shot the arrow between Dawn's teammates. "Rodes. To Rosella. Back to Rodes. Now Althena." Annias vocalized the match for those in the stands who couldn't follow the quick movements of the players. The arrow switched possession so fast that he only had time to say the names of each player as they caught the arrow. Finally, Rodes caught the light again and sent the arrow flying past Silas into the smallest hoop.

"There it is!" Annias announced. "The first score of the game. Angels-Three. Wings-Zero."

The light materialized in Silas' hand. Before either team could get situated, he launched the arrow to Titus. Dawn flew down the field, but an Angel flew beside her, ready to intercept any arrow that came in her direction. She halted her pegasus and turned back toward Titus. He flew down the field, but a magical arrow latched to his ribs, sending a shock through his body.

Titus cried out in pain and the ball flew up into the air, seized once again by Rodes. She raced toward the goal. Pulling again on her invisible bowstring, she launched toward the smallest hoop, but Silas snapped into position, snatching the arrow in his own glove and whipping a grin at the pompous flier.

"An amazing block by arguably the greatest goaltender in Hilios history!" Annias called.

Dawn continued back toward Silas. He shot the arrow toward her without hesitation. She caught it, immediately shooting toward Krom, who promptly sent it back into her hands. She faked a pass to Mae, but sent it to Krom yet again. Back and forth they flew down the field until finally Dawn grasped a hold of the ball and fired past Lyra, the Angel goaltender, and into the smallest hoop.

"A quick response from the Wings of Radiance to tie the game. Three to three!"

Titus and Mae double teamed Rodes, forcing Lyra to send the arrow into the hands of Althena. Krom and Dawn, while great at flying, could never cover the three others on their own. Rodes just being on the field was enough of a force to cause them to play on their heels. The Angels passed the arrow between them until Althena finally faked a shot toward the center hoop, pulling Silas just enough out of position to score two points.

Silas recovered instantly, sending the arrow to Dawn. She barely even turned before sending it over to Krom, but as he caught it, Rodes drove her pegasus into the side of Krom's mount. The arrow materialized into a ball and jerked out of Krom's hands as he tumbled over the side of his pegasus, barely hanging on by the reins.

Dawn ignored Rodes racing for the ball and rushed to Krom, grasping him by the hand and pulling him back up to his saddle. They glanced back to Rodes, who had pretended to pass the ball, faking out Silas again and scoring another three points.

"A tricky move by Phoenicia Rodes, but the ref seems not to have taken notice," Annias announced. "Looks like this match might get physical!"

Silas held on to the ball for a second, allowing his team to cool down. Althena and Rosella both teamed up on Dawn, not giving her any room to fly. Silas chose to send the ball to Mae.

With Dawn still swarmed by the Angels, Mae passed the ball to Titus. He flew down the field until he was stopped by Rodes, then sent the ball to Krom. Before Krom could even catch the ball, Rodes launched an arrow into his side, sending a jolt of stunning electricity through his body. Belle picked up the free ball and the Angels passed once again down the field to score another two points.

"The Angels picking up a demanding lead here, now leading the Wings Ten-three," Annias announced. "How will the Wings of Radiance respond?"

Dawn clenched her fist around her bow, scowling at Phoenicia Rodes. Silas passed the arrow to Mae, and as she feigned to Krom, Dawn charged Rodes, placing her pegasus' hoofs into her face. Rodes reeled backward, nearly falling off her own pegasus, but kept her balance in her seat.

The distraction was hardly enough as the light arrow passed between Mae and Krom down the field. Rodes pulled back on her bow and released an arrow, miraculously piercing the ball of light to the wall across the field. Rodes smiled, giving Dawn a smug wink. The Angels retrieved the ball and effortlessly maneuvered it down the field, scoring another easy two points.

A blast sounded from a horn below.

"That is it for the first half, ladies and gentlemen!" Annias announced. "The Angels leading the Wings of Radiance Twelve-Three. We will see what changes the Wings need to make to stay in the game in the second half."

The riders all retreated back to their respective locker rooms. Dawn jumped off her pegasus and pounded her fist into the wall. "I can't believe that ref!" She shouted to her teammates. "Rodes is targeting Krom like she wants him dead!"

"I'll live, Dawn," Krom assured her, drawing a cup of water from their private well.

"She can't treat you like that!"

"Dawn!" Krom startled her. "I will be fine. This is exactly what she wants. If she gets us upset, then we don't play our best. She will take advantage of every mistake."

"And we can't afford to make any more," Silas stated. "We have been on the back foot the entire match. We have to figure out how to make a move. Put them on the defensive instead."

"We've been trying, Silas," Titus complained. "Every time we get the ball, it's like they are a step ahead of us. They know our plays. What else can we do?"

"We haven't fired an aggressive arrow this whole game," Silas stated.

* * *

Kaela stormed off from the top of the stands and into the stadium hallway. Phoenicia Rodes was lucky Kaela wasn't on the field. There was no way she would have let that entitled city-girl treat Krom like that if she had been flying.

The halls flooded with raving fans, all shouting over each other their predictions for the rest of the match. Her peacekeepers stationed themselves everywhere; she couldn't even turn her head without spotting at least two watching over the crowds.

She found her way through the populace to lieutenant Erik, who had commanded his squad to sweep through the seats while the fans used the restroom and bought their snacks. He turned to lead his peacekeepers in and she continued on, marching through the crowd. The peacekeepers had taken the weapons of every person who wanted to attend the match, so she stood out to the crowd. The people moved around her like minnows avoiding a shark. She was a predator in an ocean of prey.

Kaela had never been great at blending in, though she didn't really mind. A person could never stand out while simultaneously fitting in. Ephras had made it a habit to remind her that she was made for more.

Now she had to remind herself.

A group of dark elf children from Ardglas hawked broadsheets from the corner as Kaela continued around the stadium. The hallways were a loop, wrapping completely around the building. She hadn't realized that these children had been selling their papers at each turn. She dug in her pocket for a copper coin and handed it to a little dark elf girl in exchange for her product.

To Kaela's surprise, the paper had nothing to do with the Citadel, or even Cirrane at all. It was about the wood elves in Napora, and the war crimes being committed on the southern island. She scanned the page, overlooking articles about the creatures being bred for war until she found the title story; a small dark elf village had been attacked by giant spiders. The survivors blamed the capital city of Cardya, saying they were forcing the dark elves out...

She paused, cursing under her breath. She hadn't even noticed that, while she read the tabloid, the rest of the fans had piled back into their seats. She must have tuned out the starting horn completely. With the citizens out of the way, Kaela saw clearly the symbol carved into the wall. A simple circle with a single line cutting through the middle.

And suddenly, she couldn't move.

* * *

The horn blew yet again and the teams both exited their respective locker rooms and into the air. The crowd's chanting and roars echoed loud in Dawn's ears, stirring her spirit. She wouldn't let this belligerent woman get the better of her and her team. This was Dawn's moment.

The fliers circled the rider in black once again, and he sent the light ball into the air, signaling the start of the second half. Dawn raced up toward the ball, flying faster than she ever had before. Rodes trailed behind, but Dawn grabbed the ball out of the air and flipped around Rodes back toward her goal.

She eyed Mae, who was being closely covered by Althena. She fired the arrow in between the two fliers, quickly drawing another arrow to launch into Althena's ribs. Althena reeled back in shock, allowing Mae to grasp the ball and maneuver it down the field, sending the ball through the smallest hoop.

Rodes quickly repossessed the ball, but as she passed the arrow to Rosella, Titus released a charged shot into the woman's chest, leaving the light ball flying through the air into the wall behind them. Dawn picked it up yet again, passing it between her and Krom until they scored another easy two points.

"A quick statement from the Wings of Radiance early in the second half!" Annias announced from his balcony seat.

"This game isn't over yet. Not by a long shot. The score is now Twelve-Eight."

Lyra paused for a moment, watching the teams get into position. Dawn flew near to Rodes with vigor in her veins. This was the start they needed. The crowd around them hummed in excitement as the two expert teams battled out the fantastic game.

Avoiding Dawn, Lyra passed to Althena, who carefully moved the ball between her teammates. They held onto the ball for longer than usual before finally sending it off to their star player. As Rodes aimed for the goals, Silas set himself between the two smallest hoops, leaving the only safe shot to be the large hoop. She released the arrow, shooting a glare toward Silas.

"The first single point we have seen in this whole game!" Annias announced. "The Wings have shifted their defense for this half as well! Thirteen-Eight"

Silas passed the ball to Krom midway down the field, but Rodes rushed at him, nearly knocking him off his pegasus yet again. As Rodes collected the ball, Dawn screamed and charged, causing her to dump the ball off swiftly to Rosella nearby.

But Dawn was ready. She reeled back on the reins and fired a shot at the new ball carrier, sending the ball flying into the air. Dawn and Rodes locked eyes, then raced toward the ball, glaring at each other as they soared through the sky. Before either could grab the ball, Rodes rammed her pegasus into Dawn, wrapping both the animal's wings up together and beginning a spiral freefall toward the ground.

The game continued above as they fell, Titus grabbing

the ball and leading the team down the field once again, but Dawn couldn't see any of it. The hazy blur of feathers and wings clouded her senses. She reached out her hand in a motion of pure instinct, reaching for something to grab onto to stop her fall. As she reached, Rodes' pegasus kicked wildly, cracking her right arm.

Finally, Rodes managed to pull away with her pegasus, but it was too late. Dawn continued to fall until her pegasus smashed with a THUD to the solid ground.

Dust and smoke washed over the arena, clouding everything around. Dawn's ears rang, her vision blurry. As the smoke settled, she noticed her Reflection standing at the edge of the stadium, the same wicked smirk on her face.

Dawn glanced up at her teammates, clutching at her mangled arm. Her vision was interrupted by fire. Images flashed through her mind of violence and death. The faces of her team, as well as the Angels, appeared in the midst of chaos and pain.

She forced her eyes shut, shaking her head in disbelief. Just then, everything fell silent. The crowd no longer shouted, Annias' voice went quiet. She opened her eyes and the crowd had frozen in their seats, standing or sitting in a state of suspension. The players above stopped. Their pegasus' wings no longer flapped in the air. They dropped, one at a time, through the air and crashed to the field below.

Dawn watched in horror, grasping her hand in pain. The fliers fell like raindrops, giving way to gravity. One by one they slammed to the ground in an explosion of dust.

Dawn rushed to help her friends. Krom lay under his pegasus, gasping for breath. With her good arm, she summoned an unnatural strength within her and pushed the beast off the Quarrinian.

"Krom!" She cried. "Are you ok?"

Krom pushed himself to a knee, coughing up some blood. "I'm fine. What about the others?"

Dawn and Krom ricocheted between the fallen pegasus and helped each flier back to their feet. They all gathered gazing up at the stadium full of frozen participants.

"What's going on?" Rodes muttered. "I've never seen this kind of magic."

"We have..." Krom said under his breath, glancing at Dawn.

IV

A New Enemy

As Krom spoke, particular people in the crowd began to move. They wore dark robes, pulling hoods over their heads. One by one they leapt down onto the field, slowing their fall with magical gusts of wind. They glared at the surviving pack of finalists, entering the stadium from all around. Once they hit the ground, each one summoned a blade that materialized from vapor in their hands.

Rodes grasped her magical bow and attempted to pull an arrow, but the bow's light had faded, rendering its magic useless. Dawn clenched her good fist, whispering a soft prayer under her breath. A red glow emanated from her hands.

"What do you want!" Rodes shrieked at the approaching enemy. Her voice echoed against the walls of the silent stadium.

No answer.

Dawn breathed deep. None of the others were true mages.

They had used magical items before, and even worked alongside mages. But Dawn was the only one that had been trained in using the blessings of Fos.

She tried to raise her hands, but her right hand dangled unnaturally. She could barely feel it. Shock must have taken over her body. She would be feeling the aftermath of that fall in an hour or so.

If we survive that long.

Dozens of the hooded menaces stepped forward with caution. They didn't attack, but instead allowed fear to set into the finalists. It was the same strategy Rodes had used during the match. Anything to force a mistake.

Dawn howled, shooting a blast of lightning from her good hand into one of the approaching enemies. That was all it took. Suddenly the rest charged, swords out in front of them. Dawn spun on her heels to shoot more lightning at whoever she could, but there were too many of them. Quickly, twenty or more armed attackers fell upon the unarmed group of Hilios Fliers.

The other finalists grasped their bows and attempted to utilize them as short, curved staves. They parried and struck with the rods, but barely did any real damage to the attackers. It was barely enough just to block the swings of the swords.

Dawn jumped in front of the other survivors and released a blast of wind that sent half of the attackers back toward the outer wall. She flipped again and sent another bolt of lightning into the chest of a man charging at Krom. Krom nodded thankfully to Dawn, then reached down to grab the sword from the newly deceased menace. To their shock, as he grasped the blade the entire weapon disappeared, fading into the wind like ash. Dawn turned again, hearing Krom curse.

The battlefield flashed with fire and steel. One after another, Dawn used her magic to defend her allies, but more enemies just lowered themselves into the arena.

Three swordsmen locked their eyes onto Rodes, who wildly swung her bow through the air at the heads of her attackers. Her eyes were wide. Breathing erratic. She bellowed with every swing, calling attention to herself. Dawn ducked through the array of warriors, forcing her way to her former opponent.

One of the swordsmen swung toward Rodes, but she was able to jump out of the way. The other two rushed toward her, causing her to swing her bow in response. One man snatched her bow in his giant hands, slamming his sword down on the shaft and snapping it in two. Rodes stumbled backward, tripping over her feet and gazing up at the men who would decide her fate.

Dawn rolled in, snapping one man's knee with a kick and shooting a blast of fire into another's face. The last man swung towards Rodes, but Dawn charged at him and rammed her shoulder into his gut. As the man fell, she pressed her foot against his neck and stomped, crushing his throat.

The final man found his way back to his shaky feet, holding his sword at the ready. Dawn watched him, then waved her hand upwards, casting a gust of wind from underneath him. He flew into the air, then slammed back down on his sword. Dawn offered her healthy hand to Rodes, who grabbed it and swiftly found her way back to her feet. She offered a nod of thanks, unable to put her emotions to words.

Energy within Dawn faded quickly. She could feel her life force leaving with every blast of power. Like a parasite latched onto her heart, draining her blood, she could feel her life-force escaping.

A wail echoed from across the battlefield as Lyra and Althena both fell to the swords of their attackers. Dawn called out, rushing over to assist them, but she was too late. When she got to them, the final breath had already escaped their lungs.

Her head grew light and her knees grew weak. She turned again and watched a sword slam through Titus' back and out his chest. Behind the violent chaos, her Reflection watched, unmoving. Silent. She was doing exactly as Dawn had instructed.

The finalists closed in on each other as the attackers encroached around them. Still more enemies than Dawn could quickly count. She continued to attack with lightning, but with each shot she could feel herself becoming weaker. She wasn't even sure if she was doing any damage anymore. Her vision grew dark.

A silhouette entered her sight. Was it her Reflection? It couldn't be. Her Reflection had been ordered to stay away. A decision Dawn regretted.

The silhouette darted between enemies like a leaf being carried by the wind. He fluttered from person to person, cutting through them with a spear of his own. Dawn pressed her eyes shut multiple times, trying to clear away her cloudy vision. Finally, she could see the person helping them. A hooded warrior, never taking the time to look up from the floor. He struck without looking, accurately piercing his enemies with his spear. He spun between swords like he was water, unable to be cut.

The finalists stood in awe, watching as this hooded soldier cut down the attackers one by one until finally each of them lay dead at his feet. The soldier pulled a small, dark cloth from his waistband and wiped the blood from his spear head, then tossed the cloth to the floor. He stood still, not bothering to look around at the carnage he had left.

The stadium slowly reinvigorated, shouts of terror rapidly filling the atmosphere. Dawn watched as bystanders trampled over each other toward the exits. It didn't matter who was in their way, whether it was women or children, they pushed like their life depended on it. For all they knew, it was.

Peacekeepers made their way toward the center of the stadium from all corners of the stands. They lowered themselves down the same way the attackers had, shooting a puff of wind before they landed to slow their fall. They each pulled a sword as they approached, eyes aware of each person still standing.

Kaela was among those in the crowd. She led her troop toward the battlefield. "Stranger!" She shouted. "Remove your hood. Reveal yourself!"

Dawn raised a concerned hand. "Kaela, he saved our lives!"

Kaela didn't listen, continuing her approach toward the hooded warrior with her spear raised. "One more chance, soldier! If what my friend says is true, then you will drop your weapon and come with us for questioning."

Before Dawn could interject, the hooded stranger slammed his spear into the ground. A shock wave shook the entire stadium, nearly knocking the peacekeepers to the dirt beneath them. Kaela threw her hands out to hold her balance. By the time she recovered, the hooded soldier had taken off in the opposite direction.

"Peacekeepers!" She shouted. "After him!"

The peacekeepers stormed after the escaping soldier. Dawn turned to go with them, but Kaela grabbed her by her broken arm, pulling her backwards.

"Let me go with you!" Dawn demanded. "He saved our lives. I need to help!"

Kaela held her spear up, pointing the tip at Dawn's chest. "Enough have already died under your watch, Dawn. This time, you stay behind." Without another word, Kaela turned and led her peacekeepers in the chase for the hooded soldier.

Before Dawn could chase after her, Cain made his way onto the field, placing himself between her and the chase. She pushed against him meekly. "Let me go!" But Cain pulled her gently into his arms. Dawn's muscles gave way and she collapsed in his embrace, unable to control the tears that flowed from her eyes.

"How did those mages hold an entire stadium suspended in time?" Dawn overheard Annias asking Cain and the rest of the nine council members across the room. The Sacred Order had guided the surviving finalists back to the Temple of Fos, keeping them safe from the swarming crowds.

"There is much to consider here, Annias," Taran spoke calmly. "Cain, was this Ulumbra?"

"I can't say for sure," Cain apologized. "The magic was dark, though. Fos' blessings only allow the manipulation of nature, not the control of other beings. That is the power of Seor, and I only know of one sorcerer trained in dark magic who could accomplish such a powerful time suspension spell."

"Ugh..." Taran growled. "Ulumbra. Outriders. Riots in the streets. That bloody vigilante murdering insurrectionists." He rubbed his forehead. "Did they catch him?"

"He escaped into the Old City, sir," Councilwoman Sorena responded.

"They're as good as dead, then," Annias responded. "Our Guardian keeps that passage safe since the incident in the prison last year."

"They got into the city somehow..." Taran pondered. "Was this our masked vigilante? The Butcher of Midtown, or whatever the people are calling him?"

Annias shook his head. "Our sources tell us there were some characteristic differences between the hooded soldier and our vigilante. Mainly their choice of weapon. The vigilante is proficient with a sword, not a spear. The people have already begun calling this new one the Savior's Champion."

Taran cursed under his breath. "Now there are two of them? This whole city is going into chaos!"

Dawn listened to the White Council discuss things just a few feet away from her. As she listened, a council healer fed her an herb they called toruga. It numbed her arm so the healer could reset it, yanking and pulling on the bones until it was straightened out again. Dawn didn't feel pain by it though. Just some pressure on her nerves. The council healers were legendary, and their products were incredible.

The healer gazed up at her. "I won't be able to mend the broken bone, but I can set it and cast it so it will heal on its own. Should heal itself within a few weeks. The toruga will suppress your magic for a few hours as well. Just a little side effect of the herb."

Dawn nodded, hardly regarding the healer as she listened in on the Council.

"Why were the finalists not affected by the spell?" Taran mumbled. "Even our Sacred Order couldn't break free from suspension. All our preparation for nothing. Why were the Hilios Fliers unaffected?" He glanced over to Dawn, who quickly averted her eyes, pretending like she wasn't listening and that her arm was taking up all of her attention.

"Girl!" Taran shouted, pointing at Dawn. She looked up and he motioned her over to the gathering. She slowly stood, grasping her broken arm and limping over. "What can you tell us of your attackers?"

Dawn glanced at Cain before answering the councilman. "They all bore swords that dissolved when they were dropped. But other than that, none of them used magic. They only fought with their steel."

"Can we be sure this was Ulumbra, then?" Councilman Thomas asked. "Or have the Outriders gained a powerful mage in their ranks?"

"It was Ulumbra," Cain said. "The Outriders hate magic. Everything they believe contradicts this attack. There is no way they would utilize a mage like this."

"The timing is conspicuous, Cain," Taran said. "You have to at least admit that. A year of inactivity, and Ulumbra chooses now to make a move? What did this accomplish for them?"

"It gives the Outriders fuel for their fight," Sorena said.

"How better to convince the people to join your cause against magic than by using magic in an attack like this."

"I'm telling you," Cain argued, "this was Moldolor. I don't know if they accomplished what they wanted to or if the spearman thwarted their plans, but this move did mean something to them. If we want to take on this dark magic, we need to unite the city, not divide them!"

"Division is happening, Cain," Taran stated. "Whether you like it or not. The Outriders gain followers by the day. There are riots in the streets of every district. We have no choice but to demonize the terrorists and defeat one enemy at a time. From our perspective, Ulumbra is still dormant. This must be a terrorist attack by the Outriders."

Cain grit his teeth, but stayed silent. For the rest of the meeting he sat in his chair, just listening to the plans for the next days made by the Council. A messenger jogged into the room and whispered into Taran's ear. He nodded and dismissed the Council to their own chambers while he took some Sacred Order guards and followed the messenger out of the Temple.

Dawn returned to the healer for her arm to be wrapped in a sling. Cain then escorted her out to the foyer of the temple where the rest of the survivors lay in small cots being tended to by more council healers. Remy sat with Mae as she slept in one corner of the room and Phoenicia Rodes wept in another.

Dawn rushed over to Krom, whose wounds had already been wrapped and mended. He slept quietly, gripping his pillow under his head. She knelt by him, running her good hand softly across his cheek. He startled awake, thrashing in his bed and waving his fists violently. "Kathrine!" He screamed over and over again. "Kathrine! Kathrine!"

Dawn threw her arm around him, whispering calmly in his ear. "It's ok. I am here. You are safe now."

Krom took a deep breath, nestling silently in Dawn's arms. Cain pulled over two more cots that lay nearby, tossing a couple rough pillows on them and gesturing to Dawn to lay down. "We can go home tomorrow," he said. "We're safe here. Get some rest."

Sun peeked through the stained glass windows of the great hall. Dawn awoke to a mostly empty room; the Council Fliers had all dispersed back to their stations. Cain sat upright on his cot, reading a thick book about the Great Cataclysm. "Did you sleep at all?" She asked.

Cain scoffed playfully. "I'm not the one who needed rest, D." He smiled at her, but his eyes told a different story. His grin couldn't hide his worry.

He shouldn't have to watch over me, Dawn's thoughts raged in her mind. *I need to be stronger.*

A figure materialized in Dawn's sight. Her heart almost burst from the sudden surge of anxiety until she realized it was just Phoenicia Rodes. Her eyes were red and swollen, hair a disheveled mess. Dawn had never seen Phoenicia Rodes like this.

"I just..." Phoenicia mumbled. "I wanted to... I just feel like..."

"Take a breath, Rodes," Dawn said.

Phoenicia did as she was told, closing her eyes and inhaling deep. "Thank you, Dawn."

Dawn raised an eyebrow. "Thank me? For what?"

"For saving me," Phoenicia said. She pointed to Belle and Rosella. "For saving us. We treated you terribly, but you still stuck your neck out for us."

Dawn shook her head. "I could only do so much. I'm sorry about your teammates."

Phoenicia forced a smile through watery eyes. "But you tried. You did everything you could."

It still wasn't enough.

Phoenicia sat down at the edge of Dawn's bed, resting her elbows on her knees. "I've known them my whole life, you know. Lyra and I were neighbors in Northtown as children, and Althena was kind of just always there. I don't think I remember a time where Althena wasn't around.

"But, of course, life happens to all of us. New relationships form. We look for our pathway to a bright and hopeful future, and we kind of drift away."

"It wasn't forever, though," Dawn said.

Phoenicia smiled. "No, it wasn't. I hadn't even spoken to either of them in years. Thought that season in my life was over. That I'd probably never see them again. But when my dad killed himself... You know how sometimes you can be surrounded by so many people who say they support you and say they're there and still feel alone? I had all these new people in my life, but none of them were genuine. Lyra and Althena reached out, and it was like no time had passed. They may not have been around throughout the years, but when it really mattered..." She wiped tears from her eyes, the sobs finally escaping from deep within. "And I had to watch helplessly as they were slaughtered like sheep."

Dawn put her good arm around Phoenicia's shoulder and pulled her close. She knew this pain personally. She had experienced it. She thought she had been healing, but she wasn't sure that was true anymore. Shouldn't the people dying in the arena have affected her more? Titus, Lyra, and Althena were alive yesterday, weren't today, and Dawn felt numb.

"Death is not an enemy," Cain said in his soft spoken tone. "It is just another pathway. Eventually, all our journeys intertwine on the same path. Some arrive sooner than others, but ultimately we all will cross the same finish line. It's not something to fear, but to accept when the time comes. You will see your friends again."

Phoenicia's tears slowed. She inched away from Dawn, wiping her eyes with Dawn's pillow. She smiled forcefully and stood up. "Thank you," she said, abruptly turning toward the exit.

Dawn stretched out her arms, climbing to her feet. She placed a hand on Krom's shoulder, gently shaking him awake. This time his eyes inched open slowly.

"It's morning, hon," Dawn whispered. "We should head back home where we can get some real rest."

Krom pushed himself off the cot. He watched the corners of the room, eyeing for hidden enemies lurking in the shadows. Dawn pulled him to his feet and the three of them exited the temple and made their way towards Cain's home in the Northtown District.

Dawn looked after Krom as they walked. There was terror

in his eyes still. He had been through many things before in life, but never something where he was completely powerless. Even when they had been ambushed in Port Aurora, he had snuck in his knife to retain a small grasp of control.

The arena ambush was different. If Dawn hadn't learned magic from Cain, would all of the finalists have died? Would the hooded man have made it in time to save them? He hadn't been in time to save Titus, Althena, or Lyra.

"The vigil for your fallen teammates is going to be the same day as Ephras' anniversary," Cain said as they rounded a corner. "Taran thought it was poetic to have them all on the same day. Like there was some sort of beauty to all this."

Krom was silent. That wasn't like him. Their entire time in the city, Dawn had known Krom to scoff and mock anything regarding the Council and their politics. But it was as if he didn't even hear Cain.

Before Dawn could question his silence, they rounded another corner and heard a disturbance from the road ahead. A throng had gathered on the street. One man stood on an elevated platform shouting into the crowd.

"They have complete control over us!" The man shouted. "You saw what happened at the arena! Their magic can take hold of us. Control us. They think of us as their puppets! They pull on the strings, and we respond the way they predestined us to. No more! We are no longer slaves to fear! We are no longer slaves to magic! We cut the strings today!"

The crowd shouted back to the man approvingly. They raised their voices and clapped their hands, urging the man to continue.

"This isn't going to help our cause," Cain whispered. "This

is exactly what Taran expects. They are all playing into the hands of chaos. With the city divided, Ulumbra won't have any trouble mounting an attack."

The insurrectionist continued to riot the crowd as Cain led the company away from the not-so-subtle sermon. Onlookers had gathered throughout the street to listen to his words. Hundreds of city-dwellers of all races and ethnicities coming from their minute jobs nearby.

Dawn heard her Reflection whisper in her ear. "They aren't your enemy, Dawn."

"Why do you bother me?" Dawn whispered back under her breath. "One minute you seem to actually care about my well-being. Next, you are waiting on the sidelines, watching us be slaughtered."

"I only did as you asked," the Reflection hissed. "You told me to not get involved. You weren't ready for people to know about our true power. I can involve myself more, if you would like." Dawn ignored her Reflection's words. Instead, she just continued forward with Cain and Krom, her mind set on Cain. If she hadn't told her Reflection to stay away, maybe he could have gotten some rest. Dawn always hated when others had to sacrifice for her. She was supposed to be the one who sacrificed for them. How could she protect her friends if she couldn't even protect herself?

They arrived at Cain's home, but to their surprise, the door had been cracked open. Cain halted Dawn and Krom with his hand, pulling his sword from its sheath. Suddenly, Dawn felt a breeze of cool air flowing around them. She mumbled a prayer under her breath, raising her one good hand to a fighting stance.

* * *

Cain pushed the door open to an empty corridor. Within his home he could hear the sound of flames crackling from the living area. A fire he hadn't lit. He pulled a finger to his lips and snuck to the corner, Krom and Dawn following close behind. With a swift wave of his hand, Cain jumped out into the living area, brandishing his sword.

The room was empty. The fire roared in the hearth against the wall, fresh wood crackling under the flames. A plate of unseasoned meat lay tossed aside on a table next to Cain's couch, a fork piercing a slice of the tendon.

"It's about time, Cain," a voice growled from the shadows of the next hallway. Cain snapped his fingers and a ball of light shot into the darkness. A tall, cat-like figure stood upon its two hind legs. It towered over every person in the room, at least a full arms reach taller than Cain.

"Ragnar?" Cain asked, lowering his sword.

The katze emerged from the shadows, placing a pair of hand axes onto the clips on his belt. He was wholly unkempt. The fur that covered his body matted with some areas entirely bare. A long scar traveled across his face, from his brow to his chin.

Cain pushed the look of his friend back in his mind and rushed in for an embrace. Ragnar quickly released Cain, gently pushing him back toward the two other Quarrinians. "I wish this visit were for fun, but I come on a mission." His voice was grim. "Cain, Oasis has fallen."

V

Instead of Permission

Dawn sat near the hearth, pulling a throw blanket over her throbbing legs. Cain returned to the room with four plates of food, seasoned and cooked to perfection. Dawn glanced at Krom, who sat uncomfortably next to her, gazing into the fire.

"We actually did it," Ragnar said, taking a bite of the rare cut of steak. "The Guild had no way to defend themselves against us once we attacked. We came out of nowhere. The thief's sewer system was just enough of an abstract thought to actually work."

"Does the Council know you're in the city?" Cain asked, interrupting the story.

Ragnar waved a dismissive hand. "What the Council don't know won't hurt 'em. I'm not here for Taran and his cronies. I am here for you."

Dawn eyed Cain, examining his face as he processed the

situation. She didn't know how she felt, herself. Last time she saw Ragnar he was ready to kill her. If Cain hadn't been there he probably would have. Cain's soothing effects on a person extended far beyond just her. Even a katze as intimidating as Ragnar could be calmed by her mentor.

"The battle was devastating," Ragnar continued. "We may have caught them off guard, but the rebels I gathered weren't exactly soldiers. So many lives lost. Both sides were left as a fraction of their original force.

"This wouldn't have been an issue, except the orcs had been watching the city. It hadn't even been a week since we'd forced the Guild out when they attacked. We were no match for their siege weapons and sheer numbers. They moved through the city like water rushing through a canal. No corner left untouched. I led those who escaped, nothing more than a hundred people, and took them south to Silt to find refuge. They're safe now, but Oasis is still occupied by those nasty orcs and goblins."

"That has to be Grumuk," Dawn said, glancing at Cain. "Gromoth would never leave the Port and put his people in danger just to take another human city across the continent. It goes against everything he believes."

"I agree with you there," Cain said, rubbing his chin. "I can't help but wonder though: where did the Guild go? After being forced away."

Dread filled Dawn's mind. There was an easy answer. The next largest city in Quarrine was Port Aurora. Gromoth and Dura had a fight on their hands.

"Aside the point, my friend," Ragnar stated. "I am not here to recruit a Guild hunter. I am here for help from a friend.

Oasis deserves better than orc occupation. Oasis deserves freedom. All it should take is killing the chieftain and the rest should come naturally. I've run out of options, Cain. It's my home."

Cain pressed his eyes shut and shook his head. "I'm sorry, Ragnar. There's just so much happening in the city right now. My friends... They need me."

"Your friends need you?" Ragnar growled. "*Your friends need you?* I thought I *WAS* your friend?"

"Dawn and Krom were nearly killed yesterday."

"Do you know how many times I've nearly been killed this last year?" Ragnar raised his voice slightly. Not much, but still enough to command the room. "Once again, you choose this girl over me. You choose this girl over a friend you've known for years. A friend who you helped raise. A friend who considers you a brother. She can't last a week without you? Is she that helpless? Or am I that worthless to you?"

"What you are asking is so much more than a week's journey!"

"Not with pegasus carrying us on our way."

"Cain..." Dawn interrupted. All eyes shifted to her, including her Reflection standing at the edge of the room. Her voice was soft. "We can take care of ourselves for a week. You and Silas can lend your help to Ragnar. He needs you."

Cain ruminated in silence for a moment. Dawn couldn't let him abandon one of his closest friends just for her. She needed to be strong enough to take care of herself. If she could just convince him...

"One week," Cain finally said. "And that's only if Silas

agrees. If we can't get him to join us, then we don't go. I want us to be back in time for the anniversary of Ephras' death." He eyed Dawn. "That's important to me."

Ragnar chuckled. "As long as we have the pegasus to guide us, there is no reason for this mission to take any longer. Orcs are nothing but savages, and we will have the best of the best to take out the chieftain. Once he is gone, the people of Sift can take the city again. The orcs will shatter without proper leadership."

Dawn smiled, her Reflection silently shaking her head in the corner of the room.

* * *

Pegasus riders flew across the Citadel skyline as Krom followed his friends to the Flier's Barracks in Northtown. He walked just behind the rest of them, watching the katze with his dry, restless eyes.

This seems too simple, he thought. *Why now, and why us?*

"When was the last time you were in the Citadel, Ragnar?" Cain asked.

"Hmph," Rangar said. "It's been years, my friend. I think last time I was here was when we incinerated that nest of varqors."

"Incinerated?" Cain scoffed. "You and I remember that day a little differently."

"What's a varqor?" Dawn asked.

"Scary creatures," Ragnar said. "Just one of their teeth is probably bigger than the thief's head."

"We got lucky on that job," Cain recalled. "We patrolled around the eastern coast of Cirrane and we fell into their nest. You could hardly have seen the hole in the ground even if you knew it was there. We fell a long way before hitting the bottom and finding the nest to be wiped out already."

Dawn gasped. "What happened to them? Was it another reaver?"

"I think they smelled Cain coming and they all killed themselves rather than face the stench," Ragnar grinned. "You've caught a whiff of this guy after he's been on a hunt for a few days, right?"

"Oh, yeah," Dawn chuckled. "Mighty distracting when our lives are in the balance."

"You're one to talk!" Cain said.

"Hey!" Dawn snapped, straightening her back and feigning an eloquent arrogance. "I am a lady. You shouldn't speak about my aroma like that."

Krom walked behind the company, listening as they passed back and forth light-hearted insults. Cain and Ragnar seemed to talk like they had never separated. They laughed together like brothers who hadn't seen each other in a few weeks. Dawn was just the younger sister, trying to push herself into the jokes. Krom loved that about her. She passed herself off as a recluse ever since she lost her family, but she would give anything to be involved. More than that, she would do anything to ensure her friends were happy.

Of course, she didn't need to help Cain and Ragnar find joy. They couldn't make it through two sentences without breaking out in laughter. Their infectious joy even made Krom smirk a bit.

Pegasus flew high overhead. Krom noticed a jet black

pegasus flying alongside them; Mae's pegasus. *Back to work so soon after what happened?* He had a begrudging respect for his Hilios teammates. They may work for the Council, but they had a work ethic that was unmatched by any of the other Council workers.

"I need a word with Commander Silas," Cain demanded from the guard at the front of the barracks. "Reaver business."

The guard didn't even hesitate. He simply slipped inside the door, leaving Krom's friends outside to be watched by the fliers overhead. Krom caught himself eyeing each corner nearby, watching for unfriendly eyes. He would never let someone get the jump on him again. His fingers fiddled with the hilt of the sword clipped to his waist.

Silas swung open the doors to the barracks with his sword already drawn. Cain jumped back, placing himself in between his friends and the commander.

After seeing his teammates Silas slid his sword back in its sheath, exhaling a sigh of relief. "Sorry. You can't be too careful these days..."

Cain eased himself. Krom noticed the air suddenly become warmer. *He's so powerful.*

"There is nothing to forgive, friend."

Silas peered past Cain to Ragnar, who leaned up against the side of the building with arms crossed. "Who's your friend?"

Cain's eyes widened. "You've never met Ragnar?"

Silas shrugged. "A reaver friend I'm guessing?"

Cain nodded. "Silas, we need your help..."

Krom made his way toward Ragnar, allowing Cain to

explain their situation to Silas. Ragnar didn't even bother to look at him. He simply gazed upward to the pegasus riders overhead. "What do you want, thief?"

Krom closed his eyes and exhaled a forceful breath. "I know we don't have the greatest history..."

This seemed to capture Ragnar's attention. He glanced down at Krom, who felt like a bug beneath the katze's gaze.

"You said you succeeded in retaking Oasis from the Guild."

Ragnar nodded.

"There was a member of the Guild... Someone who I am close with..."

"Ask your question."

Krom took a breath. "Director Haze. Is he dead?"

Ragnar chuckled beneath his breath. "If he is, then it happened after we took the city. Your Director escaped my axe. I have a hard time imagining him being dead, though. That man is a cockroach. He finds a way to survive anything."

Krom sighed. "Thank you, Ragnar."

He wasn't sure why he cared. Haze wanted Krom dead. He had tried to kill Krom on countless occasions. He was family, though. The only true relative Krom had left. Even if he hated the man, he wanted him alive.

The katze smiled back with his big, cat-like teeth. "Not that I wouldn't have killed him if I had the chance. I didn't stay my hand. It wasn't an act of mercy."

"Of course," Krom smiled. "I wouldn't expect anything different."

*　*　*

Dawn listened as Cain explained the plan to Silas. She

doubted Silas would go through with it. With all the chaos in the city, he couldn't risk abandoning his post for a week.

"This orc-lord," Silas started. "Some sort of tyrant?"

"He is," Cain replied. "Wants to war against all of humanity, claiming humankind as slaves to the orcs and goblins."

Silas scratched his chin. "Does Taran know of this?"

Cain shook his head.

After a moment of thought, Silas pulled a whistle from his pocket and blew on it. Suddenly, the fliers overhead dove toward the small gathering on the front steps of the barracks. A squad of five fliers, led by Mae and her jet-black pegasus, landed, surrounding the group. Dawn stumbled backwards, watching Ragnar place a paw on his axe.

"Mae!" Silas shouted. "Tonight, our squad goes with the reavers to Quarrine. Make the arrangements, but keep it quiet. The Council is not to know about this mission yet."

"Sir?" Mae responded. "We're keeping secrets from the Council?"

"They'll know eventually," Silas said. "Better to ask for forgiveness than permission, I think." He smiled at Cain. "We will leave tonight. Meet us in Barlo on Fourteenth Street, when the moon is highest in the sky."

The fliers gathered under the jet-black sky. As Dawn gazed upward, the lack of stars gave her pause. She had never seen anything like it. It wasn't like the clouds were covering the glimmering gems. The sky was clear, the stars just hadn't emerged this night.

"How is your arm feeling?" Cain asked her. Ragnar was clearing a strategy with Silas, causing the rest of them to wait under the cover of night. Remy and Mae chatted near a nearby alleyway while the two others, gentlemen named Maxie and Selvin, lounged against storefronts.

"It's alright," Dawn held her arm tightly with her good hand. "Just need to give it some rest."

Cain's countenance fell. "Just say the word, D. One word, and I send Ragnar off with the fliers. I will stay back with you. We can relax and eat some good food while we wait for Ephras' anniversary."

Dawn shook her head. "I can't let you do that, Cain. Ragnar needs you. Oasis needs you. We can take care of ourselves for a week. I will handle things over here."

"With one hand?" Cain smiled.

Dawn rolled her eyes. "Yes. With one hand."

"And she won't be alone!" Krom rushed up. "You forget that Dawn has a support system, Cain. Krom the Incredible! Ain't nothing that'll get past me."

Cain laughed, looking to Dawn. "I can take him back to Quarrine with me too, if you want. Might make it easier for you."

Krom punched Cain on the arm, but a small chuckle escaped his lips. He often used jokes and laughter as a mask. Something to hide his pain. Dawn could usually notice when he did though.

"Alright," Silas shouted. "That decides it. We should arrive after a full day of flying. We rest for the day, and invade the next night, covered by the darkness. The mission should be complete by morning, where we rendezvous outside the city and fly back to the Citadel. On this schedule, we will be back in time for the memorial."

"Seems like we will actually have time to spare," Cain said. "I like the sound of it. Let's see if we can make it happen."

Silas snapped his fingers and all the fliers under his command mounted their pegasus. Ragnar found his way atop his own beast, grimacing at Cain to follow suit.

Cain gave one last look to Dawn. "Take care of yourself, D."

Without another word, he climbed to the top of his pegasus. Silas whistled and the fliers took to the air, gliding through the sky toward Quarrine.

Dawn and Krom didn't speak again. They didn't need to. A tear rolled recklessly down Dawn's cheek. Krom placed his arm around her and pulled her close, guiding her home through the city streets. Krom walked Dawn all the way to her home in the Midtown District of the Citadel before they finally parted ways.

VI

The Rusted Hammer

Dawn found sleep difficult that night. The sight of Cain flying off with the other fliers haunted her mind.

It shouldn't, she thought. *It's only for a week. I can handle things on my own for a week.*

But for some reason this felt different. When she watched her dad leave their hut almost two years ago, barreling out the door to take on their attackers, she had thought she would see him again too. Life was always a question. No one could predict what the next day would bring. Not even a sorcerer as powerful as Cain.

She found herself plotting along on her lute. Even with an arm broken, she managed to find the dexterity to pick at the strings with some accuracy. She had bought it after her first substantial payment from a reaver hunt. It wasn't anything special, but it satisfied her craving for music. Chord after chord she played through the night, her fingers aching, until the sunlight peeked through her window.

Once the morning came, she moved to the living area where the book, *The Great Cataclysm,* lay on her table. Cain had assigned her to read the hulking manuscript early on in her reaver training. So much information about the Fallen in one single book. She yanked the pages open to a marked page and began to read:

Seor's armies were relentless. Disgusting beasts of all kinds. Some were small like children with blades for hands, others were walking mountains. Seor's gateways to the Other could appear anywhere, even within the walls of fortified cities. Human defenses offered nothing against a threat from Hell itself. Fos saw this. He watched from his throne in the Other as the Banished God moved his sights from control of the Other to control of the physical realm. Fos didn't often involve himself in the trials of men, but they could not deal with the otherworldly threat on their own. So Fos created three extensions of his spirit; one living being for each of the four islands. Kreu made his home in the forests of Napora. Krius resides above the clouds in the mountains of Ardglas. And Kytas dwells in the caverns of Quarrine. These Titans used their power to hold back the Fallen army, not allowing any new portals to the Other while they lived. Seeing the outer islands safe, Fos remained in Cirrane, making a throne for himself to sit upon where he would be able to go back and forth between the Other and the physical realm.

No one has seen Fos on this plane of existence for thousands of years, but people have made his throne the center of the human government in the White Islands. To this day, the Citadel is still the hub for all things spiritual. Nations from every island make their pilgrimage to the Citadel as a rite of passage into their faith.

Kytas. Dawn ruminated on the name. According to the history that Cain had taught her, this was a piece of Fos himself. An embodiment of his spirit. An extension of God.

And she killed it.

Whenever she asked Cain about that day he would clam up. The idea of his god being killed, and by a mortal, was an uncomfortable topic for him. Was God really God if a mortal could make him bleed?

Dawn's stomach churned. She slammed the book closed and tossed it to the table so she could make breakfast. Cain had taught her quite a bit about the art of cooking, but she still had a lot to learn. The way he prepared a meal was like watching an artist paint on their canvas. She snapped her fingers, lighting a flame to quickly boil water and tossed in a few different vegetables and seasonings. Seasonings were foreign to her, none of them being native to Quarrine. Many of the spices that were sold in the Market District came from Napora, the southernmost island controlled by the White Council. Home of the wood elves.

There was a knock at the door. Dawn jumped, nearly knocking over her pot of soup. *Krom has his own key,* she thought. *Who else could be here?*

She snuck to the living area and gripped her sword in her good hand. She peeked outside through the front window, but vision of the door was blocked by a growing bush on her doorstep. Hesitantly she approached the door, her mind racing through the worst possibilities of what could be waiting on the other side.

"Dawn! Are you in there?" The voice was Kaela's.

Dawn felt a relief wash over her, placing her sword back in its sheath and laying it on a seat in the living area. "Yeah!" Dawn shouted back. "Give me just a second!"

Swiftly, Dawn maneuvered to the front door and unlocked it. Kaela waited on the other side, her countenance distraught. "Did you know?" She shouted as she pushed past Dawn into her home.

"By all means, Kaela," Dawn groaned. "Come right in."

"They just left!" Kaela continued. "All of them! No word to the Council. No word to the peacekeepers. They all just left, and in the middle of a civil war!"

"Civil war?" Dawn mocked.

"Be serious, Dawn!" Kaela snapped. "What could have possessed them to leave at a time like this?"

"Who?"

"Cain!" Kaela shouted. "Silas and his squad of fliers!"

"Oh, them."

Kaela shot a glare at Dawn. "So, you did know."

"Yeah, I knew," Dawn sighed, shutting the door behind her. "They had important things to do in Quarrine and Cain couldn't do it on his own. Silas and his fliers will help him get there and back quicker."

"And you let them go?"

"I pushed them to go," Dawn quipped. "Kaela, Quarrine is my home. If there is a chance to make something good happen over there, I am going to push for it."

"Then why didn't you go instead?"

Silence filled the air between them. Dawn's heart sunk to the pit of her stomach.

"I guess you'll just have to fill in for Cain while he's gone," Kaela said, breaking the quiet. "You're a reaver now, right? It's your duty."

Dawn sighed. "Why do you need a reaver?"

"It's a time of civil unrest, Dawn," Kaela rolled her eyes. "And the peacekeepers are spread thin. With the fliers being on duty every day to watch the city from the skies, we need all the support we can get. Reavers are servants of the Council and have a duty to the Citadel."

Dawn scowled at Kaela, knowing there was more to her anxiety.

"Fine!" Kaela admitted. "I have a lead in the Outrider investigation and all the other peacekeepers, at least the ones I trust won't hold me back, are on duty today. I need the backup from someone I trust. You guys... I mean... You and Cain..." She trailed off.

Dawn couldn't hide her smirk. "I'm happy to help. Would you like some soup before we go?"

Kaela slumped her head. With a nod and a soft smile, she poured herself a bowl and sat with Dawn at the table.

* * *

"This is it."

Kaela led Dawn through the Market District, wary of

Dawn's arm still slung in a wrap. Even in her current state she was a reaver, and reavers were supposed to be the best. She had defended herself after the attack on the Hilios Championship, and she was just as broken then. They arrived at a building with a sign hanging on the doorframe: *The Rusted Hammer Mercantile*.

"Really?" Dawn scoffed. "This is the place you need backup for?"

The outside of the building was hardly intimidating, but Kaela had regulations to follow. "You should always have backup, Dawn," she said. "When you go in alone, people die."

The comment struck like a spear to the heart. "I thought we were past all this?" Dawn's voice quivered.

"I..." Kaela sighed. "I'm sorry. Ephras' anniversary is so close. It's bringing out some pretty fresh emotions."

Kaela had noticed the change in herself over the last year. There were times when her words would escape before she had any time to actually think through their consequences. That was how she was before she became a peacekeeper. She had thought of herself as witty, but Ephras revealed that she was actually just reckless. He had helped her change her ways.

"I wish I could go back to that day," Dawn whispered, staring at the cobblestone street. "Go back and change what happened."

"Me too." The wind whistled between the buildings, rattling the sign against the door where it hung. "I am going to go inside. Just stand out here and keep watch. Holler if you see or hear anything that seems funky. I'll give a shout if I need help inside."

Kaela entered the shop. Inside was a small room with very few people in it. Vibrant blue rugs adorned the floor, colored by brilliant foreign designs. Four tables with merchandise laid out atop; jewels, cloth, and works of literature, stood throughout the room while the owner sat on a stool behind a bar along the back wall.

Taking a deep breath, Kaela closed her eyes, concentrating and whispering a short prayer. She felt the weight of her spear acutely on her back, as well as the short sword hanging on her hip. Suddenly, with her eyes still closed, she could see the store begin to radiate with life. Each person browsing the tables emanated an aura of their own specific color; some swirled with greens and blues, while others glowed a bright yellow or orange. Kaela could also see the lingering puffs of people who had been nearby recently.

Ephras had trained Kaela in the Sight for years before he died. He had even been able to identify who had been in a room based solely on the aura that was left behind. Kaela hadn't been able to do that yet, but she practiced whenever she could.

He was so much better than me, she thought. *I need to be better. For him.*

Kaela opened her eyes, removing the aura from her sight. The man sitting in the back of the store focused on her as she browsed the tables. She picked up a small emerald brooch and fiddled with it in her fingers while covertly scanning the rest of the store. A carving of a circle with a line cut through the center was scratched into the wall near the back corner by a set of stairs.

Exactly what she was looking for.

She turned to see the owner had stood up from his chair. A scar extended across the length of his scruffy face. Kaela closed her eyes again.

"Excuse me, miss?" The man asked, approaching the table Kaela had been browsing. "Can I help you find anything?"

Kaela stretched her hands up, grazing the handle of her spear with her fingers as she made eye contact with the man. "Actually, you can." Quickly, Kaela kicked up against the table, flipping it over onto the store's owner. Screams erupted from the other patrons as they rushed out the front door. Kaela pulled the spear from its home on her back and pressed it against the trapped man's throat, intentionally not using any magic against him. "I need some information, and you are going to give it to me. Who is in charge of the Outriders organization."

* * *

Dawn leaned against the building across the street from *The Rusted Hammer*, massaging her arm. She whispered a prayer under her breath to emit a frost from her hand that iced the healing muscles.

She had a hard time recalling life without Fos' magic. It had only been a year of true practice, but that was enough time to completely change her worldview. She could heat a cup of water to cleanse it, and cool it again within the minute. Cain always warned her not to waste magic on simple things, but to save it for when the fight comes.

It's just too convenient though, she thought. *I should be icing my arm anyways.*

She wasn't sure what she was supposed to be doing to support Kaela. It had now been a few minutes since people ran out the front door, but when Dawn peeked inside, Kaela seemed to still have control of the situation. So she waited. Down the road, a group of children shared a loaf of bread. The tallest one, Dawn figured the eldest of the bunch, ripped pieces off to give to the younger ones. Their eyes met with Dawn's, but she averted her gaze.

"They starve on crumbs while the Council feasts in their magnificent temples," Dawn's Reflection whispered in her ear. "Justice is a foreign concept."

Shouts echoed around the corner. Dawn pushed off the wall and turned her back on the mercantile shop, curiously making her way through the street. A block over, a crowd gathered around a wooden makeshift stage. A man stood atop the stage, shouting down to the congregating citizens.

"Mountains only move if you are willing to pick up a spade!" The man preached. "A movement starts with a single act! Someone has to be the first to step out and do what is necessary. Something that no one else is willing to do! This is the gift that the Outriders have given us. They have lit the spark of change and we need to be the kindling that becomes the fire which will blaze through the city. We can continue their work right now, one sorcerer at a time, until a new world is formed, molded by our hands! A world where magic is absent, just as it should be."

As he spoke, a large masked man pulled a prisoner onto

the stage, throwing him to the wooden floor. Chains dangled around his hands and feet, tears rolling down his cheek. He tried to speak but only released uncontrolled sobs.

And the crowd cheered.

"The street priests are the first line of defense of the oppressive White Council! One at a time, we will take their lives until the Council is forced to release their hold on the people!"

What!

Dawn wasn't sure if it was her own voice in her head, or her Refection's outburst. She watched from the back of the crowd as the masked headsman yanked the priest to the front of the stage, pushing him to his knees and placing his head on a block with a basket set up beneath.

The crowd roared. They chanted in unison, cheering for the exhilarated speaker. Dawn couldn't hear a single opposition. Not one person wanted this man to live. What had he done that was so wrong? Was this all because he was a priest of the Council's religion? Had he ever actually done any harm to these people?

The headsman grabbed a massive two-handed longsword from a sheath at the back of the stage; the largest sword Dawn had ever seen. The speaker kept his foot on the priest's back, holding him down against the block while the headsman lined up the sword with the prisoner's neck.

And the crowd continued their chants.

"No," Dawn mumbled under her breath.

The sword raised high in the air.

"STOP!"

Suddenly, everything was still. Not even the wind was blowing anymore along the city street. The headsman's sword froze in the air. Suspended in time.

Dawn felt her breath intensify in her chest. She watched from behind the frozen crowd, waiting for time to resume, but it never did. She looked around and noticed the plants hanging in the surrounding window sills draining their color, fading to a lifeless gray.

Out of the corner of her eye, she noticed her Reflection pushing its way through the crowd. It made eye contact with each person as it made its way closer to the stage. Strangely, Dawn felt like she could see what her Reflection saw, as well as what she could see watching from behind the crowd. She saw the whites of each frightened citizen's eyes.

Before she could think, her Reflection jumped on the stage, releasing a powerful blast of energy into the headsman, as well as the speaker. Both of them flew backwards off the stage. The headsman's sword stayed frozen in the air as her Reflection moved the priest from the block and pushed him away from the execution.

Dawn watched in awe at her Reflection's concise movements. She grasped the giant sword from the air and strode toward the speaker and the headsman. Dawn could feel the weight of the sword in her broken, aching hand.

She strode forward calmly. Then, with a single stroke, the giant sword fell through the headsman's body, cutting him clean in half. Dawn gasped, throwing herself backward away from the gore. Her Reflection swung again, cutting through the preacher. Their bodies released from the freezing spell as the pieces fell to the floor.

"No!" Dawn shouted, her voice reverberating between the buildings.

Her Reflection's calm eyes met hers from across the crowd. "I am the sword you wish you could swing," it whispered in Dawn's ear. "That priest would have died if I hadn't interfered."

"You killed them..." Dawn trembled.

"You have killed without my help before, Dawn. Why do you care for these men? These murderers?"

"I..." Dawn paused. She couldn't quite put it into words. She just knew that it was wrong. The men had no chance to fight back. They weren't put on trial. There was no question. They just died.

But the priest was alive.

"You wanted the priest to be saved. Now he is." Dawn noticed that her Reflection had released the priest from the freezing spell and he was now long gone. "I did as you wished, and this is the thanks I get?"

Suddenly, Dawn was no longer behind the crowd watching the carnage. Instead, she stood over the two dismembered bodies, the heavy sword slipping from her aching fingers and clanging against the road. Her Reflection disappeared and the crowd returned to life. She could feel their eyes on her. Silence lingered in the air.

***

Kaela swung open the door to *The Rusted Hammer*, sliding a note into her breast pocket. Behind her, she left the owner alive, but unconscious, among the disastrous mess of his shop. She couldn't help but to smile.

Her grin quickly faded. Looking up, she saw an empty street. She looked left and right, but not a single soul gathered near the shop. All the civilians had evacuated, but she didn't know where.

Most concerning, Dawn had disappeared too.

She pulled her spear off her back. Closing her eyes and whispering a prayer, the street burst with color. Dawn's aura stretched from the place she lingered outside the store down an alleyway nearby. Eyes still closed, Kaela crept to the alley, her white knuckles wrapped around her spear.

Suddenly, she didn't need the aura anymore. Shouts echoed from the end of the alleyway; angry voices screaming profanity and curses. She burst out the other end of the alley, the crowd in front of her shining brilliantly with all sorts of colors. Each aura seemed to darken as the people grew angrier. She looked past the crowd, shocked to see Dawn on the other side with two dead men lying next to her.

Kaela's eyes snapped open. For a moment, she thought she saw Dawn's aura in two different places, one aura significantly darker than Dawn's normal aura. Opening her eyes revealed she was just seeing things.

I still have a lot to learn. She thought. *I am sure this never happened to Ephras.*

She couldn't say for sure, though. Ephras loved to teach her all about magic, but never talked much about his own experiences. It was hard to think that he ever struggled as much as she did.

Kaela exhaled a forceful sigh, squeezing tight around the

shaft of her spear. She knew more bloodshed would only do more damage. Two deaths was already too many.

She pushed hard into the crowd, tossing people to the cobblestone street. The shouting only grew louder as she approached the reaver who continued to stand over the bodies, her shock visible in her eyes.

The crowd quickly realized that Kaela was a peacekeeper and their shouts turned to action. One after another they swung their arms and fists toward her, but she ducked and twirled through the people. She dragged the point of her spear against the street, grabbing at ankles and tossing people to the floor. She sped up her cadence, crashing through bodies, until there was nobody between her and Dawn.

"Let's go!" Kaela shouted, shaking the stunned reaver back to reality. Dawn startled like she snapped back from a nightmare. "We will deal with this later! You have to go!"

She grabbed Dawn by the collar and pulled her down an alley, the crowd rushing after them. Kaela shoved Dawn ahead, turning to the oncoming mob with her spear. "Go to the Market District Precinct. I'll meet you there."

Dawn finally regained her mental state and nodded, taking off between the buildings. Kaela readied herself as their attackers approached. She swung her spear in front of her, blunt end out. The wooden handle smacked the rioters on their heads. If the blunt attack didn't knock them out, it slowed them enough for Kaela to focus her attention on another. She continued to swing as more and more attackers flooded the alleyway, but the length of her spear kept the distance between them.

With a final push, she poked a rioter in the chest and

turned down the alleyway again. She ran between buildings, knocking over boxes and crates that were stacked nearby the back doors to shops, slowing her pursuers. She found a larger stack of crates and climbed to the top, jumping onto the roof of the building on her right. With her spear she pushed on the crates, causing them to tumble to the ground.

She stood atop the building and looked out over the city, choosing the best path to the peacekeeper precinct.

* * *

Dawn gazed around the precinct. The workers buzzed around her in a scurry, but she hardly even noticed. The bodies of the two men, split in two, tormented her mind.

"You have killed before, Dawn," her Reflection whispered in her mind. Dawn couldn't always see her dark apparition, but it was always with her. "Why does the death of these men bother you so much?"

Dawn couldn't pinpoint why. Her Reflection was right. She had killed many people before. Always evil people. Ready to kill. She thought about the soldiers that crucified the family outside the Great Canyon Pass. She was ready to kill every one of them for the atrocity they committed.

The front doors to the station slammed open and Kaela stomped inside. "So you did make it," she scowled, glaring at Dawn.

"Thank you, Kaela..."

"Thank me?" Kaela interrupted. "*THANK ME?* For what? For stopping a riot? How about for stopping a murder? Oh no, wait. I think I was a little late for that."

"They were going to execute a priest!"

"So you executed them instead?" Kaela's words stung. "That crowd was going to kill you. Does that mean I should have murdered them? Dawn, you started a riot in the city..."

"Those men started the riot!"

Their shouts were silenced by Kaela's captain striding into the room. He didn't need to raise his voice to make his presence known. "Kaela, what is this I am hearing about a riot in the streets?"

Kaela glanced back and forth between Dawn and her captain. "Captain Belvin," she said. "Outriders staged the execution of a priest in the Market District. The executioners were killed, but the gathering mob became angry. I had to silence them by force."

Belvin rubbed his temples and shook his head. "This city is standing on the edge of a knife right now, Kaela. One move in the wrong direction and the scale will be tipped and our entire city will be at war."

"I know, Cap..."

"And you are going around today attacking civilians?"

"It wasn't her!" Dawn interrupted. "She was getting information about the Outriders."

"Quiet, Dawn!" Kaela snapped. She looked back to Belvin. "I know that today's events were unacceptable, and I take full responsibility. I was able to get Dawn out and escape without any more loss of life."

"Sir!" A peacekeeper trainee barged into the conversation. "They are looting in the Flier's Market!"

Belvin growled. "Take a team and do what you can to stop the violence. No more death today, private. Do you hear me?" He turned back to Kaela. "So, you take responsibility?"

"I..." Kaela paused. "It doesn't make up for anything, but I got information about the Outriders leader."

Belvin raised an eyebrow.

"His name is Tarik, and he lives in the Midtown District. My informant tells me that he hasn't been to his home in months, but he still operates primarily out of Midtown."

Belvin grunted. "I guess today isn't all a loss," he smiled. "We can move our operations to Midtown from here on out. Good job Kaela. Now get out there and placate those riots."

Without another word, Belvin nodded to Dawn and strolled back to the other peacekeepers.

"What are you thinking?" Kaela snapped at Dawn under her breath. "If they learn that you're the one who swung the blade, you'll be arrested on the spot for murder."

Dawn shivered. She would have been imprisoned just like Maron, not knowing when the Council would release her. It hadn't even been twenty-four hours since Cain left, and already she almost plunged the city into chaos while finding herself behind bars.

"You need to keep your head down, D," Kaela continued, starting towards the door. "It's my fault for coming to you. I guess I just forgot.

"Forgot?"

"When you get involved, people die."

Dawn clenched her teeth. "I guess I will just go home and stay there, then. Sorry."

"What?" Kaela stopped, stunned. "You can't go home. It isn't safe. You have to stay here."

"For you to babysit me?

"For us to protect you!"

"No thanks," Dawn sighed, shaking her head. "I don't need your pity, and being here around people who think so little of me doesn't exactly sound like the greatest use of my time. Don't worry, I'll keep my head down."

Before Kaela had a chance to speak, Dawn turned and slammed through the front doors. She turned down the street toward the Midtown District, her Reflection watching from a rooftop nearby.

VII

The Butcher of Midtown

Dawn gnashed her teeth, racing through the streets back toward her home. Why had she even gone out to help Kaela? It wasn't her responsibility as a reaver to lend assistance to the peacekeepers. Just because Cain had, did that mean she had to?

If I hadn't pushed him to go, she thought, *he would have been able to help, and I could have just stayed away.*

The streets were mostly empty as she hailed a coach to take her home. It made sense, after all the chaos of the last few days. Especially with the riots just a couple blocks away, most people *should* be staying home. It was the safe thing to do.

"You weren't born to stay safe," her Reflection's voice buzzed in her mind. "Those who are destined for greatness will always find their way out of isolation."

"Krom was right," Dawn whispered to herself. "There is nothing wrong with a life of boredom. Peace and quiet."

Dawn's Reflection materialized next to her, sitting in the back of the dirty cab. "Peace and quiet will have you living as the subject of beings who are greater than you. People who go out of their way to achieve greatness. To change the world, for better or for worse." It disappeared and materialized in front of Dawn. "How do you think Councilman Taran got so much power?"

Dawn waved her hands and her Reflection evaporated like a puff of smoke. "I don't care about other people's power. I just want to keep people safe."

"And how will you do that while shut up inside your home?" Her Reflection was no longer visible, but her voice still resounded in Dawn's mind.

As the sun began to set, the coach continued toward her home, letting her out in front of the stairs that led to her front door. She paused, gazing up at the building. Memories flooded her mind of that day nearly a year ago. So much had changed since then. She was more powerful, yet she still felt so weak.

Each step to climb the stairs was a negotiation. Sharp pains shot up and down Dawn's arm as she reached out to unlock her door.

But it was already unlocked.

* * *

Kaela expelled a force of wind, shoving the rioters back against the wall of the closest building. More charged at her from the opposite side, but she swung her blunt staff at them, knocking one on the head and forcing the others to slow their approach. Commander Belvin had ordered the peacekeepers to respond with no deadly weapons to try and prevent any bloodshed. Kaela was beginning to think that was a mistake.

"Death to the religious elite!" The crowds chanted as they threw stones into the surrounding windows. "Freedom in the Citadel!" She watched as a wall of unwashed and unshaven surged over two Market District peacekeepers. Soon, blood sprayed from beneath their feet and as the surge moved onward, the peacekeepers didn't get back up.

Rioters climbed in through the shattered windows of shops in the Flier's Market and ransacked the stores. They pulled magical gloves over their hands and armed themselves with the blessed bows of the Hilios fliers. Kaela cursed as a light arrow charged with electricity for incapacitation latched onto her ribs, forcing her to her knees.

Dulin came to her aid, holding up a door that had been ripped from its hinges as a shield to guard her from any more arrows. Once the electricity subsided, Kaela found her way back to her feet. She was so tired. Not only physically, but mentally. The last few days sat heavy on her shoulders. She wondered if she should have just stayed down. Stayed on the ground and waited for the madness to pass, if it ever did.

Three men smashed another window and climbed inside. But this wasn't a store. The rioters had broken into someone's home! Kaela exploded in that direction, shouting a prayer to blast herself through the same window without allowing the glass shards to cut her. She didn't know if Dulin would follow her, but at this point, she wasn't sure that mattered.

Inside, the rioters had already found the home's inhabitants.

An older woman and her daughter. Kaela recognized the woman as the street priestess Calla, which meant this was her twelve year old daughter Naomi.

The rioters tossed Calla across the room and she smacked her head against the corner of an end table. Naomi tried to run away from them, but in such close quarters she just wasn't fast enough.

"Let her go!" Kaela shouted, white knuckles wrapped around her blunt staff. She would never leave her spear behind again.

"Death to the religious elite!" One of the men bellowed back.

"Last warning," Kaela commanded. "Let her go and leave this place."

The man holding Naomi reached for a sheath on his waist, revealing a silver dagger. Kaela cursed, gripping her staff like a javelin and hurling it into the rioter's chest. She followed close behind and tackled the man to the floor, freeing Naomi from his grasp as they tumbled together.

Kaela planted her fist into the man's face as he cut upwards with the silver knife. She caught his arm and grabbed him by his wrist, slamming it back into the ground as she maneuvered her knee to his throat. With one jerking motion, the man's neck snapped under her weight and the dagger fell free.

Before Kaela could grasp the dagger, one of the other rioters ran past, kicking her in the head. Kaela blacked out for a moment, rolling off of the deceased man and onto her back. When her vision returned to her, the rioter was standing over her with the knife in his hands.

She screamed a prayer and sent a magnificent force of wind out in every direction. The man launched backwards, giving Kaela time to find her footing and locate her staff. She pulled the blunt weapon to her with a reverse gust of wind and turned toward the two remaining rioters.

They trembled before her. Belvin hadn't told them they couldn't use magic, but Kaela knew that she just proved, in the rioter's minds, that their actions were legitimate. Awful and unethical in every way, but legitimate.

Too late to change that now, Kaela thought. She whispered another prayer and started tossing random items across the room with more magic. The rioters tried to dodge out of the way of the magical onslaught and ran to the window of the house, jumping back outside into the fray.

Kaela rushed over to the unconscious Calla, where Naomi was also hiding nearby, and checked her pulse. Still beating, though that head wound was bleeding worse than she would have liked. Kaela rummaged through the room until she found a hand towel and pressed it against the priestess's head, slowing the blood flow.

Screams echoed from outside; blood curdling and deadly screams. The sounds of chaos still called out through the window, but instead of cries of revolt she heard cries of terror. She tied the towel tight to Calla's head with some nearby cloth and went to the window to investigate.

The Sacred Order had arrived.

The armored soldiers spared no time before beginning the carnage. They had come with swords already drawn and ready for blood. The rioters ran in all different directions, trying to avoid the fates that awaited them. Soon, the streets were littered with dead bodies and the Flier's Market was subdued again.

Kaela looked out over the massacre, dumbfounded. These were the people she was supposed to protect. All killed in a matter of moments.

"The White Council is dispatching Sacred Order all over the city," Dulin said, limping over to Kaela's window. His leg bled from a large gash on his lower thigh. "I guess riots like this are happening everywhere right now."

Kaela shook her head. "This isn't good, Dulin. This is going to make the Market District a war zone."

"It's not just the Market," Dulin said. "It's all the districts. Anvar just told me about something happening in Midtown."

Shock filled Kaela's thoughts. "Where in Midtown?"

* * *

Dawn thought back to the morning when she and Kaela left, trying to remember if she had locked her door. She shrugged, strolling slowly inside.

Darkness encased her home. Quiet filled her ears. She unclipped her sword and dropped it by the door, snapping a finger. Oil lamps on the walls burst to life, dimly lighting the room. Flames cast shadows that flickered throughout her living area. She slumped to her couch and started on the laces holding up her boots. She never should have left that morning. She should have taken after Krom and just stayed home, enjoying the time alone. Enjoying the isolation.

The floor creaked. Dawn snapped to attention, staring towards the kitchen of her small apartment.

It must have been the people upstairs, she thought. But she continued to stare. She glanced to the front door, eyeing her sword that leaned against the wall.

The flames continued to flicker, casting their shadows. Dawn noticed one shadow that seemed... unnatural. Almost human-like.

She jumped up, whispering a prayer and launching a blast of wind toward her kitchen. She didn't wait to see the results of her attack. Instead, she rushed to the door, reaching for her sword.

The door burst open in splinters, two swordsmen swarming into Dawn's home. They both swung at her but she leapt backwards, just out of reach of their blades. She dropped to the floor, kicking at one man's feet and tripping him while shooting a blast of lightning into the other man's chest. Before his sword could fall from his lifeless hands, Dawn had already plucked it into her own.

The other swordsman jumped back to his feet, two more revealing themselves from the kitchen. Dawn held her weapon in front of her, pressing her broken arm close to her body.

The initial swordsman shouted, charging into the living area toward Dawn. She slashed her sword upwards into his, dancing around him so that all her attackers were in front of her.

"Stop playing around!" One of the invaders shouted. "She is dangerous!"

You're right. I am dangerous, Dawn grinned. She whispered

a prayer and a current of electricity encased her hands, emanating around her sword.

All three invaders charged at once. She ducked and rolled out of the way, sending another bolt of lightning into the nearest enemy. *That's two,* she thought, finding her balance again. *Halfway there.*

Suddenly, she heard windows shatter from her bedroom. She cursed under her breath, her gaze being drawn briefly by the intrusion. With her attention drawn, the two invaders rushed again. Dawn was able to dodge one of their strikes, but she was forced to throw up her sword and block the other.

He continued his barrage of attacks, not giving Dawn a chance to think about a response. She just continued to place her own sword in front of his however she could. The man gripped his sword with both hands, slamming his blade harder and harder against Dawn's defense. She could feel her arm weakening, nearly giving way to her attacker's sheer strength.

Without thinking, she pulled her other hand up to the hilt of her sword, preparing herself for the next blow. The invader's blade slammed down against her's and an excruciating pain shot through her broken arm. She cried out, sword dropping from her hands and electricity exploding throughout the room.

The swordsman continued his attack, each swing of his blade getting closer and closer to Dawn's body as she wiggled out of the way. The other invaders entered the tiny room, beginning their own assault against her. Dawn backpedaled and tripped over a footstool, falling to the floor and gazing up at her five attackers, murderous intent in their eyes.

Without a word, the lead attacker raised his blade to strike her down, but as he lifted it over his head, another blade plunged through his back. A swordsman wearing a mask flung himself between Dawn and the four remaining men.

"You will not touch her again," the man growled. His voice was familiar, but Dawn couldn't pinpoint why.

The attackers lunged forward, but they were no match for the mysterious stranger. He danced between them gracefully, cutting down one at a time. Dawn slowly found her way to her feet, snatching a sword from a fallen enemy, but it was too late. Two attackers escaped out the windows and the stranger had already struck down the remaining invaders and stood victorious in the living area.

Dawn raised her sword at the new trespasser in her home. "Who are you? Why are you here?"

The man laughed. "That is the thanks I get for saving your life? I guess some things never change."

His voice echoed in Dawn's ears, triggering memories in her mind.

"Who... Who are you?" She asked, sword held steady in front of her.

The man turned around, a mask covering his face. "I thought I told you not to go looking for trouble, kid? Seems like you've made quite a few enemies over the last year."

Dawn's breathing stopped. She lowered her sword, eyes wide. It felt like her heart could burst in anticipation. Slowly, the man raised his hand to his face and removed the mask.

Tears erupted from Dawn's eyes.

"Dad?"

VIII

Reunion

D awn fell into her father's arms, tears streaming down her face. "I waited for you!" She cried. "Right where you told me. Boar's Head Cave. I waited until it wasn't safe to wait anymore."

"I know." Drake held his daughter close, squeezing her like he would never let go again. "I am so sorry, hon. I'm here now."

Dawn nestled herself in Drake's embrace. She felt like all of her muscles had given out and all strength had left her.

She pushed away from him, gazing up into his eyes. She half expected there to be anger in his countenance. Anger because of all that had happened. Her mother's death. Cammie's death. Dawn's move to the Citadel. So much had changed. He wanted to keep her safe and she had gone and rushed into the real world. Full of danger and chaos.

But there was no anger. Drake gazed at her with love. She

could see his desire to keep her safe. Dawn felt like a child again, still growing into her adult body. Still unable to make mature decisions on her own.

"Dawn!" A woman's voice shouted from the stairwell. Dawn pushed away from her father, readying herself for another fight.

***

Kaela rushed up the stairs to Dawn's apartment. Sweat streamed from her brow to her chin. Her limbs shivered. The rumors of an attack in Midtown seemed too close to Dawn's home, and the closer she got to her apartment, the more worry filled her heart.

She ran with her eyes closed, using her Sight to seek Dawn's aura. To her dismay, as she looked up the stairs, Dawn's home was lit up with a plethora of colors. At the top of the stairs, Dawn's door was splintered on the floor. Kaela snapped her eyes open. A body lay dead atop the destroyed wood, blank eyes staring up to the ceiling. Her heart sank.

"Dawn!" She called out, pulling her staff from her back. Curses, she wished she had her spear again. She crept forward, peeking through the door. The closer she got to the apartment, the more bodies she saw on the inside. Taking a deep breath, she jumped through the doorway. Two figures stood in the living area, swords ready.

Kaela lowered her staff, the tension in her body releasing all at once. "Thank the maker," she exhaled. "Dawn, I am so glad to see you are okay." Kaela glanced at the stranger standing next to Dawn. "A friend?"

"Kaela," Dawn gestured to the stranger. "This is my father, Drake. He saved my life tonight."

"Your father?" Kaela exclaimed, examining Drake. "I thought you were dead?"

"Only rumors," Drake smiled. "It will take more than a few bandits to kill me."

"It *was* more than bandits," Dawn laughed. "It was Ulumbra."

"Oh," Drake laughed. "In that case, maybe I should be dead."

"Don't say that!" Dawn shouted.

Kaela listened as Dawn and her father bickered back and forth. Suddenly, her attention was grasped by a mask on the ground. She recalled the drawings of the masked vigilante hanging in the precinct. The Butcher of Midtown.

"Whose is that?" Kaela asked, pointing at the mask. Drake's eyes narrowed and Kaela tightened her grip on her staff.

"Uhhhhm..." Dawn mumbled. "It's my dad's. What's this about?"

"Dawn," Kaela said. "That is the mask of the Butcher of Midtown. The vigilante that has been scouring the city. Your father is a criminal."

"Criminal is a harsh way to look at it, hon," Drake laughed. "Saving the innocent people of the Citadel from the thugs and murderers on the streets?"

"You can't stop murder with murder," Kaela snarled. Her eyes met Dawn's. "I'm so sorry Dawn, but I have to take him into custody. It's my duty."

"What?" Dawn shouted.

"He is a wanted fugitive," Kaela stated. "It's my job, D..."

"I won't fight you," Drake interrupted, sliding his sword into its sheath. "If this is what is needed, then I'll go willingly."

"Dad, no!" Dawn yelped, raising her sword toward Kaela. "I just got you back. I won't lose you again!"

Drake raised his hand to Dawn's blade and pressed it down, pulling her into an embrace. "You aren't losing me, hon. I won't be the reason my daughter is wanted by the peacekeepers. If I run, they won't leave you alone now that they know who I am. The mask was always to keep you safe."

"Then take me with you! We can run together!"

Drake smiled, placing his hand on Dawn's cheek. "Now that you know I'm here, everything will be different."

Kaela cautiously placed her staff on her back and pulled some rope from a pouch on her hip. Drake turned around and crossed his arms behind his back, allowing Kaela to tie his wrists together.

"I am so sorry, Dawn." Kaela said as she led Drake out of the house and down the stairs.

* * *

Dawn collapsed under the dimly lit lamplight, tears flowing down her cold cheeks. Her muscles felt completely limp; lifeless pieces of her body. She was so powerless. Powerless to stop her attackers. Powerless to stop Kaela. Powerless to hold onto any joy.

"You should have known," a voice said. The words may have come from her Reflection, but she wasn't sure if she had actually said them herself. "Nothing good ever really lasts. It was only a matter of time until it came crashing down again. Be glad it happened so fast."

There Dawn sat. Amongst the lifeless corpses of her attackers with her front door broken off the hinges, she sat and cried. She wouldn't have known how long she had been sitting there if it weren't for the beams of sunlight glimmering through her shattered windows.

"You really are pathetic," her Reflection took form in the room. "Life has happened. There is no spell under Fos or Seor that can turn back time. So what will you do now?"

Dawn was silent.

"Sitting here and wallowing in your own self-pity is getting us nowhere," her Reflection continued. "I can't stand to watch it anymore. Go break him and Maron out of prison. Go start another riot. Go get a cursed meat pie. I don't care. Just do something."

Dawn thought for a moment, then wiped the tears from her face and stood to her feet. She needed a friend now. Someone who wasn't her Reflection. She placed her sword in her sheath, grabbed her blessed bow to sling on her back, and made her way out of the apartment and into the streets, turning toward Northtown.

The streets were hostile. She felt as if there were enemies hiding in every shadow. Each corner was a trap waiting to be sprung. Remnants of the riots that had just recently been squashed littered the streets, coals still smoldering from the fires that had been lit. Stains from bodies that had just been removed.

More and more she saw carvings of the Outrider symbol

on the walls of the Citadel's buildings. Their influence was growing by the day.

So much had changed.

It was hardly the city she was introduced to a year ago. The life in the streets had evacuated. There were no more lively, spirited crowds. There was no more chanting for a Hilios team. She could practically taste the terror lingering in the air where it hadn't belonged just weeks earlier.

A poster caught her eye. It was large, practically taking up the space of an entire wall.

> *Due to the recent outbursts of violence, a curfew has been instated within the Gate, Midtown, Market, and Northtown Districts. Any person who is not a member of the Church of Fos must return to their homes before the sun goes down and remain in their homes until the sun comes up. Violators will be detained and held by the White Council until the threat of violence has been abolished.*

Dawn could hardly believe her eyes. She gnashed her teeth and stormed through the city until she was in the heart of Northtown. She approached a large stone building with many staircases leading upwards into multiple homes climbing high into the sky. Outside one stairway, a wooden sign hung on the wall. In nicely printed letters, it read: *Cain, the Reaver.* Underneath, scribbled in sloppy ink, it read: *and Krom, the Incredible.* A much needed smile crossed her face and she started her climb up the stairs.

Their home was only a few stories up, so it didn't take

long to ascend to the front door. Dawn raised her fist to knock, but for some reason that she couldn't explain to herself, she hesitated. She held her fist in the air just inches from the door.

Finally, she tapped on the door. A meek knock, barely enough to hear from her side of the door. She stepped back and waited, listening for movement on the other side of the door.

Silence.

She stepped forward and knocked again, this time more aggressively.

More silence.

Did Krom get up early to get something done? In her time of knowing him, he wasn't someone who rose before the sun, and generally he would prefer to stay out late than wake up early.

Maybe he is still out, she concluded. She inched over to the corner overlooking the stairs and slumped down to sit. She pulled her bow from her back and scratched at the surface of the wood, cleaning the intricate grooves carved into the design.

Thoughts of Ephras entered her mind; her first Hilios match when he bought her the bow. Even though she was now one of the most famous Hilios players in the Citadel, she had never replaced her bow with one that was more professional. She never felt like she needed it.

Sometimes she wondered if Ephras was the reason she had been so successful in Hilios. In using his bow, she allowed his spirit onto the field with her and he blessed her playing.

Of course, those thoughts never lasted long. She believed in Fos and his power, but the thoughts of spirits and ghosts were just fantasy. Death was death. There was no coming back from that.

"Now, that just can't be true," her Reflection said, knowing her thoughts. "Death didn't stop our father."

"He wasn't really dead," Dawn said. "Just because we thought he was... That doesn't mean anything."

"Oh, Dawn," her Reflection mocked. "So much you have left to understand."

Dawn continued to fiddle with her bow as she waited. Hours passed, but still she waited alone. No sign of life on the stairs. Not even the sounds of people from the streets below.

Soon the sun began to set, and still Krom was nowhere to be found. *This isn't like him*, Dawn thought. *He always wanted a boring life. Why wouldn't he come home?*

And now there was a curfew.

Dawn's heart started to race. It had now been days since she had seen Krom, and he wasn't a part of any church. While he worked with the Faithful, he was an Atheist. Would the peacekeepers have taken him into holding just for being out at night?

Dawn jumped to her feet and stormed toward the Northtown Peacekeeper Precinct.

* * *

"You can't do this!" Kaela slammed her fist on Commander Belvin's desk. "You can't punish every atheistic person for the actions of a few!"

"It's not up to me, Kaela," Belvin said, scratching a signature onto a report. "This directive comes straight from the Council."

"We can't enforce it," Kaela paced like a caged animal in the cramped office. "Isn't there anything you can do?"

Belvin shook his head, standing to his feet. "I'm sorry, Kaela. My hands are tied." He pushed past her and opened the door to the rec area.

"It's that kind of cowardice that will set this city on fire," Kaela whispered.

Belvin stopped, turning and slamming his door shut again. "You want to lead in this city one day?"

Kaela nodded, relaxing her shoulders and straightening her back.

"Then learn how to follow. Our leaders have given us simple orders. If we begin defying their rule, then others will too. That is exactly what the Outriders have done. We need to show the city that there are still some who will honor our Council and defend our people. I need your help on this, Kaela."

Kaela almost spoke back, but she just took a breath and nodded. Belvin opened the door again and led her out into the rec area, calling attention from the peacekeepers to give orders. Everyone was on duty. These people practically lived at the precinct now. Kaela was lucky to not really have family in the city because staying at the precinct didn't put her out too much, but she couldn't say the same for her teammates.

"We will be increasing our patrols during the night tenfold over the next weeks," Belvin shouted over the room. He held up a small badge that could easily fit into someone's pocket." Anyone who is out after sundown must have one of these badges on their person, otherwise it is our responsibility to apprehend them. These badges come directly from the Church of Fos. It states that a priest knows someone personally. If someone has no background in the faith, they won't have a badge and therefore must stay home."

Kaela zoned out as Belvin continued giving orders. She wondered if Ephras would have taken the orders of the White Council just because they are his leaders. He respected his role as a peacekeeper more than anyone she knew. He honored those over him, while also honoring his role as a leader of the people. More importantly, he was a leader to his family. But Kaela couldn't see her brother following through with this curfew. Just because someone was in charge didn't mean they were right.

Shouts resounded from the front of the building as Dawn crashed through the doors and stormed into the room. The peacekeepers all jumped to their feet, drawing their weapons and readying them for a fight. Kaela raced between them, holding her hands out to halt both parties.

"Where is he?" Dawn shouted. "He doesn't deserve to be in jail just because he doesn't use magic!"

Kaela placed her hand on Dawn's shoulder. "Slow down, Dawn. I can't help you if I don't know what you're talking about."

"You," Dawn scowled, brushing Kaela's hand off her shoulder. "First you arrest my father for protecting me, and now you let Krom rot in jail for doing nothing?"

Kaela turned to Belvin, who was already rummaging

through papers in a cabinet in the back of the room. "Was Krom brought in for violating curfew, Bel?"

"I don't see any records of his arrest, Captain."

Dawn's face fell, her hostility quickly turning into fear. "Then where is he?"

IX

Taken

Krom watched the pegasus riders fly off into the night. He placed his arm around Dawn and slowly guided her to her home. They didn't speak, allowing the silence to speak their emotions louder than words possibly could.

She doesn't need your advice, Cain had told him just days earlier. *She just needs a friend.* Krom knew that Dawn didn't need him to say anything. Sometimes a silent friend was the best friend a person could have.

He walked her to her home, hugged her, and parted ways. He watched her climb her stairs before turning toward Northtown and toward home. The walk back would take a while, but he still didn't try to hire a coach. Some time under the stars might be nice. There was something in him that was excited to sit at home for a day or so, not even considering leaving to go outside. With Cain being gone, he could even eat some of his landlord's expertly prepared food without any repercussions.

"'Scuse me, sir?" A rough voice feigned politeness from behind Krom. He turned to meet the stranger who stood under the flickering lamplight. He had dark skin and wore a brown leather vest over a white shirt and black trousers. "I believe I know you from somewhere."

Krom rolled his eyes. "I can give you an autograph if you supply the ink. You've caught me a little off guard."

"An autograph?" The man snickered. "What for?"

"You know me from Hilios, right?" Krom asked, slowing his breath.

"I don't think so, son," the man smiled. He hobbled toward Krom, his left leg stiff beneath him. "I think we grew up together. Back in Quarrine."

Krom narrowed his eyes, examining the stranger in the lamplight. He heard laughter. Menacing laughter, but not coming from the stranger in front of him. Suddenly, his arms were being constrained behind him. He shouted, but there was no one around to listen.

"Gag him," the man in front growled.

As he spoke, a dank cloth was shoved in Krom's mouth. He kicked and flailed his remaining limbs trying to escape, but he was overwhelmed by his attackers. He didn't know how many there were, but there was enough that he could barely move without being restrained even more.

"Take him back to the Loans Federation in the Gate District," a deep voice commanded. "They know a secret way out of the city."

Krom's eyes widened and his heart dropped. He writhed

and spit out his gag, screaming as loud as he could. Before he could form any real words there was an instant, sharp pain in the back of his head, and like a flame being smothered by a cup, the light disappeared from his eyes and he lost consciousness.

Krom jolted awake, eyes wide and breath heavy. The moon was still high in the sky. Or perhaps a full day had already passed while he was unconscious. He would never know. His hands were bound by thick twine digging a gash into his wrists. His feet were shackled, a long chain running between the two constraints so he could still walk.

"Look like the poor soul's awake," a man said. He had the same rough voice as the man from before, twisted by a strange accent. "Gotta long few days ahead'a 'im."

Krom tried to push himself to his feet, but his muscles were weak and torn. He fell back to the dirt floor beneath him.

Dirt? Krom thought to himself. Suddenly, it was like lightning struck his body. He jolted upwards and looked around at the scenery: there were six men sitting around a fire in a grouping of trees in the wilderness. *This isn't the city.*

"Who are you?" Krom demanded. "Where are you taking me?"

The men laughed. "He's got some fight in 'im, this one" another accented man said. "More like his uncle than he likes to think, I reckon."

Krom bit his tongue. If these men were sent by his uncle, then he wouldn't be able to barter with them. They were being offered so much more to retrieve him than Krom could offer for his freedom. His fame in the city wouldn't help him anymore.

"Where in Quarrine has the Director moved to, now?" The deep voice from earlier asked. "No word?"

"The Director's been waiting out the orcs in Aurora since we left," another man said. "I can't imagine they have much more fight in them. We'll pull into the port and go from there. If the Director's moved on, he'll leave a message."

The cold fall breeze bit at Krom's bare arms. His shirt was ripped and torn, barely allowing him any protection from the elements. Surrounding trees had begun dropping their colorful leaves into the wisps of wind blowing from the north.

Krom had rarely been outside of the Citadel in the year spent on Cirrane. The few times he had, it was still summer; the weather had replicated Quarrine much better. His company had also been much better then.

A howl whistled through the night. Krom's abductors snapped to attention, but the one in charge quickly reassured them. "Just the field wolves. Natives call them vargs. Shouldn't be nothin' to worry about. Tie the blout to the tree and Atreus can stand guard while we get some rest. We'll get some distance tomorrow."

Krom hardly struggled. He watched his captors wrap chains around a tree. They yanked him over and tied him snug to the trunk, hardly able to move.

The man called Atreus, a lean, skinny man, stayed awake and paced throughout the camp while the others lay down in the dirt. They pulled over rocks to use as pillows, padding them with the fallen leaves. Krom watched the night-guard until the sun came up, unable to find rest for himself. He knew he should have tried in order to preserve his energy, but his mind raced, attempting to conjure schemes to find himself free. None of his ideas were good, or even decent, but he couldn't just sit and wait to accept his fate.

Krom's captors rose with the sun. They traveled extremely light, so it didn't take long for the camp to pack up and begin the day's expedition. They pulled Krom's chains and tugged him along behind as they jogged across the Cirranian plains. The shackles around his feet tripped him over and over and one of the Quarrinians beat him each time he fell. His punishment didn't help his balance.

They ran through the day, avoiding the road. Between the trees, speeding up and down hillsides. Every now and again they would stop while one of the men lowered his head to the ground, listening for footsteps of those who might follow them. There would be no way to find them on the path they chose.

Only once did they stop for food. They tossed Krom some bread, if only to keep him upright for the rest of the day. No prisoner could keep up with their pace without sustenance. They only paused for minutes at a time before continuing through the fields.

Soon, the sun began to set again. Krom felt like his legs turning to mush. The shackles dug into his ankles. He could feel droplets of blood dripping down his feet. *Maybe this could be enough of a trail for someone to follow us,* Krom thought. It was silly. There wasn't nearly enough blood to leave a lasting mark, and the blood that was left could very well have been left by a wounded animal. He was alone.

"Get a fire going!" The commander shouted to his subordinates. It didn't take long for wood to be gathered and a flame to start. One of the men removed a bag from his back and pulled out some meat. It looked halfway spoiled, but that didn't stop them from cooking it up and scarfing it down. Krom, of course, didn't get any. He wasn't sure he would have accepted it if it was offered. Cain had ruined his pallet for bad food.

The spot they chose for camp was different from the first night. There were large stones laying all around, almost in a crescent pattern. Giant boulders gave them cover from the outside. There were hardly any trees this time, except for the one they tied Krom to.

Krom noticed Atreus sleeping while the others ate and laughed together. They wouldn't have him stand watch again, would they? He had a few hours before the others would be ready to sleep themselves, but there would be no way he could do his job effectively while running like they had that day.

Atreus was young. Very young. Krom hadn't noticed before, but this kid must have only seen fifteen years. He either hadn't been with the Guild very long, or he'd been forced to serve the Guild for his whole life. He saw the boy's face like a reflection of his own, living a life against his will.

Hours passed and the sun disappeared. The campsite was only lit up by stars and firelight. "Wake up the boy," the captain shouted. "He'll watch over the night again."

One of the men kicked Atreus in the ribs, sparking laughter from the others. He writhed on the ground for a second before jumping to his feet and bowing to the captain. He didn't speak. He didn't need to. Just the way he bowed his head to avoid eye contact told Krom everything he needed to know.

The rest of the companions laid their heads down to go to sleep, once again covering stones with fallen leaves to use as pillows. Atreus paced back and forth between the resting Guild members and the fire until each of them was snoring. Once he was sure each of them was asleep, he sat under one of the larger stones, searching for bugs and squashing them with his own rock. Krom watched him crush a few dozen, a dumb smile plastered across his pubecent face.

"Hey," Krom whispered, trying his hardest to blend his voice with the wind that slammed against the rocks. "Atreus."

The kid jumped to his feet, peering around the campsite.

"Calm down," Krom snapped, glancing at his sleeping captors. "Or you'll wake them. It would be best for you if their sleep was uninterrupted."

Atreus nodded, remaining silent.

"Come here," Krom said. "So we can talk."

Atreus shook his head violently. Maybe he was even younger than Krom had realized.

"It'll be ok, Atreus. I can't hurt you while I'm in chains. I just want to have a friendly conversation."

Atreus thought for a moment, then snuck to his feet. He tried to step silently across the campsite, but his footsteps were heavy. He sat again a few strides away from Krom, just in case.

"You know, I've been where you are," Krom whispered.

Atreus raised an eyebrow.

"My whole life, I was bullied by the Guild. I had no way out, and they treated me like dirt..."

Atreus, obviously uncomfortable, jumped to his feet, ready to run back across the campsite.

"You think about killing them!" Krom started, halting the boy in his tracks. "The only reason you don't is because you know you'll be caught. Even if you did it silently, you may still only get two, maybe three. And they won't just kill you if you are caught. It would be so much worse. You've seen the others. You wish the Guild would just kill them, out of remorse. But they're kept alive. They suffer."

"How do you know this?" Atreus finally spoke.

"I already told you," Krom said. "I was right where you are. And I can tell you that there is a way out of it all. You can have freedom."

"Only to be caught again," Atreus snapped. "Why listen to you? A prisoner? What do you know of freedom?"

Krom sighed. "I don't know anything on my own. By myself, I would still be in Quarrine, running. But once I had some people by my side, I got away from Quarrine and built a life for myself in the Citadel."

"Just to get caught again," Atreus snapped. "The Guild is always close behind."

Krom slowed down. "Atreus, do you believe in Fos?"

Atreus nodded.

"And you believe that Fos has a plan for everyone?"

Again, Atreus nodded.

"Isn't it possible that Fos brought me to Cirrane and the Citadel, only to be captured by your party, in order to give you the chance at real freedom?" Krom couldn't believe the words as he spoke them. It sounded like something Cain would say. "Fos brought us both to this moment so that we could be free. Together."

Atreus pondered this thought. It took a long while, what seemed like hours to Krom. He could see the boy praying to himself, considering this act of treachery. Krom remained silent, allowing the boy to think.

Finally, Atreus turned. "What's your plan, then?"

Krom couldn't help the smile on his face. "The plan, Atreus, is to remove my chains. And together, you and I will sneak away from this place."

Atreus let out a forceful breath. As if acting against his own will, he slowly undid the shackles and ropes around Krom's hands and feet.

"Thank you," Krom whispered, pulling himself to his feet. He grasped Atreus' shoulder. "Let's go."

The two moved on silent feet. Each step through the gravel and dry leaves crunched underneath them. This wasn't such a big deal when Atreus still stood watch and Krom was still in chains. Now, it seemed like every step took their breath away. They watched the sleeping men, who didn't even bother to cover themselves with cloaks. The cold air attacked them just the same as it had Krom.

Finally, they had reached the edge of the camp. The gravel became sparse and their steps quieted more and more. Krom couldn't believe that they were actually getting out of this mess. He would return to the Citadel and tell Kaela, who would probably post guards to follow him every day for the rest of his life.

Not like they needed to. After this, Krom wouldn't leave Cain's house for days. He would be safe there. Doors locked,

Cain's delicious food within reach. He might be able to wait it out until the next Hilios season if he was caref...

A howl. Loud. Unbearably loud. Krom could see the yellow eyes of the vargs, the giant field wolves, in the blackness of the night. They stood tall, nearly Krom's height. More eyes appeared in the darkness. The howl assembled a pack that must have been hunting nearby on the plains.

"No!" Atreus cried out. "I knew this would happen! We must go back!"

Just then, Krom heard the shouts of his captors. They hadn't gotten very far; Krom could still see the light of the flame flickering around the strange stone formation.

Before Krom could react, Atreus was sprinting away from the vargs and back to the camp. Krom called after him, but it was too late. Without another thought, Krom bolted into the night.

He could hear the snarls of the giant hunting dogs chasing him, followed by the screams of the Guild soldiers. He didn't dare turn around to see how close his captors were; not with the vargs surrounding him. If he had any luck, the Guild soldiers would take on the vargs and draw their attention, allowing him to get some distance.

A growl approached from behind him. He tucked and rolled, feeling the animal leap over him as he found his footing and sprinted the other direction. Whimpers echoed across the grassy field. He didn't turn, but he could hear the varg that leapt at him turn back toward its pack. Krom just continued to run.

His eyes grew blurry. The Guild had hardly given him any

food or water during their trek so far. His body grasped at energy that wasn't there.

But he still continued. He ran until he felt like he couldn't possibly continue, then he ran some more. He still heard footsteps behind him, but he couldn't see anything. When he looked upward, the stars were veiled in the sky, the sign of a storm rolling in.

An arrow, cloaked in flame, flew to his right. It lit up the scenery around it, catching fire on the dried up leaves. Soon, the fire expanded, illuminating the field.

Another arrow flew, this time past Krom's head. The arrow landed in the dying grass, illuminating the countryside even more. Krom finally turned. The vargs lay dead in the grass and the Guild soldiers sprinted across the plains toward his position.

New energy filled him. As if the almighty himself breathed into his lungs. He turned and ran, faster than he'd ever run before. In all the times he had evaded capture, escaping guards and the Guild alike, he had never felt this kind of energy.

But his legs failed him. As if they had transformed into jelly they collapsed underneath him and he tumbled through the grass. He didn't have time to feel the pain. He tried to jump back to his feet, but it was already too late. He pushed himself to his hands and knees just as one of the Guild soldiers ran by, kicking him in the side of the head. His vision blurred as his captors quickly surrounded him.

One by one, the men beat him. They kicked and punched, never using their weapons. They didn't need to. Krom could nearly feel his life leave him. That fresh wind that filled him, snuffed out in moments.

"Enough," the deep-voiced captain shouted. "Bring him back to the camp to be punished."

Krom spit blood on one of the soldier's feet. He wasn't sure if it was an act of spite, or survival, trying to remove the blood from his lungs. In reality, it was probably both. His captors grabbed him by his hands and feet, one person per limb, and carried him back to camp.

The fire spreading across the field lit up the varg corpses. It didn't matter how large a beast was, a well placed arrow could drop almost anything. Each animal had been shot only once, right through the eye-socket. An instant and painful death.

These aren't just any soldiers, Krom thought. *No normal soldiers can make that shot every time. This is Haze's personal guard.*

When they entered the camp, Atreus' body was there, flayed open for the elements. Just a couple cuts, efficient and effective. At least he wasn't kept alive for a torturous punishment.

"Now, what to do with you," the captain pondered. "Normally with a runaway we would break your legs, maybe take one of your feet. But your uncle wants you alive and I don't really feel like carrying you all the way to the ship." The captain looked to his men. "Take his hands."

Krom gasped. He cried out, trying to kick and punch his way free but he had no chance against the number of soldiers. They pushed him face down into the gravel, extending his arms out on each side. He tried to pull them back into his body, but the soldiers were too strong. They pressed a knee against his forearms, locking them in place.

Fos, Krom prayed. *If you are there, make yourself known right now. Interfere. Do something!*

Swiftly, a pair of axes came down, severing Krom's hands from his wrists.

X

Clash of Ideals

"Last time I saw him he was walking me home," Dawn said as she and Kaela ran through the streets. "He dropped me at the front door and went back to Cain's house."

"If he ever even got there," Kaela said.

They stopped at the staircase leading to Dawn's home. She looked to Kaela to speak again, but Kaela had already closed her eyes. Dawn had heard a little bit about Kaela's special Sight. She wondered if Kaela had ever seen her Reflection with it.

She would have mentioned something if she had, Dawn thought.

Kaela's eyes stayed closed, but something snapped her to attention. She took off down the street, nearly leaving Dawn behind. Dawn tried to follow as Kaela turned down different roads. It seemed like she was just following the normal route from Dawn's home to Cain's.

Kaela stopped, her eyes snapping open. She bent over and picked up a small piece of twine covered in splatters of blood.

"This is where he was taken," Kaela said.

Dawn's heart dropped. "Kaela... I..." She tried to speak, but she couldn't get words out.

"It's ok to be afraid," Kaela's voice quivered too. "Ephras always told me that. It is ok to be afraid, as long as you clear your mind and continue to think with logic." She grabbed Dawn by the shoulders. "We are going to find him, D. It's not too late."

Dawn wiped tears from her eyes and nodded. "What do you need me to do?"

Kaela smiled. "Stay close."

She closed her eyes again, but this time it didn't take long for her to take off down an alleyway. Dawn followed close behind as Kaela led her between buildings and down paths that she didn't even know existed. It made her think that Krom's kidnappers were Citadel natives with how well they apparently knew the landscape of the city.

They moved from district to district until Kaela led them to a scummy looking building in the Gate District with no signs outside. She cursed loudly and raced out the front gates of the Citadel, making their way toward Barlo. Dawn couldn't help more tears from flowing. She had at least hoped his kidnappers had stayed within the city, but she felt foolish for expecting something so ridiculous. Why would city-dwellers want to take him? She knew exactly who was responsible.

She could even see his face.

***

Kaela grit her teeth. She couldn't bring herself to tell Dawn how many auras she had seen, or the name of the building that the auras had led them to. The path had been painfully clear until it disappeared underground. Krom wasn't just taken by a small group of people but instead what seemed like an army. She could almost put together the scene in her mind. She didn't want to, but she couldn't help herself. She'd been a peacekeeper for too long.

They sprinted through the woods toward the city of Barlo in complete silence. Neither could bear to speak the images that flashed through their minds, to bring to life the nightmares in their thoughts. Instead, they focused their energy into their legs and plowed through whatever would enter their path.

Even though the auras had disappeared underground, Kaela knew exactly where she was going. She didn't know Barlo as well as the Citadel, but she knew this path like the back of her hand. She had taken it many times before.

Finally, she halted her sprint and opened her eyes. The building in front of her had luxurious marble archways, but she knew better than the facade of the exterior.

"What is this place?" Dawn asked.

"The Citadel Loans Federation," Kaela growled. "Debtors of the Cirranian underworld. I have a sort of... history... with them." She glanced at Dawn. "Don't pay too much heed to their words. The men who run this place are scum."

Dawn nodded and Kaela stepped forward. The doors were locked, as she expected, so she slammed her fist against the oak. Three aggressive knocks would do the trick. She closed her eyes and saw the auras of people inside scurrying to hide their suspicious activities. The only people that would be intruding on them would have been the peacekeepers. Kaela opened her eyes as the doors swung open.

The katze on the other side wore a fine suit, regal and expensive. He eyed the two women standing outside his door before scowling. "What do you want? We don't have any appointments in our books today."

Kaela smirked, whispering a prayer under her breath. The man flew back into the room in a gust of powerful wind. Kaela waved Dawn inside where four other men, two dark elves and two humans, drew their swords, shouting all sorts of curses in languages not native to Cirrane.

Dawn reached for her blade with her good hand, but Kaela waved again. "A friend of ours was brought through here from your Gate District passageway. Tell us where he's gone and we'll be on our way."

One of the dark elves narrowed his burgundy eyes. "Well, well," he snickered. "If it isn't little Kae herself. It's been quite some time since you showed your face around here." He grinned a disgusting, toothy smile. "How's your brother?"

Dawn growled, finally drawing her blade, but Kaela held her back with an arm. "We haven't come to exchange pleasantries, Cher," she growled. "We are just looking for our friend. Quarrinian. Twenty years old. You probably would have known him from Hilios posters around town?"

Cher grunted. "Now, Kae. You know I would do whatever I could to help you out, especially now that your debts have been paid. We don't want your head anymore." He dug the tip of his sword into the wooden floor and leaned on the hilt. "But the boy you speak of is long gone from here. The Guild is probably back at their boats and sailing to Quarrine as we speak. I'm afraid you're too late."

Kaela could hear Dawn's breathing intensify.

"What is your business with the Guild?" Kaela asked. "Why would you want to help them?"

Cher laughed. "The Guild pays a pretty penny for minimal work, hon. We provide passage and they provide payment."

"But they would be your competition."

Cher huffed. "You really are a lot like your brother, hon. He trained you well. If only you could have helped him stay alive. How does it feel to be responsible for the death of two siblings?"

Kaela whispered under her breath. A blistering gust of wind threw each thug back into the furniture around them. Their swords flew through the air as Kaela pulled her spear from her back. She rushed forward and pressed the tip underneath Cher's chin. Dawn followed suit and held her sword against a thug's chest.

"I'll ask one more time, Cher," Kaela growled. "You don't need to die today. Now, tell me. What business do you have with the Guild?"

Cher raised his hands above his head, trembling in his fine suit. "We have no business with them. I swear!"

Kaela pressed her spear a little harder, pulling a drop of blood from Cher's neck.

"Really!" He wailed. "The only reason we helped them is because they traveled with an old friend. Someone we knew from before the war. Hadn't seen him in twenty years. Thought he was dead!"

Kaela pulled her spear back. "And who is that?"

Cher coughed. "Why do you care?"

Swiftly, Kaela pressed her spear against Cher again. "He might be able to lead us to our friend. Now, stop making me ask twice."

Cher cried out. "His name is Drake!"

* * *

Dawn winced at the sound of her father's name.

"He was an Ulumbra captain during the war," Cher continued. "We thought he died during the assault on Seor's Temple. I was relieved to see him alive again."

Dawn's sword slipped from her fingers. She glanced at Kaela with tears in her eyes, then bolted out of the building, pummeling through the door. She ran without restraint, not caring about her exhaustion or the pain in her muscles. She even plowed through the people on the streets. Nothing could stop her.

She ran out of Barlo and through the wilderness again toward the Citadel. Kaela shouted from behind, but Dawn didn't slow. Too many thoughts raced through her head. She didn't even pay heed to her Reflection as she raced by.

The Citadel gates opened for her without her needing to stop; the benefits of being a celebrity in the city. Even the guards knew of the Hilios star from Quarrine.

Dawn raced from street to street, district to district, until she finally forced her way to the Temple District. She didn't even glance up at the temples, where a crowd had begun to congregate. Her sights set on the prison entrance. The oak doors would lead down underneath the temples, where the most dangerous prisoners were guarded by the best of the best. Maron was down there, and Dawn knew that her father would be too.

Rain began to fall as she approached the doors. Two soldiers wielding spears stood guard outside, their steel armor clanging with the sound of raindrops. They both pointed their spears at Dawn.

"Let me in!" Dawn shouted, reaching for her sword. She stopped. Her sword was still on the floor of the Loans Federation. The guards glared at her.

"It's okay," Kaela shouted from behind. "She has business inside. Let us through."

"Lady Kaela." The soldiers lowered their weapons and saluted. "On your orders, we will let her in. But Councilman Taran has been looking for you. We are to escort you into the Temple of Fos."

Kaela raised an eyebrow, looking at Dawn. "Go. I'll see what this is about, and then I'll come and find you. Take a right and follow the corridor to the very end. Past Maron. You'll find him there."

Dawn nodded. The guards opened the prison door and she pushed past them, the doors closing behind her. Torches lined the walls of the prison. She had come this way to see Maron numerous times. Starting down the corridor, she followed Kaela's instruction and turned right at the first chance she could.

Normally, the prisoners that inhabited the cells on either side of her would grab her attention, but her vision was focused. Nothing could distract her from her task. She continued down the corridor until the torches grew more and more seldom.

"Dawn!" Maron's voice called after her. She flipped to see him at the edge of his cell. "You don't seem okay. What's going on?"

"He lied to me, Maron!" She shouted. "He has been alive this whole time, and he might have killed my best friend!"

"Who?" Maron asked.

"My father!" Dawn shouted.

Maron nodded. "I thought I saw him being escorted in here. If someone was going to live through the attack on our village, it was going to be him."

Dawn turned to rush back down the corridor, but Maron reached out and grabbed her by the arm.

"Go easy on him, Dawn," Maron said. "People do crazy things for their family. Things they wouldn't normally do. Things they may even consider to be evil, all for the sake of seeing their family safe."

Dawn exhaled, then nodded. Maron released her arm and she continued down the hall. Finally, in a cell at the very end of the hall, she found her father sitting in a corner eating a bowl of cold soup.

"Dawn?" His eyes brightened. "What are you doing here?"

Tears threatened Dawn's eyes, but she took a deep breath to control her emotions. "You know, I actually came to ask you the same question, Dad."

"I told you," his voice lowered. "I came for you. What's this about, hon?"

"You know what this is about," Dawn's fists clenched, almost outside of her control. "How did you get here?"

"I took a boat," Drake said, leaning back and taking another spoonful of soup.

"The Guild, Dad!" Dawn's emotions burst. "They escorted you here!"

"Ah," Drake set his soup down, drying a dribble from the corner of his mouth with his sleeve. "That's what this is about."

"You led them here," the tears finally erupted from Dawn's eyes. "And now my best friend might be dead, and it's your fault."

"You are always involving yourself with people who are beneath you. First, Maron the Moron, now this char skinned man. He was a common street thief. Nothing more."

"He was a good man!" Dawn snapped. "Who are you to talk? You were a commander for Moldolor. For Ulumbra."

Drake gazed into the floor. "I guess I couldn't keep that from you forever. I'd gotten out. But, just like your thief friend, sometimes the past catches up with us."

Pieces snapped together in Dawn's head like a puzzle. "You're the reason they're all dead," she mumbled to herself. "Mom, Cammie, everyone. They were there for you. The raiders wanted you."

"That isn't true."

"Then tell me the truth!" The torch light flickered on the walls.

"You aren't ready!" Drake sighed. "It's... Complicated, Dawn. Everything I've done has been to protect you. Getting away from Ulumbra. Fighting my way through Quarrine.

Finding my way here no matter what the cost, even if it meant selling out your friend. I needed to protect you. There are some really bad people who are looking for you and I needed to be here to keep you safe. That's what a good father does."

Suddenly, Dawn's Reflection appeared next to her. "You aren't my father," Dawn felt her lips moving, but she could recognise her Reflection's voice. "You have no place in my life. You partner with evil. Giving your life to Ulumbra, selling your soul to the Guild. We will find our way with people who are good at heart, like the reavers or the White Council."

Drake frowned. "Be careful, hon. The White Council isn't as clean as you may think. Councilman Taran and Moldolor..."

"Dawn!" Kaela rushed down the corridor. "Taran needs to see you. He found the terrorists who attacked you in your home."

Dawn's Reflection disappeared. Drake inched backwards in his cell. "Just... Be careful."

"Goodbye, Father," Dawn snapped. Without another word, she followed Kaela back through the corridor and out of the prison.

On the surface, the rain continued to pour from the sky, the red moon illuminating the Temple District square. Dawn could hear thunder rolling just outside the city, masked by clanging church bells resounding from the temple.

People had continued to congregate around the foot of the temples. Now there were hundreds of citizens all responding to the call of the bells. Two young katze boys pushed past

Dawn and Kaela and disappeared into the growing crowd. "What is this about?" Dawn asked, pushing her wet hair out of her face as she followed Kaela into the crowd.

"You'll see," Kaela answered in a rushed tone.

The plaza was a solid mass of people from every sect of the city. They all yammered and strained to draw closer to the front of the crowd. Even with the nasty rainfall, the atmosphere seemed more excited than anything else.

Kaela and Dawn squirmed their way through, pressing past one person at a time. It was like trying to push into another organism. Dawn gasped for air as the bodies seemed to constrict around her. She grew frantic. Following Kaela, who continued to force her way to the front of the crowd, Dawn was pushed off balance. She couldn't even fall over with the sheer amount of people pressing in. It was like a cage, and the walls had closed in on her.

Finally, a hand shot out of the press and closed around her arm, yanking her forward through the crowd. Kaela's strength surprised Dawn as she was wrenched off her feet and farther into the crowd. Kaela pulled again and again, leading Dawn one step at a time through the congregation until Dawn stumbled out of the fray at the foot of the temples.

A covered stage had been set up between the two massive towers. Sacred Order guards stood at each corner. Standing in a line at the back of the stage was the White Council, each of them wearing a long white robe with gold patterns running up and down the garments. One wore a crown of gold and crystal that sparkled in the flickering lamplight of the temple streets.

Seven prisoners kneeled in bonds; two men, two women, and three children.

The bells stopped ringing. Once the noise dampened, the crowned councilman stepped forward. It was Taran. "Today, we show everyone what happens to those who wreak terror on the Citadel!"

The crowd roared.

"The people on this stage are known conspirators for the insurrectionists known as the Outriders!"

Dawn examined the prisoners. She recognized the two men as the ones who invaded her home. Men that she almost killed herself. The two women were strangers though, and the last three were just children. She could see the fear in their eyes. She had seen a similar fear when she watched Cammie die.

"No!" She found herself shouting. The plaza hushed, all eyes now fixed on her.

"Dawn," Taran smiled, extending out a welcoming hand. "So glad you could make it. Please, come up here."

Dawn hesitated, but Kaela nudged her forward. Taran reached out a hand and helped her up onto the stage.

"These are the men who escaped the raid on your home," Taran explained. "As well as their families. We tracked them down once we got word of the attack."

"Those are children," Dawn whispered. "They have nothing to do with this."

Taran chuckled. "Oh, no my dear girl. We don't plan to kill their children, or their wives. They are here so they will know firsthand what happens when you oppose the White Council."

Dawn's fists tightened and her knuckles turned white. "You would murder their fathers right in front of them?" She tried to keep her voice down, but it was getting difficult. "What kind of justice is that?"

The crowd grew restless. One at a time the people started to yammer until the plaza was full again with shouts and curses. Dawn could hear them clearly.

"Take their heads!"

"Kill the traitors!"

"The Outriders are too dangerous to let sentimentality cloud your vision," Taran's eyes narrowed. "Don't you see? This is what the people want. The families of these terrorists must witness firsthand what happens when you fight against the White Council, or they may turn against us later. Would you have me kill their families?"

Dawn reeled back. "No!"

"Then," Taran interrupted. "This is the only way. Justice is administered, and we are assured peace in the future." Taran gestured for a guard to come over. The Sacred Order soldier pulled a longsword from a sheath on his back and handed it to Taran.

Then Taran offered it to Dawn.

"You are the one these terrorists attacked. You should be the one to pass the judgment."

The two men were dragged to the front of the stage and thrown to their knees.

Dawn took the sword from Taran's hands. It weighed heavily in her one healthy hand. She heard the words of Cain in her mind. *There is easy, and then there is right.*

"No," Dawn looked the men in the eyes, then back to Taran. "If the power of judgment is in my hands, then I choose mercy. Let them go."

Taran shook his head. "You know I can't do that."

Dawn's grip tightened around the hilt of the guard's sword. She watched each Sacred Order guard turn toward her, grasping their own blades.

Taran held up his hand, halting the guards. "I thought you would be happy about this, girl."

Annias rushed to Dawn, placing himself between her and Taran. "You have to understand, Dawn," he pleaded. "This is about more than a couple families. This is about more than you, or us. This is about making a statement to the terrorists in our city."

"These children aren't terrorists!" Dawn cried out. She felt fire welling up within her.

A grin flashed across Taran's face. "The work of the Council isn't always pretty," he said. "I thought you were someone who could eventually become one of us. But if you can't handle the dirty work..." He closed his eyes and shook his head. "If you aren't one of us, then we can't protect you."

Suddenly, Taran nodded to the guards at the edge of the stage. She tried to raise her blade toward them, but a strong gust of wind pulled it from her hands. Dawn glanced up to see Kaela extending a hand out toward her, her eyes trembling.

Dawn looked back up just in time to watch the Sacred Order executioner slam his sword through the two men who attacked her home. Swiftly, the steel separated their heads from their lifeless bodies.

Everything went quiet. Dawn could see the children

crying, their mothers doing whatever they could to comfort them from the confines of their bonds. She looked out over the crowd and saw the pressing throng cheering and shouting. A sharp ringing blared in her ears. Her Reflection stood next to the executioner, her eyes glowing a deep maroon, matching the light of the moon. Her hands grew hot, like fire had engulfed them.

"Take the rest of them to the third floor chambers with the other insurrectionists," Dawn could barely hear Taran's voice give the command over the ringing in her ears. He approached Dawn slowly, laying a hand on her shoulder. "I expected more from you." He turned his back to her, followed by his Sacred Order, and strode into the Temple of Fos.

The bells rang again and the crowd dispersed. Everyone but Kaela left, leaving Dawn alone with the bodies of the two headless men.

XI

Siege of Oasis

Cain landed his pegasus a few miles outside of Oasis. He had missed the arid landscape of Quarrine. Cirrane was beautiful in its own way, but there was something about the desert country that provoked a sense of joy to his heart.

"Nice to be home, isn't it my friend?" Ragnar smiled, slapping Cain on the back. "I don't know how you can live in a place where it rains so much. You city folks are strange creatures."

"Not all of us are cats, Ragnar," Cain responded. "Some people actually like water."

Ragnar chuckled as they guided their pegasus to a bundle of Quarrinian yucca trees and tied them off. The fly over hadn't taken too long, but a full day of flying would take its toll on anybody, especially the pegasus. They would need rest before their strike on the city.

"Thank you again for this," Ragnar whispered. "I wasn't

sure if you would actually come over here and help. With everything going on in the Citadel..."

Cain smiled back, though his mind raced with thoughts of the city. He wondered how Dawn was doing. Had she kept her head down during his flight?

"Hopefully," Silas interrupted the conversation, approaching with the rest of his crew, "we won't be gone for long. The flight gave me some time to plan out a strategy that I would love some help perfecting."

The hot sun had risen not too long ago, rising from behind them as they flew. Cain was happy that they didn't have to fly into the setting sun again. The glare in his eyes was just too frustrating.

"Anything I can do to help," Ragnar stated. "This is my city. I know it better than anyone here, including Cain."

Cain caught his mind as it wandered. The ache in his back made it difficult to focus, even on something so important. He shook his head and forced his eyes wide, inhaling a deep breath. Silas gestured for them to sit under the shade of a tree, circling around each other.

Ragnar drew a rough picture in the sand of Oasis with a stick he found. It wasn't pretty, but he clearly marked the important portions of the city that would need to be dealt with, circling a facility in the center. "The orc chieftain will be holed up in this building, directly in the center of the city. He hides here while the rest of his tribe patrols the streets and keeps him from danger."

"We don't need to eliminate all of the orcs in the city," Silas pondered. "If we cut off the head, history tells us that an orc tribe will fall apart. Kill the chieftain and the city will be yours again in just a few days."

"Ragnar," Cain said. "Are the sewer systems still an option for us?"

"Doubtful," Ragnar sighed. "When we attacked from underneath the city, we ensured a surprise attack wouldn't be able to happen again by setting patrols and guards in the sewer systems. I am sure the orcs will have done the same."

"We have one advantage, then," Silas stated, pointing to his pegasus. "We have the skies. They can't be expecting an air assault on their fortress. We can fly directly into the center of the city, take out the chieftain, and fly back out before they even realize we're here. The orcs won't know what hit them."

"We will be vulnerable to their archers," Mae spoke up. "Fliers need to be careful against archers. I really don't feel like freefalling again."

"Mae is right," Remy said. "That was the first thing they taught us at Oceanview. A good archer with feasible cover can take on a battalion of fliers if their quiver is full enough."

Silas nodded. "So we attack under the cover of darkness. Minimize the risk of being seen by their archers. Even the flames of their torches shouldn't expose us too much."

The other fliers considered the thought. Cain knew most of them, but not all of them. Silas and Mae were the most vocal during the planning, with Remy chiming in with her fresh expertise. There was also Caprica, a gal he had met before but hadn't really had much conversation with. According to Remy, they had graduated from Oceanview at the same time. He had never met the final two, but Silas had introduced them as Maxie and Selvin. They were just boys, hardly Dawn's age.

Barely older than Roy was.

He had been on Cain's mind a lot lately. It had been years since Roy had been killed, but recently Cain couldn't stop thinking about him. About what he would be doing if he were still alive today.

Cain shook his head again, refocusing on the strategy meeting. "It's a good idea," Cain said. "As long as we have a way out. The orcs won't let their chieftain be murdered without giving chase. If anything goes wrong, we need a fallback."

Silas nodded. "Max and Sel," he gestured to the boys. "Stay back and rest, but keep your eyes open. Be ready to assist in a quick escape." Silas looked back to the rest of the group. "Let's take the rest of today to rest. When the sun goes down, we strike." The group nodded and each soldier found a spot to lay their heads.

Cain rested against the tree where his pegasus was tied. Even the beasts took the time to sleep through the day, nestling their heads underneath their vibrant wings. He watched Ragnar pace around the campsite, never even sitting down in the shade. He strolled alone in the baking desert sun as Cain slowly closed his eyes.

Cain startled awake. The cool, nighttime desert air bit at his skin. The moon glowed red in the sky that night, stars veiled by its glow. Even with the freezing air, Cain's hands felt clammy. A pit grew in his stomach. He glanced around the camp to see each of the other soldiers beginning to untie their pegasus from the trees.

"You're up," Ragnar chuckled from behind. Cain flipped to see the katze sharpening his hand axe with a common sandstone. "Still having nightmares?"

Cain closed his eyes and sighed. "Was it that bad?"

Ragnar shrugged. "Not to them. They don't know you like I do. They haven't seen what we have." He looked up to the sky. "You noticed the moon, I assume?"

Cain nodded. "I have a bad feeling, Ragnar. I can't explain it, but it feels like we're missing something."

"We always miss something," Ragnar laughed, standing to his feet. "Never stopped us before."

"I guess."

Silas found his way to the reavers as he was tying a sack to his back. "You guys almost ready?"

Ragnar slid his axe into its holster and smiled, his big yellow teeth shining in the moonlight. "Always ready, friend."

The soldiers each mounted their pegasus, Maxie and Selvin staying back and lighting a fire. "You two, keep your eyes on the sky," Silas whispered the command. "The rest of you, stay in formation. We all go home tonight. Watch each other's backs and this mission will be quick."

Silas directed the pack of fliers into a trot. One at a time the pegasus took to the skies, Cain flying in the back of the pack. Silas and Mae flew in the front with Remy, Caprica, and Ragnar flying in the center. They trekked through the air like a flock of birds, silently coordinating their movements and following the suit of their leader.

Oasis twinkled in the distance. The city lit up with flamelight, but not enough to make Silas' strategy ineffective. Between the fires of the Oasis torches and the red moon, the entire landscape of Quarrine glowed a deep maroon color. The sand of the desert wasteland looked like a sea of blood.

Within minutes, the fliers were at Oasis. As they approached the walls, Cain could hear the chatter and calls of the orcs from below. Arrows zoomed past them, coming within inches of hitting their marks. The darkness veiled them as the extra layer of defense they needed.

A horn bellowed from below. Suddenly, like a flash of lightning, powerful lights erupted from the city rooftops. Magical lights, unnatural and blinding. Silas cursed from ahead. He shouted back toward the rest of the team, but Cain couldn't make out his words.

Arrows continued to launch toward the fliers. Silas and Mae turned their pegasus back toward the city walls to retreat and regroup, but the orc's bolts swarmed them. Arrows pierced both of their beasts in the chest, dropping them into a freefall.

"Down!" Cain screamed, watching Silas and Mae crash to the hostile city streets. He sped his pegasus to the front of the pack, attempting to lead the rest of the fliers to a safe landing spot. They couldn't make it all the way to the center of the city anymore, nor could they safely turn around.

Arrows continued to whiz by the fliers as they circled the city. Quickly, they descended to the first street where they could land, now many blocks away from the city center.

Cain jumped off his pegasus, pulling his sword from its sheath. He counted the rest of the riders that followed him down, but there were only two: Remy and Caprica.

"Where is Ragnar?" Cain shouted.

Remy and Caprica looked at each other, unable to form words.

Cain growled. "Silas and Mae went down just a few blocks from here. If we can find them, we will have a better chance, but we have to move."

"What do we do with our pegasus?" Remy asked, finally finding her words.

Cain cursed under his breath. "Remy, you and I are going to push a couple blocks over where I will use my magic to draw some attention to us." He looked at Caprica. "When you see the signal, you take the pegasus and get them away from the city. Go back to Maxie and Selvin and wait for my signal to come back and pick us up. Remy and I will find Silas and Mae."

"I can't go back up there!" Caprica cried out.

"The pegasus can't stay here." Cain snapped. "And neither can we. This is our only chance to get everyone out of here. We need the other pegasus, and we need to ensure these ones stay alive."

Caprica shook her head violently.

"Please, Cap," Remy said. "We need you."

Caprica met eyes with Remy, then nodded. "Be fast."

Cain smiled. "Watch the sky. When you see my magic, go as fast as you can."

Cain and Remy locked eyes, then bolted through the street. The magical light glared between the buildings, nearly blinding them with its brightness. Goblin chatter came from the roofs as Cain led Remy away from their landing zone.

They weren't trying to be quiet. Every step resounded off

the walls into the blushing night sky. Each echo they made gave Caprica a better chance of escaping with her life.

Cain rounded a corner, then stopped, raising a hand in the air and whispering a prayer under his breath. Just then, an enormous fireball erupted from his fingertips into the sky. As it ascended, it slowed, until it settled in the sky above the city. It sat for just a moment until finally it exploded into a thousand bolts of lightning crashing down on the city rooftops.

"That should do it," Cain said to Remy, who gazed dumbstruck into the sky. "Let's move. It won't take long for the orcs to descend on this location."

As he spoke, arrows fired from the windows of the buildings surrounding them. Cain tackled Remy into a nearby alleyway, removing her from the line of fire.

"Focus!" He shouted as he pulled her to her feet. "One mistake will cost you your life."

Remy nodded. Cain quickly maneuvered to the end of the alleyway toward where he thought Silas and Mae had crashed. He didn't know exactly where they had been hit, but he knew they had to be close. Him and Remy continued to rush through the streets, never stopping even to look around at what enemies may have been in pursuit.

They pressed their way into an opening. Goblins and orcs alike crowded the center of the square like a swarm of gnats. He guided Remy behind an abandoned food cart, pressing his finger to his lips. Peeking over the cart, he could barely see the bodies of two pegasus being torn apart by the scavengers. Just the sight made Cain's stomach twist. This was abnormal behavior for goblins.

"No matter what happens," Cain whispered to Remy. "Stay here, and stay alive."

Without waiting for a response, Cain jumped out of hiding, summoning a gust of frozen wind against the bloodthirsty creatures. The gust knocked many of them off their prey, revealing even more of the mutilated pegasus' bodies. Cain thrust his fist out and a tempest of ice and lightning swirled throughout the open space. He rushed forward, swinging his blade into any creature that attempted to stop him.

Once he finally reached the fallen pegasus, he reached deep within himself and exhaled a powerful rush of wind that knocked back any creature approaching. The tempest died down, revealing many dead goblins left in his wake. He could feel the energy leave him like water being squeezed from its pouch. He could only do something of that magnitude so many times.

To Cain's relief, he didn't see the bodies of Silas or Mae. He scanned the surrounding square for signs of their escape, but his recent carnage had covered up any tracks they may have left. He sprinted back to Remy, who still held her blade tightly in her hands. Her face was washed white.

This girl must never have seen battle in her life. Cain concluded.

"Silas and Mae weren't here," he said. Remy's eyes darted up to him, then relaxed slightly. "They must have started toward the center of the city. We're already here, so we might as well finish the mission we came here to accomplish." Cain held out a hand and helped Remy to her feet. "The city center isn't far. Keep your eyes up and head on a swivel." He placed his hand on her shoulder. "We will make it through this, Remy. Just stay with me and I will get you through this."

Remy nodded blankly. Cain forced a smile to his lips, then turned toward a nearby alleyway. The streets would be a faster way to their destination, but the alleys would help give them cover from unwanted eyes. If they were caught, the confined space would render their enemy's numbers useless. Two could survive against an army in the small corridors.

They snuck from shadow to shadow, avoiding any wandering eyes. Cain stopped them at the road, waiting for patrolling orc troops to pass their alleyway before racing across to the next. The disrepair of the city became one of their advantages, offering them many hiding places. Cain wondered if the city could ever be inhabited again. Three sieges in one year is a lot for a single city to withstand. People may never be willing to live here again.

As they approached the orc chieftain's central building, they heard shouts from ahead. Human shouts. Cain locked eyes with Remy, then raced forward to find Silas and Mae fending off a horde of goblins and orcs alike. Silas was a storm of steel bouncing between enemies. His fighting was like a dance; elegant and fluid. Even though he was young, he had accomplished much in his years of training. Even when Mae struggled to defend herself, Silas easily made up for what she lacked.

"Silas!" Cain shouted, leading Remy into the fray. His distraction opened Silas up to easily finish off the rest of the orcs. "You're alive!"

Remy ran into Mae's arms, her breathing erratic and tears streaming from her eyes.

"It's okay, Rem," Mae said. "We're okay."

"It will take more than a fall to take out your sister," Silas smiled. He shifted his attention to Cain. "Where are Caprica and Ragnar?"

"Caprica went back with our pegasus to keep them safe while we found you," Cain responded. "Her, Maxie, and Selvin should be awaiting my signal to pick us up. We will have to terminate those lights first."

"And Ragnar?"

Cain shook his head. "He disappeared in the fray. Lost him after you guys went down."

Silas pursed his lips. "This is the building, right? You know the city best, after your katze friend."

Cain nodded. "This should be it. Directly in the center. This is where the Guild held their operations when they took residence here. Easy to send out orders to anywhere else in the city."

"Then let's finish this," Silas smiled, leading the team through the front door.

XII

Isolation

Dawn stared at the headless bodies laying on the stage in the Temple District. She didn't know how much time had passed since they had been slain. She didn't know how long she had been sitting in the rain. She had no way of knowing.

Kaela stood next to the stage alongside her. Dawn couldn't even look at her. She couldn't comprehend what had just happened. These were supposed to be the good guys. The heroes. They were supposed to be the ones who kept people safe from the monsters in the world.

"How could you?" Dawn grumbled, her voice cloaked by the heavy rainfall.

Kaela looked up, eyes puzzled.

"How could you support that monster?" Dawn howled. "I could have saved them. I could have stopped this."

"Stopped this?" Kaela asked. "*Stopped this?* You were about to take on seven Sacred Order guards *AND* the White Council all at once. With a broken arm, I might add. I saved your life."

"I didn't ask you to!"

"What was your plan, Dawn?" Kaela snapped. "To kill them all and run away like before? Maybe you could have killed a few of them. Maybe you could have even killed Taran, but what would have happened after that? You would be dead, the prisoners would still be dead, and I would probably be dead too!"

"They are murderers," Dawn interrupted. "Our fearless leaders are nothing but killers."

"So were the people they executed," Kaela responded in a cold, harsh tone. "So am I. So are you."

"Exactly," Dawn said. "What right do we have passing judgment on those men when we are just as bad?"

"There needs to be justice in the world, Dawn."

"They had families, Kaela!" Dawn grimaced, looking deep in her friend's eyes. "Children, who are going to grow up with that image burned into their memories. The image of their fathers' corpses."

Dawn tried to storm away, but Kaela reached out and grabbed her by the arm, pulling her around to make eye contact. "What Taran did might not have been great," she said. "But there is never a perfect leader. Sometimes we have to choose the lesser of two evils, and right now, the White Council is better than the Outriders."

Dawn pulled her arm away. "And who do those children think is the 'lesser of the two evils?'"

Kaela paused.

"Taran is no better than Moldolor."

"Dawn, stop."

"Murdering Ephras in front of us. In front of his family. In front of his sister."

"DON'T!" Kaela cried. "Don't use him as the basis for your own political confusion! Moldolor may have cast the spell, but *YOU* are the real reason Ephras is dead. *Your* amulet brought the sorcerer back. *Your* friend led Ulumbra into the city. You have to ask yourself; would these men be dead if *you* hadn't murdered that executioner yesterday?"

Dawn shoved her finger in Kaela's face, but she held her tongue. She looked down and noticed a cool breeze emanating from Kaela's hands. "If you are going to do it... Just do it." Dawn lowered her hand and turned away. "If you hate me so much, then maybe I deserve it. But don't waste our time with empty threats."

She stormed away again and this time Kaela didn't follow. Instead, her Reflection pursued silently. As Dawn scampered through the damp city streets, her Reflection didn't say a word. A rare experience.

She hurried through the city until she found her home. She opened the splintered door to the massacre from before. She hadn't gotten a chance to clean up the mess and she didn't have the energy to do it now. The odor of the rotting flesh would have to wait. Instead, she surrendered herself to the darkness.

Drawing the curtains to her room, she lay down in bed and tried to sleep. Even in nightmares, sleep helped her escape from the world. She woke up with tears already in her eyes and tried to sleep some more. She was alone. Cain was gone. Krom was taken, probably dead, headed back to Quarrine. Kaela was against her. Maron and her father were in prison. Surrounded by enemies with no friends in sight.

She tried to sleep through the night, but her slumber was leaden, dreamless, and brief. How long had she been in bed, now? When she was awake she held back tears, laying under her blankets and shivering in anguish.

She was just so exhausted. Cain had taught her about a body being drained of life through using magic, and she expected this to be how that would feel. Her eyes weighed heavy and she woke from her momentary slumbers even more weary than before.

That was where she wanted to be. Asleep. Away from the real world. Away from the terror and the chaos. When she slept, she felt peace. When she slept, she felt whole.

Maybe it would be better if she didn't wake back up.

Dawn found herself slinking toward the outdoor stairwell and out to the roof of her building. At six stories high, it wasn't the tallest building in the Midtown District, but it would do the trick.

Would death really be so bad? She wasn't sure what the afterlife would be like, but anything would be better than this life. Even if there was nothing waiting for her once she died, at least she wouldn't hurt anymore.

She closed her eyes, feeling the wind consuming her, waiting for it to hurl her over the edge of the roof.

Her Reflection appeared next to her shaking its head.

"This is how you plan on getting out of this? By running away from the real issues in the world?"

"What am I supposed to do?" Dawn snapped. "You were right. Everyone I get close to ends up either dead or hurting. I make everything worse. The world would be better if I wasn't around."

"Look," her Reflection said, pointing. Dawn glanced up from the street below to a nearby rooftop where Phoenicia Rodes was also standing near the ledge.

A sudden surge of adrenaline filled Dawn's body. She whispered a prayer, launching herself across the gap between buildings with an intense gust of wind. She jumped recklessly, slamming to the adjacent rooftop in a loud *THUD*. Phoenicia Rodes turned from the ledge to see her as she climbed back to her feet, but quickly turned back.

"Rodes!" Dawn called out. She didn't know what else to say, but she knew this was where she needed to be.

"Go away, Dawn," Phoenicia said. "I'm not worth the effort. Go back home and leave me be. Pretend like you never saw me."

"I can't do that," Dawn said. "I'm not going anywhere without you."

"You suddenly care for me?"

"I saw you," Dawn said. "I may not have seen you before, but I do now. And now that I'm here, I'm not going anywhere."

Dawn's Reflection boomed in her mind. "Why do you care?"

Rodes shook her head. "Just let me be alone. It will be no

different than how you've lived the rest of your life. I just need to be by myself for a couple more minutes."

Dawn took a small step forward. "I know what you're planning, Phoenicia. I can read your thoughts like a book. I know the last few days have been hard, but this kind of ideation doesn't seem like you."

"You think you know?" Phoenicia whipped around with tears in her eyes. "Because you haven't seen me act on it, you think you know my thoughts? You think you know my life? You think you know my pain? You don't!"

"Help me understand," Dawn said, taking another step forward. "I want to understand. Explain it to me."

Rodes was silent for a moment, but Dawn looked her right in the eyes. She couldn't risk blinking.

Dawn winced as her Reflection spoke again. "She deserves what's coming to her. Do you remember how she treated Krom? You are wasting your energy."

"What's the difference?" Phoenicia finally said. "If I wasn't here anymore, nothing would change, and I wouldn't have to..." She choked on the words.

"Phoenicia..."

"It doesn't matter. I tried to make a difference and only ended up doing more harm. I thought I could use my influence, but I'm nothing."

"You aren't nothing," Dawn said. "You are one of, if not *the* best, Hilios players in the world."

"And that's it," Phoenicia said. "My entire life and identity has been defined by Hilios. The prodigy. Living legend.

Greatest to play the game. One single match and that all falls apart. My life. My identity. My friends. All gone.

"I tried to do something more. I tried to calm the rioters, but they wouldn't listen to me. I tried to stop them from looting and violence. When Sacred Order came out and started cutting through people, I just hid inside, listening to the butchering happening a few feet away. I listened to them scream and I did nothing. I just hid like a coward. Same as when Althena and Lyra died. I just watched. I couldn't do anything. I just watched."

"Sometimes there is nothing anyone can do," Dawn said. "That doesn't mean you're worthless."

Phoenicia turned her back on Dawn and looked out over the city. She stepped up onto the ledge with one foot and Dawn felt her heart drop. She reached out with her good hand, a prayer beginning to form in her mind. Would she be fast enough?

But Phoenicia hesitated. She left one foot on the ledge, her golden hair blowing in the cool breeze. "I thought about what your friend said. The reaver. He said that, eventually, everyone dies. We're all on the same path toward the afterlife, some of us sooner than others. If death is the final finish line, then maybe it's time I crossed it."

"You're still here," Dawn said. "You aren't dead yet. Which means you still have more race left to run. If your story was over, you would have died with the rest of them. But you're still here. You're still breathing. You're still fighting. That means you still have a part to play. You may not see it right now, but you will."

Phoenicia broke into tears, pulling her foot away from the

ledge and dropping to her knees. Dawn darted over, throwing her arms around the Hilios champion.

"I'm just so tired," Phoenicia sobbed. "I..."

"That's okay," Dawn said. "You don't have to do this alone."

"I'm insignificant, Dawn," Phoenicia said. "I don't want to be insignificant. I used to think I was so important, but that just isn't true."

"If you make the picture big enough," Dawn said, "we are all insignificant. The world will continue to turn after we're gone. Mountains will rise and fall. The wind will still blow. Civilization will build and diminish. Later generations won't even remember us."

"This is supposed to help?"

"You have to focus your picture," Dawn said. "We may be insignificant on a larger scale, but if you focus on the smaller picture, you will see that you are important. You matter, Phoenicia. Think of Belle and Rosella. They need you. They are going through the same thing you are and need your guidance."

Phoenicia dried her eyes, then nodded with a forced smile. "I'll go to them now. Just to check in. Make sure they're alright."

Dawn smirked, helping Phoenicia to her feet. "I'll go with you."

The streets were still empty as they wandered through the Market District. Phoenicia's eyes fell as she passed the signs denoting the city's curfew. Dawn often forgot that most of the Hilios contenders didn't use magic. Phoenicia and her teammates would have to adhere to the new barbaric law.

"My father never would have allowed something like this," Phoenicia mumbled.

"Did he have some sort of authority?" Dawn asked.

"He did. Councilman Taran might have the absolute power right now, but he used to have a support system. People that would give him council. My father was one of them. He and Taran were really close, to the point that I grew up calling him Uncle Taran instead of Councilman."

Dawn couldn't help but grin. "What changed?"

Phoenicia looked away, staring at her shoes as they passed through the District Gates. "He struggled to stay happy as the Outriders rose to power. He never reached out to anyone, though. I guess he wanted to be strong enough to handle it on his own. He was the strongest person I've ever known. He never scrimped on his family but still was the best worker the city had. My mother reached out for help and support, but none ever came.

"One day I come home from academy and he is hanging from a rope in our living room. The people we think are the strongest still struggle, just in secret."

"I'm so sorry, Phoenicia," Dawn said. "How did Taran respond?"

"He finally gave my mom support afterwards, but the damage had already been done." Phoenicia looked at Dawn with tears in her eyes. "Why does someone need to die before people are willing to listen?"

They arrived at a stone building set at the corner of the street and Phoenicia came to a stop. She turned to Dawn and wrapped her arms around her neck, squeezing tight. "Thank you, Dawn."

Dawn awkwardly hugged Rodes back before gesturing for her to make her way to her friends. She watched Phoenicia climb the stairs to Rosella's home and embrace the young girl as the door swung open. Dawn was glad Rodes had come back to reality, but part of her felt... strange. She had said all those things, but she wasn't sure if she really believed them. If she was honest, she felt the same way Phoenicia did. She had been ready to make the same decision moments before.

At least she has people, Dawn thought.

"You're pathetic," her Reflection said.

"I don't want to talk about it," Dawn whimpered, turning back down the street. She didn't know where she was going, so she just walked.

"Poor Dawn," it continued. "All alone. Nobody around and still you want to be rid of me. I am all you have left."

Tears welled up in Dawn's eyes. She didn't know how to respond, so she didn't. She imagined her breathing was keeping a leaf afloat to hold anxiety at bay, just as Gromoth had taught her, while she made her way through the Citadel streets towards the Temple District Prison.

Her Reflection didn't follow.

The prison was guarded by the same two guards that had let her in the day before. Or maybe it was days before. They held out their spears as Dawn approached.

"It's okay," Dawn waved her hand. "I'm with the peacekeepers, here to see a prisoner. Let me in."

The guards shook their heads.

Dawn exhaled in frustration. "You let me in yesterday. Lady Kaela left orders to allow me access."

"We have new orders," the guard replied. "Direct from the White Council. No one sees the prisoners."

Dawn clenched her fists, but then sighed, turning away from the prison entrance. She glanced up at the Temple of Fos, where peacekeepers escorted dozens of apprehended citizens inside to await their punishment for breaking curfew the night before. Taran watched her from a window a few stories up, his eyes smoldering.

Dawn wandered back through the street, waiting for her Reflection to mock her. It never came. There was silence in her mind and she was useless again.

She never thought she would miss that menacing voice in her mind. All it ever did was attack her, scorning and ridiculing her every move. Now that she was alone, sitting in silence, the quiet was violent. She couldn't hide behind the noise anymore. She was alone with her innermost thoughts. Her fears, anxiety, only amplified by the emptiness in her soul.

Ducking away into an alleyway she sank to the floor, wiping tears from her eyes. At least she could still cry. There was still emotion to prove that her heart continued to beat. She dreaded the day when the numbness would take over again.

"Fos," she whispered under her breath. She opened her mouth to speak again, but she couldn't find the words. She felt her lungs fill and deflate, listening to the sound of her heartbeat in her ears.

"You are supposed to know what is going on in my life," she continued. "You are supposed to care. You give us this incredible power but you don't guide us in how to use it. You just leave us to our own devices."

She waited. Listening, but there was no response.

"COME ON!" She screamed. "Talk to me! Where are you!"

The sound of rolling stones shot through the alleyway. Dawn jumped to her feet, staring toward the noise. She searched up and down, looking for who, or what, might have been in the alley with her.

Suddenly from behind, a bag shoved over her head. Both her arms were pulled behind her back and tied with coarse rope. She wrestled, but pain shot through her broken arm like knives slicing into her skin. She tried to scream, but she couldn't find her voice.

"Take her," a man's voice said as they shoved her forward through the alleyway.

XIII

In the Shadows

Krom felt his fingers tingle. It was a strange feeling, since they were no longer attached to his body. Even when he looked at the tips of his severed arms he felt like he could feel his fists clenching and relaxing.

The pain had diminished, which was a relief. Krom wasn't sure if the wounds had actually stopped hurting, or if he had finally become fully numb. He wasn't sure he cared.

He walked with his captors for days. They couldn't bind his wrists anymore, so they tied a rope around his neck instead, irritating him as the scratchy material rubbed his skin raw. Each night they would tie him to a tree, leaving one of the senior members to watch after him. It was pointless, though. He wouldn't try to run again.

Krom had been wounded before, but never like this. He thought back to prayers he had learned growing up. Prayers to both Fos and Seor. It all seemed nonsense now. He still prayed, but instead of asking for Fos to help him, he cursed the creator. His entire life had been an orchestration of tragedy. When he finally found a way to have joy, it ripped away from him. Sometimes, he would even find himself weeping until he heard his captors laughing at him. Then he would make his eyes go dry and his heart go dead. He forced all his pain to go away.

Each day the sun rose they would continue toward the coast. Krom's legs ached. They shouldn't have. He had traveled much farther at faster speeds before. His energy drained into his severed arms. Blood and puss seeped from the mis-managed wound and his missing hands throbbed to the rhythm of his heartbeat every time he took a step. He could smell the infection setting in. His captors had cauterized the wound quickly with burning sticks, but that was hardly a sterile medical instrument.

As they crested a hill, Krom could see the coast in the distance. "Still another day's travel," the captain said, pointing to a small ruined outpost between them and the sea. "We stop there for the night and set out at first light." He pushed Krom forward down the hill.

The ruins were abandoned. Based on the ivy and shrubs that grew within the rock walls it had been abandoned for a long time. One of the soldiers started a fire in the center of the outpost and tied Krom's feet to a post. They hardly needed to even tie the knot. Krom wouldn't be able to untie anything anymore.

He laid on his back and gazed up into the sky. A stone walkway lingered over him, a loose boulder sitting on the edge. He imagined the stone falling from its place and crushing him beneath its incredible weight. He wouldn't get that lucky. He pressed his pain down until he could hardly feel it, even forcing the tears away. His eyes were as dry as his soul.

The sky was strangely beautiful. A graceful crescent moon blessed the atmosphere. Stars decorated the black canvas. Krom had never seen so many stars. *How could a night like tonight be beautiful?* He wondered. *Why would the stars bless me?*

As if he was blessed. He knew better. It wasn't that there was no God. Krom believed in Fos. He believed in the power Fos gave to his followers. He had seen the evidence. He had seen the magic and the power. He had also seen the pain. The heartache that touched the lives of the people in the world. If someone believed in Fos being loving and all knowing, planning each day of the people he'd created, they would also have to believe that Fos orchestrated the pain they experienced.

Krom passed in and out of consciousness, always passing into a nightmare. When he slept, Ulumbra closed in around him, and when he awoke, the Guild was still there. He couldn't escape. There was nowhere to run. Normally, waking from a nightmare would be like escaping captivity. Now, he would wake up into another nightmare. It was never-ending.

Fos, Krom prayed. *If you hate me so much, just end it. I don't want to do this anymore. Let me die.*

"'Ay," one of the men laughed. "You think the boy is 'ungry?"

Krom's eyes shot open. He could feel his heart beat in his stomach. They had been feeding him less and less every day. He tried to push himself up without pressing his wounds into the dirt.

"We 'ave extra, right?" Another man asked.

"Oh, yes," the captain smirked, smirking at Krom. "We do."

He tossed a piece of meat toward Krom, landing in the dirt. Krom crawled the best he could toward the food, but it was just out of reach of his severed arms. The men all roared in laughter, one even falling back out of his seat.

"Just wait 'til you see your uncle, boy," the captain said. "You're gonna miss our charming hospitality."

Krom scooted back against the post where his feet were tied. He leaned his head against the solid wood, resting his stubs on his legs. His wounds would get even more infected if he wasn't careful. Though, at this point, he wasn't sure it mattered. With any luck, he would be dead by the end of the week.

He continued to sit with his eyes pressed shut. When he wanted to find sleep, he couldn't, but when he wanted to stay awake, he dozed off. There was no control over his body.

"What was that?" One of the soldiers asked, hushing the rest of the laughter.

Krom opened his eyes. He didn't look around, but he listened. A rock tumbled over the wall to his right. Was it a bird? Maybe some sort of rodent. Surely nothing that these soldiers would have to worry about.

But then he heard it. Footsteps. Slow and steady, just outside the ruins. The Guild warriors stood to their feet and drew their swords, some of them nocking arrows to their bows. They watched the entrance where gates had once kept the ruin safe from the world outside. Now it was just a hole in the wall.

A hooded man appeared in the doorway, a spear slung on

his back. He had an empty gaze, as if he were looking through the soldiers.

"Keep moving, stranger!" The captain shouted. "We have nothing for you here."

The hooded man remained silent.

The captain cleared his throat. "You deaf, boy? Or just stupid? I ain't 'gon tell you again!"

A smile flashed across the man's face.

The Guild captain waved nonchalantly to one of the archers, who released a bolt toward the stranger. He slid out of the way and raced into the ruin toward the soldiers. The captain shouted for the rest of his men to fire, but the stranger dodged the arrows like a leaf being carried by the wind. Without drawing his spear he ducked under a bolt and planted his foot into one man's knee, snapping the bones under the weight of the kick. As he fell screaming, the hooded soldier slammed his fist against the man's temple.

The rest of the soldiers rushed in with their swords, but the stranger was too fast. He pulled his spear from his back and spun, whacking two with the blunt end and sending them backward.

Krom watched as the man ducked and dodged out of the way of the expert fighters. Before his opponents could even start to swing, he was already moving out of the way of their strikes like he knew how they were going to attack before they even started to move. It almost seemed as if he was dancing. His movements, while violent, were beautiful.

He kept his distance, sliding out of the way of the soldiers' swords before ramming his spear through their chests. One after another he challenged the Guild henchmen, making quick work of them. The captain's face fell, watching his men die in front of him. Soon, he was all that was left.

The captain feigned a strike, trying to pull the hooded soldier into a mistake, but he didn't budge an inch. Finally, the captain charged, swiftly striking with his blade. The hooded man sidestepped the sword, planting his spear into the captain's gut.

Krom watched, trembling. The stranger yanked his weapon from the captain's body and turned his empty eyes toward him. Pulling a cloth from his waistband, he wiped the blood from the tip of his spear.

Krom squirmed. He tried to claw at the rope on his neck, but it was no use. He instinctively pressed against the post where he was tied, trying to escape from the menace. The stranger walked unhurriedly toward him, extending his spear out.

When he finally reached Krom, he pressed his spear against his neck. Krom whimpered but didn't speak. If this was the end, he would gladly accept it.

But then, the stranger sliced the blade carefully against the rope, freeing Krom from his bonds. Krom gazed up as the man slung his spear against his back.

"Hello, Krom," he smiled, reaching down and helping Krom to his feet. He gestured to the fire the Guild captors had created. "You should eat. Your journey is far from over."

"But..." Krom stuttered. "I mean... How... Why... Who are you?"

The man removed his hood. His long, dark hair nearly hid his glazed eyes. They were milky and white, foggy and dry.

"My name is Fen," the man said, grabbing a plate of the

soldiers' food and offering it. He never made eye contact. Instead, he gazed past Krom, almost as if he were peering into his soul.

"Wait a second," Krom paused. "I've seen you before. You were there that day. At the championship! You've saved my life twice now."

"Fos guided me here to find you and take you back to the Citadel," Fen said. "It seems he still has plans for your life."

Krom scoffed. "I doubt it. The author of life himself has plans for me in this tragedy?"

"Fos sees you, Krom," Fen took a bite of food. "He sees you and he is concerned."

Krom's eyes narrowed. "How do you know my name..."

Fen grinned. "Fos told me. He knows you well."

Krom raised an eyebrow, working his way to a seat. He balanced the plate of food on his severed arms and leaned his face down to take a bite. Curses, life was going to be difficult moving forward.

"You're pretty big on the whole religion thing, huh?"

"No," Fen stated. "All your religious rituals do me no good."

"Oh, no," Krom said. "I'm not religious at all."

"You don't believe in Fos?"

"Don't get me wrong," Krom said. "I believe in Fos. You don't lose both your parents only for you and your sister to be raised by your crime-lord uncle, and not believe. You don't lose your little sister practicing dark magic to try and find an escape from this present reality and not believe. Life isn't just a series of coincidences, friend. I believe there is a higher power, and I hate him."

Fen shook his head. "He doesn't hate you, Krom."

"What do you know?"

"I know Fos. He speaks so highly of you. He calls you a splash of sunshine in a dark world."

"Great," Krom sighed, mumbling to himself. "He saved me twice, and he's a nut job."

"He told me that you are the reason Dawn is still alive."

Krom stopped.

"Cain may have given her purpose, but you have given her life. You helped her develop her joy."

"You've been watching us?"

"You aren't listening, Krom." Fen said. "Fos has been watching. He sees you, and he loves you. He led me here to save you."

"Save me?" Krom growled, tossing the plate to the ground and raising his severed arms up in front of his face. "If he wanted to save me, he would have saved me days ago. He wouldn't have let this happen. I asked him for help..."

"And he sent it."

"He was too late!"

Fen gently set his food on a rock, wiping his mouth. "You know, life doesn't need to be impossible now that you don't have your hands. My sight was taken from me years ago. And while yes, I still don't have my eyes, Fos has given me the ability to see. He can give you the ability to live with this affliction. Not just to survive, but to thrive."

Krom paused. "He gave you sight?"

Fen shook his head. "He gave me a new way to see. He didn't give me my eyes back, and he won't give you your hands. But he will give you a new way to live."

"And you can show me this?"

"Fos can show you this," Fen said. "Ask him to show you."

"I have!"

"Ask him," Fen held up a hand. "And then listen. He will give you what you need."

Krom sat, maneuvering another plate of food onto his arms again so he could continue eating. "You said Fos sent you to save me. Why?"

Fen grimaced. "Because your friends are in trouble, and Dawn needs you."

Krom pursed his lips. "What kind of trouble?"

XIV

Fallen City

Cain blasted open the barricaded doors with a powerful explosion of icy magic, revealing the makeshift throne room of Grumuk. The chieftain stood in the back of the room surrounded by orc and goblin bodyguards. Clad in plate armor and wielding warhammers, the orcs were menacing. The goblins aimed their bows at the door, waiting for their masters to give the word.

"Grumuk!" Cain shouted. "Your reign is over. Leave now and avoid any unnecessary bloodshed."

Grumuk chortled. "Avoid unnecessary bloodshed? How many of my tribe have you killed tonight?"

"Only because you first slaughtered the people of this city!" Silas responded. "When you act in violence, don't be surprised when violence responds."

Grumuk removed the war axe from his back. "Consider this my violent response."

Cain exhaled a prayer, shooting a gust of icy wind at the goblin archers. As they released their arrows, the blast slammed into them, throwing the arrows off course. Silas shouted, leading Remy and Mae headfirst into battle, Cain following close behind.

Red moonlight illuminated the storm of steel swirling throughout the room. Cain guided the squad with his magic, creating openings in their enemy's defense.

The armored orcs charged forward. They swung their hammers at the humans, but the humans ducked and dodged out of the way. Wood shards exploded from the floors and walls as the hammers missed their targets.

Cain rushed the goblins as they readied their bows again. He cut down two before the others had their arrows nocked. Rolling under one arrow, he whispered another prayer. He found his footing again and blasted a bolt of lightning into one of the armored orcs.

The lightning strike exploded against the orc's chest. Blasts of energy exuded from it, throwing Remy and Silas off their feet. Another orc rushed forward, sending his hammer down toward the defenseless humans.

Cain rushed at the attacker, slamming his shoulder into the brute and knocking the hammer away. It fell to the floor right next to Silas, who quickly jumped back to his feet. Cain sidestepped out of the way and Silas slammed his sword into the orc's neck.

Cain helped Remy back to her feet as Silas and Mae charged the remaining goblins. He turned to Grumuk, who stood wide-eyed in the back of the room, watching the battle.

"Enough!" Grumuk screamed. He chanted in a foul language as his eyes shifted to a bright blue.

"No..." Cain mumbled, tightening his grip on his sword.

Blazing red lights appeared behind the chieftain. Suddenly, they expanded and burst open, like a door leading to another world.

"You think you have power?" Grumuk's voice was distorted. "You don't know power. This is my city. I won't let you..."

As he spoke, a giant beast burst from the portal, tearing through Grumuk like a hot knife cutting through butter. Remy cried out, recoiling in terror. Cain stepped forward, readying himself.

The beast that emerged was a kemage; a creature that Cain had only encountered once before. It had batlike wings and giant, razor-sharp claws. Standing nearly nine feet tall, it hardly fit inside the chieftain's throne room.

"Get behind me!" Cain shouted. Silas and Mae stayed where they were, but Remy rushed behind Cain, nearly dropping her sword in terror.

The creature growled, baring its disgusting teeth. Huge flies swarmed its triangular head as it glared at Silas and Mae.

"Silas!" Cain shouted.

Suddenly, the kemage leapt at Silas, but he ducked out of the way, slicing upward at the demonic being. His blade clanged against the creature's armor-like skin, not even a scratch appearing on its carapace shell.

"Get back!" Cain shouted. "This creature is beyond any of you!" Mae helped Silas back to his feet.

"Get to the roof," Silas responded, focusing on the kemage. "Cain, call in the others."

"You can't do this on your own!" Cain said.

"I don't plan to," Silas said. He rushed at the kemage again, passing it and racing to the room's entrance. "Go!"

Cain nodded, grabbing Remy by her hand and leading her and Mae toward the stairs. He glanced back to Silas, who led the kemage out of the room.

Fos, guide him.

* * *

Silas raced through the corridor, listening to the creature crashing into the walls behind him. The wooden planks that held the floor together nearly fell away as he sprinted across them.

The kemage must have been barely ten steps behind. It wasn't stealthy. Silas glanced over his shoulder to see the monster hardly fitting in the narrow corridor. Walls crumbled around it as it slammed its giant claws and wings through the solid wood.

Silas approached a set of stairs and leapt over the railing. He dropped to the floor beneath them, rolling to his feet. Lightning flashed in the windows, the clash of its thunder masked by the beast crashing down the stairs. It roared as it chased Silas further through the building. Silas could feel his heart beating in his throat. His legs could have given out at any moment, feeling like jelly from the prolonged exertion.

But he couldn't stop. He allowed the rain beating against the window panes to be his cadence. Each aching step was faster than the last. Even if he didn't survive, he would have done his job.

He turned a corner and quickly ducked into a side room. The creature slowed when it lost sight of its prey. It sniffed, seeking a scent. Silas held his breath.

A low growl rumbled his bones as the kemage entered the room. It must have been used as a writing room at one point, maybe for the city news. Tables littered the room with ink spilled over the floor. This wasn't the first conflict to happen here.

Silas hid under a splintered desk, listening and watching. He heard the creature's heavy footsteps slam right next to his hiding place. Claws scraped against the top of his table, gouging a hole into the wood.

The footsteps cracked farther into the room. Silas exhaled slowly, as quiet as he could, watching through the holes in the table for signs of his hunter. Rain beat against the window leading outside.

It roared, rushing back to the hallway and slamming through another wall. Silas winced, releasing a small whimper from the depths of his being. His eyes shot open, pushing the table over and rushing toward the window. The kemage had already begun to crash through furniture behind him, swiping its claws close enough for Silas to feel the wind nearly knock him off his feet.

Finally, he slammed into the window and crashed down to the streets below. He landed on his shoulder, writhing in pain.

To his dismay, the kemage followed. With a crash, it landed on the street beside him, bellowing in the night. It walked toward Silas, but before it could crush him with its giant claws arrows descended down on it. The beast growled, looking up to the multitude of orcs and goblins that fired at it from the windows and rooftops of the surrounding buildings.

The kemage flapped its wings, releasing a tempest of wind as it jumped up to the rooftop of the nearest building. It slashed through multiple goblins at a time, tossing them down to the street as they died by its hands.

Silas pushed himself to his feet, limping to a nearby alleyway. Suddenly, another portal opened in front of him, red eyes glaring at him through the abyss.

* * *

Cain took off in a dash, followed by Mae and Remy. The walls had shifted and cracked, allowing the rain to seep in and wet the floor beneath them. It was slick and even one slip could have been fatal.

They found the stairs and strode up them two steps at a time. The passage led directly to the rooftop, where a dozen goblins were perched with bows in hand.

Cain was upon two of the goblins in a flash, cutting them down with a slash of his blade. The others cried out, scurrying across the rooftop, but Remy and Mae charged them. By the time they all knew what was happening, their lives had been taken.

Cain glanced over the rooftops to assess the situation. Each building was manned with a squadron of archers ready to shoot down any fliers that would approach the city. The brilliant magical light that had revealed their mission had disappeared. Now the red moon illuminated the city, along with the flames that quickly engulfed the streets below.

The kemage leapt up onto the rooftop across from them, slaughtering the goblins that had been positioned there. Remy yelped. Cain tackled her to the floor and covered her mouth with his hand, silencing her.

A blood-curdling screech echoed across the city rooftops. Cain reached back into his studies about the kemage, trying to recall its weaknesses. It was no use. Its diamond hard skin could repel any blade that tried to pierce it. It would take an incredible force to...

Their rooftop shook. It was so sudden that Remy yelped again through Cain's hand.

Fos, Cain prayed. *Grant us victory.*

Quickly, he jumped to his feet and leapt across the rooftop away from Remy and Mae, shooting a blast of lightning into the sky. The creature turned to him, crouching low. It dug its claws into the rooftop, scraping them in a horrible sound.

It charged. Cain leapt out of the way, expelling a blast of wind to push him faster. He landed on his back on the other side of the roof, rolling to his feet with just enough time to jump away from another charge.

He landed on his feet and flipped toward the kemage. A cool breeze encased his body. The creature charged him again, but this time he charged back. He slid underneath the monster and shot a blast of frosty lightning up into the kemage's gut. It squealed, flying across the rooftop and slamming into the door that led back downstairs.

The kemage slammed its claws through the door in a rage,

screeching in the night. Cain readied himself for another charge, feeling energy fade within him.

But it turned.

Cain followed its eyes to see Remy and Mae sneaking to the side of the rooftop. He looked back to the kemage. It was smiling. Its demonic lips curled in an eerie expression.

"No!"

The kemage stormed toward Mae and Remy, flapping its wings to launch it through the air. Cain expelled a burst of air behind him, pushing off against whatever he could to throw himself in between the monster and its prey.

But the kemage was faster.

In a single terrible swipe of its claws it tore Remy's body into two pieces. The force of its strike knocked Mae backwards and she reeled over the edge of the rooftop, falling to the city street below.

Cain watched in horror. The pieces of Remy's body lay in a scarlet pool of blood.

The kemage roared. Cain clenched his fists, fire burning inside. As the creature turned back toward him, he blasted it with a hurricane force of wind, throwing it up into the sky. With another twist of his body he pulled the creature back down to the rooftop, cracking through the wood to the floor below. Cain released a gust beneath him, launching himself into the air. Once he was directly over the beast, he screamed and unleashed the rest of his energy into the monster's chest in a blast of magnificent frosty lightning. The kemage's chest exploded, discolored gore flying in every direction.

He tumbled back down to what remained of the rooftop. All the energy inside him had evacuated his body, and he passed out of all thought as the red moonlight glared down upon him.

* * *

Silas snatched a sword from a fallen orc nearby. The creatures that exuded from the portals were something he had never seen before. Demons from another time. He had heard stories of the Fallen before, but never believed them.

They ravaged the streets, tearing through the orcs and goblins that occupied the city by sheer numbers. Many were reptilian in appearance, standing on two large back legs and slicing through enemies with their massive front claws. Others had twisted flesh, coated by dark armor. Almost human-like.

Almost.

Silas snuck between shadows, hiding behind crates, debris, and even fallen corpses. He could hardly even hear the rain beating around him over the screams of the battle. How had it come to this? It was supposed to be a simple mission. In and out with no trouble.

Mae's body fell to the street in front of him. She writhed on the ground, squirming in pain. Creatures closed in around her.

A shout escaped Silas' lips. He raced into the street in a maelstrom of steel, cutting through anything that got in his way. The reptilian creatures were susceptible to the sword, unlike the beast from before. Heads turned toward him, claws and swords following close behind. He jumped out of the way of a charging reptile, slashing into another and quickly raising his blade to block one of the humanoid beasts.

Something swiped at his legs as he fell backwards to the ground. He kicked upward in a reflex, knocking a humanoid creature back away from him.

One of the reptiles jumped onto his chest, snarling in his face. Its breath stank of rotting flesh, its sharp beak dripping blood. Silas squirmed, but it was no use. The creature pinned him with its muscular legs. It raised its claw into the air.

A flash of white knocked the creature away from Silas. He rolled and found his way to his feet, seeing four more pegasus tackling the rest of the monsters.

"Commander!" Caprica shouted. "Jump on and let's get out of here!"

"Not without Mae!" Silas said. He turned to Maxie and Selvin. "Cain and Remy are on the roof of that building."

They didn't even wait for the order before taking off to pick up the others. Silas rushed to Mae, throwing her on Caprica's pegasus. She cried out in pain, but there was no time to be careful. They needed to leave. Silas jumped on the back of his own pegasus and they flew off into the night, Selvin and Maxie flying close behind.

XV

Beneath the Citadel

Dawn's knees burned as she was pushed to the ground, masking the pain in her broken arm. Her captors removed the sack covering her head revealing a dirty backroom around her. Water seeped through the floorboards and pooled into muddy puddles throughout. Only one door adorned the room with four guards standing in front of it. One way in, one way out.

"It's nice to finally meet you, love," a man sat with a smile in a janky wooden chair. "I apologize for any harm my men may have caused in getting you here. I did tell Maraxis to take care of you, but I didn't think you would come if you knew who had invited you."

Dawn eyed the man. He wore a suit, but that didn't disguise how dirty he was. His hair grew past his shoulders in knotted curls weighed down by his own body oil. A man stood next to him, small and scrawny. Maraxis, Dawn guessed.

"And who is it that's invited me?"

The suited man laughed. "My apologies, love. The name is Tarik. I lead the Outriders in their fight for freedom against the religious tyranny of the White Council."

"You..." Dawn cringed. "You are the reason everything is falling apart!" Her wrists rubbed raw as she squirmed in her restraints.

Tarik chuckled. "You have been hanging around the peacekeepers too long. Always jumping to conclusions. Now you see why I couldn't trust you to come on your own. You see me as the big bad guy. The terrorist. If you were to think rationally for a moment, unlike your friends, you would realize that we are only here to adjust your perspective."

"You intend to recruit me?"

"No! Not at all. I'm not delusional, my lady. A simple alliance, temporary, is all I ask."

"An... alliance?" Dawn raised an eyebrow. "Like you made with Ulumbra?"

Tarik gasped dramatically. "You think so little of me? That I would partner with the dark sorcerer himself? I am offended. Downright hurt by the accusation alone!" He leaned forward, voice suddenly low and serious. "We intend to free the world of all magic. Light and dark. That includes your little cultists."

Quickly, he jumped to his feet, a smile reappearing on his face. "You're different, Love. I feel like you and I could have been friends. Maybe in another time."

"I doubt it."

Tarik grabbed a cup from a counter, downing its contents.

"Perhaps you're right," he smiled. "Don't have to be friends with someone to work together, though."

"What makes you think I would work with you?"

"You saw what they did," Tarik said. "The White Council is no better than Ulumbra. Murderers, the lot of them. They killed those fathers, and now the rest of their families lay in a dungeon, awaiting the same fate."

"They plan to kill them?"

"What else would they be planning to do with them? They can't release them. Not after that scene."

Dawn remained silent.

"I saw the whole incident," Tarik continued. "We watched from afar. We watched you stand up to Councilman Taran and his servants."

"Then why didn't you do anything?" Dawn snapped.

Tarik returned to his seat in front of Dawn and shrugged. "What good would it have done? Me and mine rushing into a fight that would most certainly have ended in our deaths? Those men were dead the moment the Council captured them. Wasn't anything we could have done to stop that. Their families, on the other hand... Their fates are not yet sealed."

"I can't help you," Dawn said. "They took away my access to anything in the city. My part in your game is over."

"If I wanted to get in the easy way, I wouldn't have come to you," Tarik said. "Together, with our planning and your magic, we can get them out of their confinement without the..." Tarik cleared his throat. "Allowed access."

Dawn narrowed her eyes. "You expect me to believe that you want to do this out of the goodness in your heart? After all the evil you have done? One good gesture doesn't excuse years of terrorism."

"You are the ones who labelled us as terrorists. We prefer to think of ourselves simply as activists."

"Your activism brings terror into the heart of the people."

"Sometimes freedom has a high cost," Tarik sighed. "But I have not brought you here to argue motives. Nothing you will say can dissuade me from my mission, as nothing I can say will change your mind about me and my organization. Our agreeing on policies and politics is not necessary for the mission I have planned for us. What matters is that we both want to see those children free. Can you work with someone you disagree with in order to see justice?"

Dawn thought for a moment before finally speaking. "Yes."

* * *

"I want you to stand watch in the Market District," Captain Belvin raced through peacekeeper headquarters in the Northtown District, Kaela following close behind. "With the Butcher in custody, crime has skyrocketed within the district. And of course, that is where Taran wants to make his statement to the city."

"It has the largest population in the Citadel," Kaela said, obliviously.

Belvin shot her a quieting glare. "He wants the entire city to know that he is not afraid of the terrorists, yet he pulls the Sacred Order all back to the temples like a child hiding behind his mother's skirts."

"Does he plan to have the Order at the rally?"

"He wouldn't go anywhere without them."

"But you don't think that will be enough."

Belvin shook his head. "You are the best we have, Kaela. So much of your brother in you. I need you to be in the crowd looking for anyone suspicious. Use your Sight to pick out any would-be assassins." He stopped, making eye contact with Kaela. "Can I trust you for this? After what happened with your friend?"

Kaela nodded. "My allegiance is to this city..."

"And to the Council?" Belvin interrupted.

"And... to the Council. You can trust me with anything."

"Good," Belvin said. "Keep it up, and you will see much more authority come your way."

Kaela smiled, saluting before exiting the headquarters toward the Market District.

***

People raced through the Citadel streets toward the Market District. Tarik, however, led Dawn against the flow. It was like trying to wade upstream through a river, people bumping into her, not caring at all.

I guess we are the rude ones, she thought, holding her broken arm close to her body so it wasn't accidentally bumped.

"That blasted announcement," Maraxis grumbled.

"Leave it to the Council to say a single word and expect the entire city to rush to hear it," Tarik said, pushing his way through the crowd. "Their self importance could not have been what Fos intended for his faithful."

"Statement?" Dawn asked, trying her best to keep up with the activists. "What statement?"

"Have you been living under a rock?" Maraxis scoffed.

"Councilman Taran put out an announcement after the executions at the temple that he would be making a statement to the city regarding the 'terrorists and the safety of the people'," Tarik explained. "He's just trying to save face. Gives us a good opportunity though. The Councilman would never go anywhere without his Sacred Order. The Temple should be mostly unguarded."

Before Dawn could process Tarik's words, he pushed himself out of the crowd and down an alleyway. Finally, they found a set of stairs leading down underneath the city.

The same ones she had fallen down a year ago.

"We're going into the Old City?" Dawn asked.

"Well, we can't just walk up to the front door and knock, now can we?" Tarik laughed.

"What about the Guardian?"

"One single beast," Maraxis said. "If we're careful, it won't even know how to find us."

Tarik gestured Dawn down the stairs. "Maraxis and I have been planning a way into the temple for months," he said. "Didn't know when we would need it, but we knew the opportunity would arise eventually."

"The Temple of Fos has a passageway that leads into these tunnels," Maraxis said. "I guess Taran wanted a way of escape that wasn't into the streets should trouble come his way."

Tarik smiled. "Maraxis has been down here a dozen times, at least. With him by our side, we have nothing to worry about."

As they descended the stairs the light from the world above faded. Dawn snapped her fingers to reveal a small magical light that illuminated their path. She glanced around, her heart pounding in her chest. This was a place she had never wanted to visit again. Emotions filled her as if she were there again, watching Ephras' life being drained from his body.

"Keep your light dim," Maraxis said. "Don't want nothin' drawing in any unwelcome eyes."

Dawn nodded, whispering a prayer under her breath to diminish the light. They walked through the dark streets like three silhouettes. Shadows hiding from the light. Occasionally, Dawn saw a fourth shadow. Her light would flicker and her Reflection would appear for a moment before disappearing back into the darkness.

* * *

Crowds packed in tight outside Champion's Field in the Market District. Kaela pushed her way through the people, making mental notes of anyone who looked suspicious. She didn't exactly know what she was looking for, but she knew her instinct would tell her when she found it.

Even when she closed her eyes and used her Sight, the auras of the people were mostly the same color; a smoldering orange that indicated nerves and excitement. That wouldn't help her at all.

She pushed her way to the edge of the crowd and climbed up a banister to enhance her vision. There were thousands of people waiting to hear from Taran. She wasn't even sure if they could have all crammed into the Champion's Field if they had tried.

A shimmer of obsidian and silver flashed at the front of the crowd. Kaela squinted to see a squadron of Sacred Order guards pressing their way to a wooden stage. It was rickety and must have been constructed that same day.

Once Taran stepped out from behind his guards, the roar of the crowd silenced. Two other council members stepped onto the stage with him. *They must have left the rest of the Council back at the temple,* Kaela thought. She saw him mouth a few words before his magically amplified voice covered the entire crowd.

"Thank you all for gathering here today," Taran started. "Recent events in our city have brought us terrible grief and pain. The Outrider scourge has done so much damage in such a small amount of time. Our hearts go out to anyone who has been affected by the awful events."

The crowd began to murmur. Kaela looked out over the people, focusing on those who didn't speak. The ones who tried to draw no attention to themselves. There were too many to pick out. She couldn't make a move yet.

"After much deliberation, we have decided to focus the attention of our peacekeepers, as well as our military, on the Outrider presence. No longer will we live in fear of their attacks. We will strike fast, and we will strike hard against any movements made by the terrorists."

The crowd roared in agreement, though still no movement.

"Through thorough investigation, we believe there to be only one enemy in our city."

Kaela's attention snapped away from the crowd and to the Councilman.

"The rumors of Moldolor and Ulumbra are completely

unfounded, and have been used as fuel by the terrorists in order to create more fear of magic. All the dark magic that we have seen over the last year is just a tactic. An attempt to recruit people to their vile cause. I must be very clear to the people of our great city. Moldolor is dead, and Ulumbra is gone."

Kaela couldn't believe her ears. After everything she had gone through. Watching as her brother was murdered. The grief that followed. Was it all worthless? She grit her teeth, drawing her lips to a point.

The crowd had no such reservations. They cheered and chanted in approval, raising their fists into the air. They were so loud, Kaela almost missed the shouts of terror midway through the crowd.

Immediately she closed her eyes, seeing the aura of orange turn black. Her eyes shot open to see a group of people pulling swords and bows from underneath coats and cloaks. One readied an arrow, leveling it at the stage.

As it released, Kaela whispered a prayer, expelling a blast of air to throw the arrow off target and into the closest building. She pulled her spear off her back and leapt from the banister with another gust of air, launching herself into the center of the crowd.

The attackers swung their swords at her, but she easily parried their blows, keeping them from wildly hitting any bystanders. She waved her spear through the air and swiped at the terrorist's feet. Quickly, each of them was knocked to the ground. Kaela kicked their weapons away as more peacekeepers pressed in to bind their hands and legs.

"Take them to the Market Precinct," Kaela commanded. "We need to ask them a couple questions."

She studied the group of attackers. There were only five of them and none of them seemed to know how to fight. She was able to take care of them all with ease, by herself, while no civilians were even injured. The whole attack seemed sloppy.

Too sloppy.

* * *

"We never meant you harm, love," Tarik said as they walked through the old city streets. The loose cobblestone grasped at Dawn's feet, attempting to trip her in the dark.

"Never meant me harm?" Dawn scoffed. "You sent assassins to my home!" The light exuding from her fingers flashed.

"Quiet!" Maraxis said. Their voices carried throughout the cavernous caves, echoing off the walls. "Put out your light."

Dawn extinguished the magical light. Drops of water crashed into concrete all around them, covering the party's breathing.

That's when they heard it. The snarl of the beast. Guttural and terrifying. Suddenly, the earth shook violently, loud crashes echoing from deep within the caverns. Dawn felt wind brush her face as debris fell around them.

"We gotta go," Maraxis mumbled. "Now."

Dawn whispered a prayer to reignite her light, illuminating the rubble around them. Maraxis bolted through ruined buildings, climbing through shattered windows and busting through doors. Tarik and Dawn followed close behind.

Maraxis and Tarik had drawn their swords, but Dawn kept hers in its sheath in order to keep the light up.

Giant crashing footsteps resounded again in the undercity. This time they were louder, like they were getting closer. Dawn tried to climb through a window, but the shaking of the earth had shifted the foundation of the building. She fell through the loose wood, splinters scratching at her arms and drawing blood.

The footsteps grew louder and faster as they ran. Their feet ached as they pounded them against the stone pavement. Everything around them shook.

Maraxis stopped at a window inside an empty building, throwing his hand up to halt his companions. Dawn stopped, dimming her light until they could barely see outside the window.

The creature that sniffed around outside was massive. It was hard to believe that its canine body was small enough to even fit beneath the Citadel in the Old City. As it walked, it slammed into the sides of the buildings, knocking debris loose.

It lowered its head to sniff around a nearby building, revealing four dark red eyes. This creature wasn't anything natural. Dawn could hear Cain's voice in her head calling the canine beast an abomination.

Maraxis silently mouthed to Tarik and Dawn, pointing back through the house. They tip-toed across the floor, eyeing the creature that stalked them. As it sniffed, gusts of rancid air swirled around them. Rotting flesh nested within its mouth, packed between its teeth.

They snuck out of the house and around a corner away

from the beast. Unfortunately, this also led them away from their destination. Dawn watched Maraxis and Tarik closely.

"How do we get around it," Tarik whispered.

"I've never had to," Maraxis admitted. "I've always been quiet enough that it didn't even know I was here."

"What if it doesn't know we're here?" Dawn asked. "Can we just wait it out?"

"That creature is of canine descent," Maraxis said. "If it doesn't know we're here yet, it will quickly catch our scent and track us down."

"Then we use that to our advantage," Dawn said, recalling monster hunting lessons with Cain. "This thing will find us with its nose? Then let's lead it out of the way and rush through when we have an opening."

Tarik rubbed his chin. "Maraxis. Is there a passage or path through the city that leads us back to this spot? An easy circle we can traverse?"

Maraxis nodded. "I don't like this."

"Neither do we," Tarik said. "But our mission has been compromised. It's time to improvise."

Dawn snuck between buildings silently, listening for the creature's footsteps. The magnificent architecture of the Old City was something to behold. She wondered how something so beautiful could be kept hidden underground. Even with the ivy and weeds growing out of the rocks and cracking the foundations of the streets, this city was majestic. The orcs could learn something from the ancient Cirranian builders.

She reached a building around the corner and whispered a prayer, flashing her light on and off in a brilliant illumination.

It brightened and dimmed until finally she heard the footsteps of the guardian pounding through the caverns. They accelerated quickly, growing louder and louder. Dawn bolted out of the building and back toward their destination.

Suddenly the crashing footsteps were right behind her. She leapt behind a piece of rubble as the guardian charged into the street, slamming into buildings as it ran. Her light diminished quickly, the only thing lighting the city being small cracks at the ceiling of the cavern letting in slivers of sun.

The beast's fur shimmered a glossy silver splattered with specks of gray and red. Its tail slapped into the surrounding buildings. Dawn could hear the stone foundations cracking beneath its enormous weight.

Suddenly, her foot slipped out from her hiding place, a rock rolling away and into another pile of rubble. The guardian stopped sniffing. Dawn listened, pulling her foot back in and inched herself as far under the rubble as she could. Without even realizing it, she held her breath like she was trapped in a bottle. A stream of drool dropped in front of her, pooling in the dirt by her foot.

A shout echoed from deeper in the city. The guardian grunted, stepping over Dawn's hiding place and peeking its head between two buildings. Another shout, and the creature howled, racing off toward its new target.

Dawn counted to five in her head before rolling out from under the rubble. She reignited her light, running back toward her destination. More shouts echoed in the cavern, followed by the creature's bloodcurdling snarls. It was no longer on top of her, but the noises were still too close.

Dawn knew she was close to her target when she saw Maraxis sprinting around a corner. "Let's go!" He shouted.

"Where's Tarik?"

On command, Tarik leapt through the shattered window of a nearby building with a sword in his hand, rolling to his feet as he landed.

Dawn heard the crashing footsteps before she saw it. The guardian blasted through the building after Tarik, stone exploding in every direction. Tarik stood to face the creature as it snarled at the three trespassers.

"So much for avoiding the thing," Maraxis cursed.

The guardian barked, lunging forward at Tarik, but Dawn blasted a bolt of lightning at it. With a whimper it stumbled away from them but quickly regained its footing and charged again. Tarik screamed as the guardian raced toward him before leaping out of the way at the very last second, attempting to cut it with his sword.

The guardian flipped back toward the humans, growling and baring its teeth. Its four red eyes glistened in Dawn's magical light. "Come on!" Tarik shouted, pounding his chest. "Come and get me!"

Suddenly, the guardian charged, but this time toward Maraxis. His eyes widened, tripping over a piece of rubble as he backed away from the creature. He chanted something foul under his breath and a dark energy exuded from his hands; purple and black tendrils. The color seemed to fade from the wood and stone around him as the tendrils slapped against the canine, but it didn't work. The guardian continued to charge.

Dawn shouted, blasting another bolt of lightning at the

beast. As it was about to chomp on Maraxis the bolt hit, startling the creature.

The beast's momentum was too great. It continued and slammed into Maraxis, its claws cleaving into his chest. He fell back into the debris, unmoving, as the guardian crashed into the building behind him.

But Dawn didn't relent; she continued to fire magical blasts at the creature. One after another, her attacks found their target. The guardian whimpered, backing away as Dawn cried out, throwing her energy at the monster before her. She felt the power of her Reflection flowing through her as she attacked, hatred and anger filling her. Everything that had happened. Everyone she had lost. All the people who had been killed. Justice filled her veins. Finally, the guardian climbed to its feet and raced away, whimpering as it ran.

Dawn turned to Tarik, who was standing over the body of Maraxis. Only, as she approached, she noticed that it wasn't Maraxis. It was someone else. Someone who seemed familiar, as if she had met him at some point before.

"I can't believe I trusted him," Tarik growled. "All this time, coerced by a dark mage."

"What is this?" Dawn asked.

"Dark magic is a powerful thing, love. Allows you to play with things that shouldn't be in your control. Lets you play with other people. Freeze them in time. Influence their emotions. Sometimes, it even allows you to wear someone else's face." Tarik turned away from the stranger's body. "We need to move. Our window will be closing here soon."

Dawn followed Tarik away from the scene of the battle, looking one last time at the fallen mage. Where had she seen his face? She didn't know any dark sorcerers, and the ones she did know she would have recognized.

"I want you to know, love," Tarik said as they found the rope ladder that led upward into the Temple of Fos. "We never sent anyone to your home. You will find that magic has many unnatural tendencies. Those men who died on that stage had never seen your home before. I doubt they even knew who you were." He looked into Dawn's eyes. "There is another player in this game. One that is trying to frame my Outriders as the enemy. I swear to you, love. I am not the villain here."

XVI

Sting

The ladder ascended into the dungeons of the temple, still beneath the city streets. Tarik led Dawn into the dark corridors until they reached a small set of stone stairs that ascended up into the rest of the tower.

Dawn stepped in front of Tarik, shoving a hand against his chest. "Let's be very clear before moving on," she whispered. "There is one mission here, and that is to free the prisoners of the executed families. There is not going to be any death, and we shouldn't need to use swords."

"Of course, love," Tarik smiled, pushing her arm out of the way.

Dawn pushed him back again, holding out her hand. "If we don't need swords, then you should be just fine leaving yours here."

Tarik laughed. "You expect me to walk into the fortress of the enemy unarmed?"

Dawn nodded. "That is exactly what I expect you to do."

"And if I refuse?"

"Then you won't enter," Dawn glared, her hand moving to her own blade.

Tarik looked at her sword, then looked to the door that was just ahead of them. Suddenly, he burst into a fit of laughter. "I like the way you do things." He pulled his sword from its sheath and set it against the wall, his hand remaining on the hilt as he pointed at hers. "I'll expect the same from you."

Dawn thought for a moment before removing her sword and setting it next to his.

"Such trust," Tarik smiled. "I hope I don't regret bringing you along."

Dawn and Tarik continued up the stairs toward the temple door. "Why *did* you bring me?"

Tarik pulled two thin metal pins from his pocket and fiddled with the lock until it clicked and he could push the door open. "Maraxis seemed to believe you were necessary to the cause. Didn't think we would succeed without a magic user's help, and you seemed like our best candidate."

"And what do you think?"

Tarik shrugged, walking nonchalantly into the temple. "You definitely helped with the guardian, but I think we would have figured something out."

Dawn glared at him, but remained silent. Her Reflection lingered in the shadows as they pressed deeper into the temple, chandeliers and beautiful designs decorating its expansive hallways. The temple was mostly empty, something Dawn had not seen often. They would hear a voice coming from down the hallway and duck into an empty room as the person passed before continuing on their mission.

Soon, they found the staircase, quickly gliding up them until they reached the third floor. The Temple Dungeon, where the Council would keep people before they were sent to the prisons within the city. People who weren't as much of a threat as most of the criminals that rotted behind the bars. Maron had been kept in the Temple Dungeon for a few weeks, but it didn't take long for Taran to have him moved to the city prisons. Her father never even saw the Dungeon.

A voice shouted from down a hall and Tarik pulled Dawn into a nook in the wall.

"You're sure that nothing is going on?" A woman's voice asked.

"It has been this quiet here since Councilman Taran left," another voice said, this time a man. "If anything was wrong, we would have signaled the Sacred Order with the bells."

Tarik smiled, turning to Dawn. "It's your peacekeeper friend."

Dawn immediately recognized that he was right. It was Councilman Annias and Kaela who were talking. Quickly, she pulled Tarik into a nearby room, searching for another door they could use.

"What was that about?" Tarik asked.

"She uses a magic called the Sight," Dawn said, finding another door to go through. "If she looked down the hallway, she would be able to see us even if we were hidden." Dawn wasn't sure that she couldn't find them, even now. "We have to keep moving."

Tarik smiled, following close behind. "I guess Maraxis was right. You *are* useful."

The door led into another room where Dawn listened hard to anything happening in the hallway. These two rooms had been connected, but didn't lead them anywhere else. They would have to wait for Kaela to pass by or leave on her own.

"How have you been doing?" Dawn heard Annias ask. "Regarding recent events with your friends?"

Kaela sighed. "They aren't as bad as everyone is saying, Annie. It's just been such a hard few weeks."

"They're nice enough people," Annias said. "I'm not arguing that. I've known Cain for years. He was like a brother to me. When Roy died, we traveled together to Ardglas to spread his ashes. But once the fuse is lit, true character is revealed. Pressure reveals what is real. Under the pressure of the last few weeks, they have chosen to abandon reason and join the enemy."

Are they talking about Cain? Dawn thought. *What does he have to do with any of this?*

"They aren't our enemies, Annias," Kaela stated. "Just because Dawn doesn't entirely agree with you or Taran, doesn't mean she is a villain."

Tarik placed his hand on Dawn's shoulder. "She is distracted. We should take advantage of the moment and head deeper into the temple. There must be another way to the dungeon."

Dawn nodded, moving her ear away from the door. They peaked their heads outside and scurried back down the hallway and turned down another corridor. Kaela and Annias' voices faded the farther they got, even though their passion was quickly escalating. Tarik moved them quickly and efficiently, stepping between artistic pillars and beautiful sculptures. Finally, Tarik peered into a room and stopped in his tracks.

"What is it?" Dawn asked, noticing his astonishment. She pushed past him to find a room filled with jail cells that were packed full of people. Sickly looking women and children sitting shoulder to shoulder, overflowing waste buckets rotting in the corners.

"The curfew..." Dawn muttered.

"You still think I'm the bad guy?" Tarik asked, stepping into the room. "This is what I fight against, love. These people have done nothing wrong. Now, if you please?"

Dawn whispered a prayer and froze the locks on the cell doors, Tarik coming behind her and kicking them in. The frozen, fragile metal shattered and the doors swung open. Prisoners flowed out of their cells like water, hardly even expressing their thanks before bursting out of the room and down the hall.

"Do they know where they're going?" Dawn asked, continuing her way through the room.

"They'll figure it out," Tarik said.

"They'll be caught again!"

"Some of them will, but with how little people are here right now, many of them will be able to escape and find freedom. Our mission will still be successful. It's a numbers game, love. For every ten people that find their way back into a cell, seventy more will maintain their freedom."

"What about the ones whose freedom I owe," Dawn paused.

Tarik rolled his eyes. "You think their lives are more important than the rest of these?"

Dawn stayed silent.

"Fine," Tarik sighed. "We can see about taking them back through the Old City. Probably safer for them to try and get through the front doors, you know."

"We get them to safety. That was the mission I agreed to. The children on that stage who watched their fathers die." Dawn continued freezing locks for Tarik to shatter.

"That was the case for all of these children."

Toward the back of the room, Dawn recognized the family that had been on the stage the previous day. The three children still cowered while their mothers held them close. As Tarik kicked in the cell's lock, they jumped up and ran to Dawn, wrapping their arms around her. "Thank you," the two women pleaded. "You came back for us. Thank you."

"Of course," Dawn smiled. The children clung to her legs.

"As much as I love a good reunion," Tarik said. "It's time to go. We'll be escorting you personally out of the facility."

The women nodded, peeling their children off of Dawn as Tarik led them back out of the rancid room. Prisoners continued to pile through the hallways and rush to the stairs. No one tried to stop them.

Where is Kaela?

Screams echoed as the flood of people poured down the stairs all the way down to the first floor. Tarik stopped Dawn and the families on the steps, listening to the chaos on the bottom floor. The screams were screams of terror.

"They're back," Tarik cursed under his breath. Bells started ringing outside the temple walls. At the bottom of the stairs a soldier clad in obsidian armor sliced his way through the crowd, uncaring of age or gender. His heavy blade cut through the prisoners like a hot knife through butter.

"You have sentenced them to death," Dawn's Reflection spoke in a deep, otherworldly voice.

"Let's go!" Dawn shouted, leading their smaller group back up the stairs. "There has to be another way down."

They retreated back up the stairs and into the hallway. Dawn pushed ahead of the prisoners, magical energy radiating from her hands. She heard it before she saw it. The clanking of steel plate against the marble floors. She pushed the families against the wall behind a pillar, hushing them with a finger.

Dawn closed her eyes, listening to the soldier approaching. She waited until he was close, then leapt out from their hiding place, shooting a blast of magical energy at the obsidian plated guard.

He moved so fast. Unnaturally fast. Faster than anyone in heavy plate armor should have been able to move. He ducked out of the way of Dawn's blast and leveled a sword at her.

"Run!" She shouted, motioning Tarik to lead the family away. The Sacred Order soldier laughed menacingly under his helmet. He charged Dawn, swinging his sword terribly fast through the brittle air. Dawn jumped out of the way, but the soldier swiftly followed up with a punch to her shoulder blades with his other hand. Dawn fell to the ground in pain.

She whispered a prayer and expelled a gust of wind against the wall, pushing her out of the way of the imminent follow up strike of the soldier's sword. It chipped away at the marble floor. He struck again, Dawn rolling as fast as she could away from her attacker.

What had she gotten herself into? This soldier was trained to fight against mages. She had no chance.

She expelled another gust of air into the ground, launching her back to her feet. The soldier swung at her gut, but she dodged backwards just in time. The blade sliced through the cloth in her shirt, shearing right through it. She shot a blast of fire at the attacking soldier, but he was too fast. He ducked out of the way and laid a shoulder into her, sending her back into the wall.

Without thinking, she expelled against the floor again, shooting her over the head of the soldier and into the center of the hallway. She looked both ways down the hallway and noticed that Tarik had led the families away from the fight.

Time to go.

The obsidian soldier charged again, grazing Dawn's arm with the tip of his blade. She jumped out of the way and expelled a gust of air all around her, trying to push everything backward. She hadn't practiced this maneuver much, but she had seen it work when Cain and Kaela had tried it, so it was worth a shot.

The soldier hardly moved. He threw his hand up over his face and positioned his feet to stabilize his balance. Dawn grit her teeth, taking off down the hallway. It was no use. The soldier encroached on her quickly, tackling her to the ground.

Dawn thrashed as they fell, kicking the sword out of the soldier's hands. They wrestled for advantage, each of them reaching for the steel weapon that flung across the corridor. The soldier smashed his gauntleted fist into Dawn's face and she lost consciousness. It was only for a second, but once she regained her presence of mind, the soldier stood over her with the blade in his hand. She backed up against the wall as the soldier swung his final strike.

Suddenly, Dawn's Reflection appeared behind the soldier and he froze, suspended in time. "Why do you always insist on doing things yourself?" Her Reflection asked. "One of these times, I won't interfere."

The soldier didn't struggle. Dawn couldn't tell if he was even breathing. He was just stopped, stuck in a moment in time while Dawn stood to her feet. She grabbed the sword from the soldier's hand and gripped it with her good hand.

"Finish him," her Reflection said. "I can't do everything for you, Dawnie. Just swing the blade."

Dawn held the blade tight, but then shook her head, throwing the sword through a nearby window. "He was just doing his job. He isn't the bad guy here."

"You're right," her Reflection smiled. "You are." The apparition disappeared suddenly into a puff of smoke as the soldier released from his suspension, falling unconscious to the floor.

Dawn exhaled a sigh, racing back down the corridor after Tarik and the imprisoned families. They had left a door open leading to a separate staircase, away from the massacre happening just a few doors away. She barreled down them two at a time, listening for any signs of additional soldiers that guarded the temple. Most of them had congregated at the bottom of the other set of stairs to stop the mass breakout.

She bounced between pillars, silent on her feet. The screams from the other side of the building haunted her, but there was nothing she could do. One of Cain's first lessons to her, back in Oasis, was to weigh the odds. A lesson that Kaela had...

Two bloody corpses lay in the corridor in front of the Old City entrance. Dawn nearly jumped out of her skin. Tarik stood over them with a nasty grin on his face, blood dripping from a knife in his hands. Dawn's eyes widened, looking down at the bodies. It was Councilman Annias and Thomas. She glared back up at Tarik.

"The families are in the Old City, just like I promised," he shrugged, gasping for breath. "Our mission is complete, love."

"No..." Dawn cursed under her breath. She could feel the heat rising up within her. The rage of her Reflection running through her veins.

Tarik wiped the knife on his trousers. "I still have a mission to my city and my people. This is only the beginning."

As he spoke, Kaela charged into the clearing with her spear in hand. Her eyes burst open, locked on the dead councilmen in front of her.

Tarik lunged at her, but she jumped out of the way. Dawn whispered a prayer, blasting Tarik into the wall with a gust of blustering wind. His head slammed against the marble and he fell unconscious on the floor.

"Kaela," Dawn sighed. "This is Tarik, the leader of..."

Kaela screamed, tackling Dawn in an act of pure rage. Dawn thrashed, trying to break free, but Kaela wouldn't let go. They rolled around in a blur of marble and steel, throwing fists at each other whenever they had a chance. Finally, Dawn kicked Kaela off of her and they climbed to their feet.

They stood, glaring at each other in silence. Dawn tried to put words together, but she couldn't.

Two more Sacred Order soldiers rushed into the corridor with swords drawn. Kaela held up her hand. "Arrest them," she commanded, looking back to Dawn. "Taran will want a public trial."

The Sacred Order soldiers lowered their swords and bound Tarik's unconscious body. Dawn backed away slowly. "Kaela, I swear, this wasn't the plan."

"Dawn," Kaela growled. "Don't make this any more difficult than it needs to be."

Dawn sighed, putting her hands behind her back. The soldiers quickly bound her and led her into the dungeons below the temple.

XVII

Trial

Dawn had seen the temple's prison many times. Visiting Maron had brought her there almost weekly. At least, that was before this last week. It was different now. Now she was on the other side of the prison bars.

She found herself whispering prayers under her breath, seeing if she could summon any magic to aid her. Nothing happened. She suspected the food they fed her was laced with toruga, which suppressed any latent magical abilities. There were two options: starve and get her magic back, or eat the disgusting food they provided.

Of course, without her magic, she hadn't seen her Reflection. She wasn't sure how the apparition was connected to her religious thoughts, but moments like this only proved it in her mind. She just sat in silence, waiting for anyone's words to comfort her.

"Who would come?" Dawn found herself mumbling.

"Everyone is gone. Cain left. Krom is probably dead. Kaela put me in here."

She had no one.

Dawn listened to the sound of her lungs filling and deflating, pondering the purpose of each breath. Her eyes pressed shut. She tried to find sleep, but it eluded her. She tried to scream, but it did her no good either. So she just sat, listening to her lungs toiling to give her breath.

The torches barely lit up the prison this deep into the dungeon. Even when Dawn inched her eyes open she couldn't see to the far end of the cell, so what was the point?

When Dawn kept very still, her arm didn't ache so much. The toruga kicked in and sent needles and a stinging sensation to her nerves, but the pain went away. So she tried to sit, unmoving. She had no idea how long she had been in the dank cell, but it seemed like an eternity. Were they feeding her extra portions to keep suppressing her magic? It felt like they were feeding her more than just three meals a day. Or had she just been in the cell for longer than she initially thought? If she counted correctly, she had been brought food by a guard eight times. Waiting for three days to decide her fate after the debacle in the temple seemed like a strange move for Taran.

She was finally half asleep when she heard the footsteps in the hallway. A glowing red light encroached on her darkness, penetrating it with its light. At first, she thought she was dreaming, as she often had. She expected her Reflection to appear, disparaging her.

Kaela appeared in the flamelight, her face downcast. She opened the food hatch on the cell door and tossed in a jug of water. "It's clean," she said with a heavy voice. "Should taste better than what they've been feeding you."

Dawn glanced at the jug but shrugged it off. "How long is he going to make me wait?"

"There's not much to deliberate here," Kaela said. "You killed two councilmen."

"I didn't kill anybody," Dawn said. "Tarik killed the councilmen. The Sacred Order killed the prisoners. I only wanted to save people. To save those families."

"Dawn... The families you helped escape were found dead in the Old City. The guardian got to them."

Dawn's eyes flashed with grief, but tears couldn't fall. What had she expected? All that bloodshed, all for nothing.

"Sounds like you have already made your decision," Dawn said. "I imagine Taran has, too. Why keep me waiting?"

"This is about more than just *your* sentence, Dawn."

"Kill us both, then," Dawn said. "Tarik deserves it too."

"Not Tarik," Kaela said. "Dawn, this is bigger than you realize."

Guards led Dawn by the chains through the dungeon, her ankle shackles clanging against each other with each step. She remembered the chains of the orcs back in Quarrine all that time ago. How had she managed to find prison twice in two years?

The closer they got to the outer door, the more torches and lamps lined the walls. Criminals gazing at her felt different now. Her chains completely changed her perspective. She was helpless.

Her eyes burned as the guard opened the door to the world outside. After days of nothing but dim torchlight, the setting sun pierced aggressively into her eyes. She reached up to shield herself, but the guard continued to pull her toward the Temple of Fos. She didn't need her vision to notice the crowds roaring all around her, waiting for the trial. She stumbled up the steps, unable to see as they quickly found their way back indoors.

The trial was to be held on the first floor in a large rectangular room at the other end of the temple. Taran and the four other remaining members of the White Council sat upon thrones in the back of the room with other important people lining the sides; mostly business owners, priests, and military commanders. Kaela sat among the crowd on one side, while Silas sat on the other. None of his squad was there with him. None of Dawn's former Hilios team.

Cain was nowhere to be seen, either.

Positioned in the center of the room were three small wooden platforms with built in stocks and chains. The guard pulled Dawn onto one and locked her chains onto the platform's circular shank. She looked to the platform on her left where Tarik leaned, still wearing his disgusting suit. It was now covered in the blood of Annias and Thomas.

The crowd murmured as they watched Dawn get locked in place. She felt their eyes staring at her, awaiting her inevitable conviction. Taran waved his hand and the crowd quickly silenced. He glared down at Dawn and Tarik. "You two have made quite a mess of things, you know. Would you like to make a defense?"

"We have nothing to defend," Tarik said.

"Oh! Well, that's a relief," Councilwoman Sorena scoffed.

"Dawn?" Taran redirected their attention.

"*Now* the Council believes in giving prisoners a defense?" Dawn mocked. "While you just murder men in public? And you cut down every person you could who we tried to help escape."

"You admit to it?" Taran grinned.

"You've already made up your mind!" Dawn said. "Nothing I say will convince you otherwise. Why prolong the process?"

Taran waved his hand at the guard in the back of the room. "You're right, Dawn. Your sentence is already final. His, on the other hand, is not."

The guard opened the door and led in another prisoner. He was disheveled and weak, needing to be dragged most of the way to the stand. The guard locked him into place and backed away. Dawn gasped as the prisoner looked up at her.

Cain.

Dawn frantically looked around the room, pulling on her chains. "No!" She shouted. "He didn't do anything!" She looked at Kaela, who just buried her face in her hands.

"Quiet!" Taran commanded. Dawn clenched her teeth, drawing her lips to a line. "Here is how this is going to work. You will give us your testimony, and we will decide if this man deserves death, the same as you two."

Dawn tried to lock eyes with Cain, but he just stared at the marble floor.

"You can go first, girl," Taran said.

Dawn could do nothing but sigh and nod. "I don't know

exactly how long I have been prisoner under the temple, but I didn't meet Tarik until the day we infiltrated the Temple of Fos. Our plans, at least the plans that I knew of, was just to free the prisoners in the dungeon on the third floor of the temple. The prisoners that had done nothing wrong except not believe in Fos. Children who had to watch their fathers die only to be held captive in that disgusting place you call a prison.

"We had almost succeeded, until the Sacred Order returned from your rally. They began to cut down all the escaping prisoners, so we took a small group back around to the other set of stairs. One obsidian guard stood in our way, so I sent Tarik onward with the prisoners while I held off the guard. I left him alive." She tried to make that very clear. "Even when he threatened me with violence, blood was not shed."

"Your intentions are not of importance to me," Taran stated. "Whether you intended it or not, blood was shed. Because of your actions, two councilmen are dead."

It was true. Dawn knew it. Annias was dead because she helped Tarik. Tarik may have swung the blade, but Dawn still had blood on her hands.

"You only care about the death of the councilmen?" Tarik spat. "What about the innocent people you slaughtered as they were trying to find freedom."

"They would still be alive," Sorena said. "If you had not interfered. It was your acts that led to their deaths."

"I have accepted my responsibility in this tragedy," Dawn said. "I have made a terrible mistake and am ready to take whatever consequences I have earned. Cain had nothing to do with it."

Taran shook his head. "That is not your place to decide, girl. During this time, where was your mentor?"

Dawn glanced at Cain, but he continued to gaze at the floor. "He was on a mission in Quarrine. Nothing abnormal for a reaver of his status."

"Indeed," Taran said. "Which is what makes it a good story." He averted his glance to the downcast reaver. "Tell me. Why does a reaver need an elite team of pegasus fliers for a simple mission to Quarrine?"

"The mission," Cain finally spoke, "was anything but simple. The free city of Oasis was besieged by a monster who held an army. This was too much for a single reaver to handle, so I asked for backup."

"Why not bring more reavers, instead?" Sorena asked.

"I did. The mission was originally another reaver's plan. Ragnar the Wrecker. He was asking for my assistance. Dawn had just been attacked at the Hilios Championship, so I thought it would be inappropriate to bring her on such a dangerous mission."

Taran rubbed his chin. "Let me make sure I understand what you are trying to tell me. There is an attack against your friend here. You say the attack is Ulumbra, though there is no evidence that it isn't this man and his Outriders." He gestured to Tarik. "Then, another reaver appears, wanting to take you, one of the Citadel's most experienced fighters, as well as the most skilled squad of fliers we have, across the world. He wanted to take protectors of the White Council and remove them from their positions for upwards of a week. He wanted to do this during a time of civil unrest, when there are attacks from terrorists happening daily at high profile targets. And you thought this was a good idea?"

Cain didn't answer.

"He only left because I pushed him to!" Dawn interrupted.

Taran waved his hand. "I don't want to hear from you again, girl. I understand that you will say whatever you can to save your friend." He looked back at Cain. "This is a clever story, reaver. Even with your known conspiracy regarding Ulumbra, this story just paints you as naive. Naivety does not deserve a death sentence."

Dawn exhaled a sigh of relief.

"It's too bad that's all it is. Just a clever story. A coverup for your own deception and acts of terror."

"What?" Dawn shouted.

"Another word, girl, and we will have all your heads here now, and this trial will be over." Taran's voice commanded the room. "Here is what I think happened, reaver. You have been partnered with the Outriders for a while, which is why you have been trying to divert attention away from the Outriders and towards that ancient cult, Ulumbra. Once we debunked the conspiracy, you wanted to remove those who opposed you. So you cleverly schemed to remove our pegasus fliers from the city while setting up your protege to assassinate councilmembers while the city was defenseless."

"Ragnar came to me!" Cain shouted. "He informed us that Oasis was under siege by orcs and he needed help to take out the chieftain. He is a good friend, and I wanted to help him. So I turned to Silas for help."

Taran sneered. "You think the White Council is blind, reaver? You think we are unaware of the goings on in the world around us? That we don't see the chaos in the world outside these walls? We know about Ragnar's siege against Oasis, where he pushed the Guild away from the city. Word has reached our ears about the tragedies that took place there nearly a year ago when your reaver friend assaulted the city. We are also aware that the katze known as Ragnar the Wrecker perished during this invasion."

Cain was silent.

"I don't need to hear anymore," Taran said. "Due to recent events, and piecing together the evidence that has been presented to us, I hereby sentence the three of you to death by beheading. The execution will proceed publicly at sunrise tomorrow. Councilmembers and peacekeepers will begin spreading the word to the citizens, and this insurrection will finally be over."

Taran continued to speak, but Dawn stopped listening. His voice faded as she stared at her mentor, his face fallen.

XVIII

Keeping the Peace

Kaela sat on the steps of the Temple of Fos, fiddling with her necklace. It was a simple piece of jewelry, hardly expensive. A ruby set into the back of an engraved slate of silver. "Remember who you are," the engraving said. It was a gift from her brother after he helped her pay off her debts to the Citadel Loans Federation. A reminder of so much more.

She didn't even glance up at the crowd that flowed around her under the fresh moonlight. The people who had watched that farce of a trial. It was still unbelievable. Cain was one of the most honorable people she had ever met. When Ephras died, he was there for her. He was a mentor to so many more than Dawn. How could he have orchestrated the murder of Annias?

"I thought I saw you leave."

Kaela jumped. Taran stood behind her at the top of the

steps. "I thought about going home, but that just seemed so... lonely."

"As opposed to sitting alone on the steps of Fos' temple?" Taran laughed. He sat down next to her, looking out over the rest of the Temple District. "What do you see when you look at our city?"

Kaela shrugged. "It's just a city. A lot of people gathered together. Doing life together."

Taran nodded. "Sure can be lonely, surrounded by all these people."

Kaela chuckled.

"Doesn't need to stay that way, though," Taran said. "The Citadel is a sea of people hiding behind stone walls. Most of them are trying to find isolation, but fellowship is possible for anyone with the mind to seek it out."

"I did find fellowship," Kaela sighed. "I had such a great life here. Even when Ephras died, I thought I had lost everything, but Fos gave me more. He gave me people. He..." She stopped herself.

"They were close to you," Taran said. "That much is clear. What are your thoughts about their sentence?"

Kaela drew her lips to a line. "Can you still love someone when they mess up so badly? As a peacekeeper, is it okay for me to still wish the best for them, even though they did so much wrong?"

"Sometimes you need to do something that looks evil in the sight of others in order to maintain what is good."

"A necessary evil is still evil."

Taran placed his hand on her shoulder, sending a shiver down her spine. Suddenly, a wave of nausea overwhelmed her. A feeling in her heart she had only felt one time before; in the prison with Ephras. "You made an oath to this city, same as I have. To keep the peace. To protect those who can't protect themselves. Everything I have done has been in service of that oath. You can be loyal to your friends, as long as your loyalty to your purpose always comes first." He knelt in front of her, staring into her eyes. "I need to know I can trust you, Kaela. I need to know that your loyalty remains with the Citadel and with the White Council. Put first things first. Before family. Before friends."

Kaela averted her eyes, exhaling a sigh. "Ephras didn't do it that way," she whispered. "He always put me before his work. That's why I am still here."

Taran frowned. "You can be even greater than your brother, Kaela."

She pondered the statement, then nodded, forcing a smile.

Taran stood up straight and descended the stairs with his shoulders high. "I expect to see you at the execution tomorrow. Don't disappoint me, Kae."

His words stung like a knife in her heart. Only Ephras called her that. That name was reserved for him.

As Taran walked away, she couldn't get rid of the dark feeling in her stomach. It was the feeling that something terrible was towering in front of her. Like she was watching someone she loved die. Her heart had been infected by the evil of the last few days. As Taran moved through the gates into the Northtown District, Kaela inched to her feet and closed her eyes.

Suddenly the dark city burst to life. Even in the nighttime her Sight helped her see exactly what she was looking for.

Taran's maroon aura shone on the other side of the Northtown District gate, moving slowly outwards to the edge of the city. He was surrounded by purple auras, probably his personal Sacred Order guards. The man would never go out into the city in its current state without them.

Kaela maneuvered to a dark corner and whispered a prayer under her breath, expelling a gust of wind underneath her as she jumped up onto the wall dividing the districts. She leapt to the nearest rooftop and continued to move toward Taran. He and his posse moved slowly. Too slowly. As if he was trying to not draw any attention to himself. Trying to keep himself from being followed.

Kaela wouldn't give him that luxury. She continued to push herself from rooftop to rooftop while Taran led his guards through the city. Eventually they reached the edge of the Gate District and exited the Citadel.

Why would he leave? Kaela asked herself. She waited for them to put some distance between themselves and the gate before exiting the city herself. Best to keep herself hidden.

The moon grew bright as the night continued, but Kaela hardly noticed it. While using her Sight, brightness didn't matter. As the landscape illuminated more, Taran moved faster. Being out of the Temple at night really disturbed him now that people weren't around to watch him.

They pushed through the wooded path until they arrived at Barlo. Kaela wasn't sure that she had ever seen a council member in Barlo. It was technically still under White Council jurisdiction, but peacekeepers hardly even made their way out this far. At least, not until Ephras punched a hole in the criminal empire that ran underground there.

She moved into the city slowly and followed Taran from a few blocks behind. Barlo was still a big city, but not nearly as massive as the Citadel itself. Less places to hide.

Taran crossed the bridge that led from the Upper District to the Lower. Every block he walked surprised Kaela. How far would he go? Had he come out this direction before? Do his guards know where they're going? Finally, he stopped. Kaela climbed onto a nearby rooftop to get as close as she could without drawing attention to herself. She opened her eyes to see the councilman and his guards outside the Other Observatory. He whispered a couple words to the Sacred Order and quickly disappeared inside.

* * *

Dawn sat in her damp cell without saying a word. Cain was imprisoned just down the hall across the breezeway from her, but she couldn't muster the courage to speak to him. It had been hours since they were thrown back down in the disgusting cells beneath the Temple. Hours of silence.

It gave her time to think, though she wasn't sure that was a good thing. Prison cells were supposed to be something that protected the public from dangerous people, but instead it locked her in with the most dangerous person of all. Herself.

Even with her Reflection quiet, her mind raced. She missed those harsh words. While that piece of her could be mean and spiteful, her Reflection was generally honest. That might have been why she hated it so much. Sometimes honesty hurt.

"He was there, right?" Cain's voice suddenly broke the terrible silence. "You saw Ragnar. I'm not crazy. He was there, in my house, asking us for help."

Dawn shook her head. "When I was in the Old City with Tarik, we saw something I didn't think was possible. One of his henchmen was killed by the guardian, and when he died his face shifted into that of an entirely different person. His skin was more shriveled, his face was shaped differently. It was like someone underneath was wearing the facade of Tarik's friend."

Cain grunted. "I can't believe I let this happen. I should have been more careful. I knew Ulumbra was out there, but I didn't know where."

"Cain..." tears threatened Dawn's eyes. "I am so sorry. You left for a few days and everything fell apart. It's all my fault. You should have been able to trust me, but no matter how hard I try, everything always ends in tragedy."

"No," Cain stated. "You are a victim, just like me. But we don't bask in our victimhood. The past is the past. It's gone and cannot be regained. Now we look to the future with expectation."

Expectation? What was Cain expecting from the future that wasn't already written in stone? In a few hours, Taran would have their heads, and their story would be over. The future was bleak and hopeless. Silence crept back into the prison and suffocated the dark cells again.

A familiar melody entered Dawn's mind. She didn't dare sing it; not in her current circumstances. It was the melody of a song her father had taught her long ago. The song she sang for Kaela after Ephras died.

I am fall leaves under the frost.
The chill is in my blood.
I'm unsure if what I feel is pain.
I'm unsure if it is not.

The melody bounced around in her head as if it were being sung to her by an experienced musician. She could hear her father's voice singing it in her mind, alongside two or three lutes playing in harmony with each other. Beneath her eyelids, she imagined herself by the warmth of the hearth in her home in Quarrine. Her mother stirred a pot of soup over the fire, sprinkling in some desert herbs. Her mother's soup, while good, was nothing compared to Cain's eloquent cooking. He had spoiled food for her for the rest of her life.

Her father sat on a ratty cushioned chair in the corner with a lute in his hands. She swore she could actually hear every pluck. Every note he played resonated in her mind.

His singing voice was soft, almost defeated. She could hear the pain in his timbre, trembling at every word. Cammie rushed into the hut, followed by Maron, both of them grinning from ear to ear. Maron laughed like she hadn't heard in a long time as Cammie tried to help her mother cook. He didn't know what he was doing, but he was having fun and that was what was important.

Suddenly, the vision grew dark. One at a time the figures of her family and friends vanished into a thin vapor. Her father's voice grew deeper as the flame in the hearth spread throughout the hut.

Can I endure this hopeless winter?
Will I be sleeping through the night?
Or will my heart stay cold and bitter?
Even as darkness turns to light.

Dawn's eyes burst open, tears staining her shirt. Her teeth clenched in her mouth until her jaw hurt. She had lost everything. Everyone and everything. Gone.

Her father's voice continued, only now without music.

For now, I wait for spring.
Where the sun will return and glow ever bright.

"That song was beautiful," Cain said.

Dawn scratched at her head. "You... heard that?"

"Well, of course he did," another voice chuckled. "I wasn't trying to be quiet." Dawn inched to the edge of her cell, peering out into the dark hall. She couldn't see him, but she knew her father's voice. He sat on his crusty bed in his own cell adjacent to Dawn's. "I used to sing that song to Dawn when she was little. It was one of her favorites."

"Ah," Cain laughed. "I remember now. You're the father?"

"Your deduction skills are immaculate," Drake scoffed. "If monster hunting didn't work out, maybe you could find work in the field of peacekeeping."

Cain sighed. "I wish it were that easy."

"People always say that." Drake said. "It *IS* that easy. You build up the courage to do it, and then you do it."

Cain sat silently, as did Dawn.

"I did want to tell you, reaver," Drake continued. "Thank you. You did a lot for my daughter, getting her into the city safely. Keeping her alive. Teaching her how to be a warrior. Thank you for everything."

"Of course," Cain said. "I just asked myself what I would want for my son if he were in Dawn's position."

* * *

Kaela raced back through the Citadel to the peacekeeper headquarters. She whispered prayers to try and get her feet to move faster, but her magic couldn't do that.

Peacekeepers and priests shouted the announcement through the streets about the execution scheduled for the following morning. Civilians poured out of their homes to discuss with each other what it meant. Was the time of unrest finally over? Kaela knew it wouldn't be that easy. There was still a long time until the execution.

She pushed through the doors of the peacekeeper headquarters where it was bustling with her fellow keepers. "We need four squads of seven in the morning, one squad per corner of the crowd." Captain Belvin shouted from the top of a set of stairs. Three men nodded at him, taking notes on small pads of paper. "After that," Belvin continued, "I want fliers over the execution. See if you can recruit Commander Silas and his squad. I am sure Taran is expecting them there anyways."

Kaela rushed up the stairs as Belvin dismissed the three

men. They raced off in separate directions to accomplish the tasks they were given.

"You!" Captain Belvin shouted, pointing his finger in Kaela's face. "Where have you been? That execution announcement came out of nowhere! Weren't you at the proceedings? We have so much to prepare to ensure the safety of the people. You..."

"Belvin!" Kaela interrupted. "I need a word. In private."

Captain Belvin furrowed his eyes. "Remember your place, Kaela."

"Please, Captain."

Belvin nodded, leading Kaela into his office and shutting the door behind them. "Make it quick," he snapped. "There is still so much to do."

"Captain," Kaela sighed. "After the trial, Taran talked with me. Something about his tone just made me... uncomfortable. I don't know how to explain it, but I trust my instincts."

"I can't believe this," Belvin rolled his eyes. "Your instincts are telling you that our leader is up to something? And you expect me to believe this after he sentences your friends to death?"

"Captain!" Kaela shouted. "Please, just listen to me. I followed him out of the city and into Barlo."

Belvin leaned forward, narrowing his eyes. "Go on."

"Last I saw him, his Sacred Order had led him to the Other Observatory."

"And he went inside?"

Kaela nodded. "The Observatory was shut down when Ephras and I followed that mage assassin into his hideout, wasn't it?"

"We've had a couple peacekeepers sweep the place to discourage squatters," Belvin said. "But it has been a while since our last patrol."

"Captain. Something is happening. Something we need to be ready for."

Belvin nodded. He opened the door to his office and clapped his hands. "Anvar and Dulin! With me!" The two peacekeepers leapt to their feet as Belvin turned back to Kaela. "You're coming with us, too. If what you are saying is true, then I want us to be ready for anything. Taking my three best keepers seems like the best course of action." The four peacekeepers equipped themselves with their best weapons and rushed out of the Citadel.

***

"You never told me you were a father," Dawn said, inching closer to the cell door.

Cain sighed. "Memories of a time long lost, D."

"What's his name?"

Cain was quiet for a moment. "His name was Roy. He was about your age when he died."

"No father should outlive his own child," Drake grunted.

"I would have given my life for Roy to live," Cain said. "Seems to be a common thread of my life. When I go out of my way to care for someone, they always end up in jeopardy. Everyone under my care dies."

"Cain..." Dawn said, but she didn't know how to comfort her mentor.

"I did everything I knew how to keep Roy alive," Cain said, his voice breaking. "He still died. Taken by the Fallen.

I left home to live in a foreign country and helped Ragnar become the warrior he was destined to become, and now he's gone, too. I swore to myself I'd get Remy back to this city alive, and that... Beast... took her. And now look at us! Sitting in a cell, waiting for death to descend upon us. The fingerprint I leave on people's lives is the very fingerprint of death. You'd be better off without me."

Silence overtook them. Dawn had never seen Cain this way. From the moment she met him, even when everything went awry, he was the voice of confidence. He was the voice of reason. There was never anxiety in him, instead being calm, cool, and collected. Sometimes the strongest people are the ones who love beyond all faults, cry behind closed doors, and fight battles nobody knows about.

"A touch of gray for every shade of blue," Drake said. "There can't be light without some darkness. But the darkness doesn't extinguish the light. They exist together. Alongside each other. You can't see the shadows if there isn't a source of light. On the contrary, the shadows are proof of the light's presence.

"There may be darkness in your past, but you are the reason Dawn is still alive today. The next few hours aside, thank you for buying a father the time to say a proper goodbye to his daughter."

* * *

The Sacred Order remained outside the Observatory as the peacekeepers approached. Commander Belvin led them through shadows. Best to remain out of sight until they knew what was going on.

"If something really is happening," Belvin whispered. "Three Sacred Order guards might be too much for us."

"We can distract them," Kaela said. "One of us can pull them away while the others move into the building."

"I volunteer," Dulin said, raising his gauntleted hand.

Belvin shook his head. "Have you ever witnessed the Sacred Order in a fight? Your magic won't give you an advantage."

"I don't need to beat them, Cap," Dulin said. "Just survive long enough for you to get inside."

Belvin nodded. "You'll need to make enough of an impact that all of them abandon their posts to go after you."

Dulin smiled. "I got this." The young peacekeeper strolled out into the moonlight with a sword in each hand. The guards seemed like they didn't even notice him as he walked by. Dulin shouted, screaming a prayer to Fos at the top of his lungs. Suddenly, lightning struck between him and the guards, one of the largest bolts Kaela had ever seen. Stone flew about the street and slammed into the heavily armored guards, throwing them back into the Observatory wall. Another bolt crashed into the wall of the Observatory, blasting a hole into the building.

The guards leapt back to their feet, but Dulin had already rushed to a nearby alleyway, summoning another lightning bolt toward the nearest guard. The heavily armored soldier moved like wind, flashing to the side to allow the bolt to hit the side of the building. Stone crumbled to the floor, creating another clear opening into the Observatory. The Sacred Order guards cursed loudly at each other, the three of them pursuing Dulin into the dark alleyway. Belvin nodded, signaling Kaela and Anvar to move into the newly created entryway.

Darkness radiated within the structure. An unnatural shadow engulfed each corner. Last time Kaela had seen this place it radiated color. The plants and fauna that grew in each room had glowed a brilliant bioluminescence. There was hardly even a need for lamps and torches because the wildlife that grew here would act as a light that reached wherever it was needed.

That was no longer the Other Observatory. All the life that once grew here was now dead. Rotting gray vines hid underneath shadows of what used to be estranged trees and bushes. Dry branches crunched under their feet as they crept from room to room. Something like a thick fog filled the wide open corridors.

Kaela tried to use her Sight, but nothing sprang to life as the world normally would. Belvin and Anvar's auras even stayed hidden to her, something she had never experienced since she learned she could use this power.

The building was a labyrinth, but it was nothing the peacekeepers couldn't navigate. They snuck between rooms, bouncing from wall to wall to hide in the shadows. The stone set within the floor was scorched, stained a deep black. How could this place change so much in a single year?

They continued onwards at a slow pace, passing different rooms and countless passages. Some hidden doorways had begun to crumble, revealing the secrets of what they guarded. Finally, they made it to the final room; the center of the sprawling facility. It was blocked by a massive granite door engraved with familiar carvings. Belvin scanned the door while Kaela ran her hands across the grooves in the stone. One carving in particular caught her eye. A teardrop set atop a cross.

A nervous rumble filled her stomach. She reached for her spear and yanked it from her back. Anvar unhooked the two axes clipped to his waist, glancing back and forth around the corridor. "What is it?"

Kaela hushed him, placing her ear against the door. There were voices; more than one. Two men and two women speaking in whispered tones.

"Please, just give me another twenty-four hours," one man's voice trembled. "All the blame for the chaos will fall to this man and to the Outriders, and you will have the girl's power. She will be dead by midday tomorrow, and the rebellion will be quashed. The city will be yours. There will be nothing that can stop her fate this time."

"You best hope you are right, Councilman," the other man said. Kaela shivered when she heard his voice. It was a familiar voice; one that sent sickness into her mind. "If I have to watch this city crumble and burn to see her dead and my power returned to me, I will do so."

"No one else needs to die, my lord."

"I wish that were true."

Belvin growled. "Enough." He whispered a prayer and blasted the door open with a hurricane force of wind, throwing the granite from their hinges.

Three hooded figures stood in the center of the massive circular room, alongside Councilman Taran, who stood on his own nearby. It was the same room Kaela and Ephras had chased the assassin into a year ago. The same room that had begun their journey to Quarrine. It was the only room that hadn't changed over the years, still springing with unnatural life.

"Councilman," Belvin said. "Care to tell us what you are doing here?"

Kaela studied the three other figures. She had seen them sometime before...

She gasped, tightening her grip on her spear.

It was Moldolor.

XIX

The Other

The night dragged on in the prison. Dawn lay on the mat, reminiscing about the last year. Even amidst hardship, life had always turned around. It was generally Cain that saw to that.

"The mission," Dawn asked, recalling Cain's words about Remy. "To Quarrine. What happened over there?"

She could hear his audible sigh like pure pain escaping his lips. "It was nothing like it was supposed to be. Ragnar, or whatever it was that wore his face, had disappeared and the orcs were waiting for us. But even that we could have handled. We *did* handle that. It was the chieftain, dabbling in things he didn't understand.

"Once the first portal opened, the floodgates broke. The barrier between our world and the Other was already weakened by the red moon, and he released the Fallen upon the city like a tidal wave. There was nothing we could do. He killed them all. I used every ounce of my energy to destroy just one of them. So much energy, I should be dead. When I woke up, Silas had me tied up. Mae was on the verge of death. Remy's body was left behind."

"Silas blamed you?"

"I would have done the same," Cain said. "Everything was stacked up against us, D. We left it alone for too long and Ulumbra got the better of us. With Kytas dead, it was only a matter of time before the Fallen broke through. Fos' defense was broken and the enemy exploited that fracture."

* * *

"You shouldn't have come here," Taran cursed, removing a sword from a hidden sheath. "I had this under control. Everything would have been so much simpler if you would have left well enough alone."

Kaela felt rage boil up inside her until she screamed uncontrollably. A blast of wind expelled from her feet to launch her at the councilman. He danced out of the way, slamming his blade down. Kaela raised her spear and kicked at his feet, but he backpedaled away.

The dreary atmosphere clouded Kaela's mind. Taran slashed again with his sword, but Kaela slammed her spear against the blade and checked him with the blunt end. He fell to his back and she held her spear at his throat, but deep purple tendrils wrapped around her and tossed her back against the far wall. She pressed her eyes shut to get a better view of the arena, but darkness shrouded everything. The auras of every fighter blended together into a single messy color palette.

She snapped her eyes open and jumped to her feet to see the witch Ariyah taking her place among the fighters. Kaela recognized her from the Old City Prison too. She was the one who brought Moldolor back in the first place. She didn't, however, recognize the final figure; a young orc girl with deep blue eyes. Not the normal green of an orc.

Belvin and Anvar leapt into the fray in a flash of fire and wind. Elements engulfed the room like a blazing tempest. Kaela rushed forward to assist the peacekeepers' onslaught of attacks, but Ariyah expelled a blast of radiant darkness, pushing back against their powerful blasts and kicking up smoke and dust throughout the room.

Taran emerged from the settling smoke, swinging his blade toward Kaela. She ducked, slamming the butt of her spear into his chest. As he curled in pain, Kaela stepped up onto his back and jumped off toward Moldolor, who hadn't moved once during the fight. He just stood with a menacing smirk on his face, watching the violence. She slammed her spear at the murderer's head, but dark tendrils slammed her down against the floor, this time from the orc girl.

Kaela glanced up as the young girl jumped on top of her, glaring into her eyes and speaking words in a disgusting dialect. It wasn't orcish. It was darker than that.

Suddenly, Kaela couldn't move. Just like the Hilios match, she was suspended in time. Magic continued to flourish around the room, but she remained still, watching the orc girl snarl above her. Darkness encroached on the light in the room. It was unnatural. Terrifying.

The girl glanced back to Moldolor, who simply nodded.

She looked at Kaela and smiled, reaching out and touching her cheek with her nasty hand.

Kaela felt a surge in her body. An instant, grueling pain from her head to her toe. She gasped for air, but her lungs failed. She directed prayers toward Fos, but she was unsure if he could hear her. All the energy in her body was escaping like water out of a cistern.

Just then, Captain Belvin laid his shoulder into the orc girl, tackling her to the floor. Kaela gasped a breath of air as life began to refill her body. She pushed herself to her feet, stumbling as her legs turned to jelly beneath her.

Taran and Ariyah cornered Anvar, who spun violently to keep on his feet. Taran unleashed a barrage of strikes toward the peacekeeper's steel while Ariyah attacked him with her own magical blasts.

The orc girl had found her way back to her feet and was attacking Belvin with everything she had. The commander backed into a corner, sweat pouring from his brow.

And Moldolor just watched from the back of the room.

"Fos," she spoke as she set her sights on the dark sorcerer. "Give us strength to expel the darkness."

Suddenly, a burst of energy flowed through her body. She screamed, charging again toward the foul sorcerer. He spoke a word she didn't understand and Ariyah turned, leaving Councilman Taran to fight Anvar on his own. The witch released a blast of darkness, but Kaela's light radiated all the more, engulfing the darkness in its brilliance. Dark spells continued to fly towards the peacekeeper, all for naught.

Kaela ignored Ariyah, her eyes set on her brother's killer. The murderer. Images of the prison flashed through her mind, his face the center of them all. Ephras' lifeless, empty eyes staring up at her. Grief welled up inside, but it quickly turned to rage. A blazing fire roaring in her soul. Once her fire had started, ordinary water couldn't extinguish it.

But Moldolor was no ordinary enemy. She rammed her spear toward his head and he ducked out of the way. He was chanting something, Kaela realized. Foul words that had been filling the air for the duration of the battle. Kaela swiped again, following up with a blast of icy wind that threw the mage against the back wall, but it was too late.

As Moldolor climbed back to his feet, a portal opened in between him and Kaela. She could see his blue eyes behind the dark abyss for only a moment before a figure materialized in front of her. Two freezing eyes stared at her with pure hatred, a deafening wail escaping from its jagged mouth.

The creature emerged from the portal, its blubbery head sitting atop a towering, stringy body. Scars and still-open wounds covered most of its torso. It advanced toward Kaela on four hulking legs, a vine-like tail scraping the floor beneath it. Two immense wings extended out from its body, each one the length of at least two grown men.

Kaela watched as the creature approached, its eyes never once moving from her small, frail frame. Her fire faded, extinguished in a moment. The rest of the fighters ceased in order to watch the behemoth escaping from its captivity, ready to pounce.

* * *

A crash echoed from down the prison corridor, followed by deafening shouts. Dawn recognized the voices. It was the prison guards. Something was happening. Their cells shook and there was silence again. Dawn gazed beyond her cell door as darkness seemed to encroach on their minimal torchlight.

"What is this devilry," Drake asked, his voice low.

Chattering resounded from the entrance. There was a consistent tap against the stone. A dreadful rhythm from the depths of Dawn's worst nightmares.

"Cain?" Dawn muttered.

Cain sighed. "Our fates may have caught up to us."

* * *

The demon jumped at Kaela and she rolled swiftly out of the way. It didn't stop though, racing directly toward Anvar. The peacekeeper didn't stand a chance. He could only wave his axes once before the creature crashed through him and the outer wall in quick succession. The demon turned back toward the facility's center, carelessly slamming its hulking hoof through Anvar's skull.

Kaela winced and turned back toward the portal, but to her dismay, another had opened a few feet from the original. Smaller reptilian creatures emerged from it. Moldolor's laugh resounded throughout the room, a guttural and inhumane laughter. "The girl will die," he said. "One way or another."

Kaela drew her lips to a line, tightening her grip on her spear. As she took a step in rage toward the monster of a man, Belvin leapt in front of her.

"Go!" He shouted, slicing through one of the smaller demons. "We've lost. We have to regroup."

The larger beast burst back into the room, roaring a

terrible roar. Belvin pushed Kaela out of the way with a blast of heavy wind as it charged past them.

"I will hold them off!" He said. "Just go!"

Just then, the rage she had for Moldolor transformed into something else. Fear. A primal terror that gripped her heart and wouldn't let go. She flipped back toward the two doors where they entered from and ran. She could hear Belvin slicing through the little creatures that surrounded him, but she didn't look back. She just kept running.

* * *

Dawn whispered a prayer under her breath, but it was no use. The drug was still in her system, diminishing her powers. It would be the same for Cain.

A large, bipedal beast emerged from the shadows. It glared at Dawn with three horrible eyes set in the back of its horrid bony skull. It tapped the floor with the claws on its lizard-like hind legs as it grasped Dawn's prison door with shorter front arms. The creature sniffed and wind blew around the cell, nearly knocking Dawn to the floor.

The creature roared, rattling the scales on its back before grasping a single prison bar with its disgusting mouth and snapping it between its enormous teeth. Each one must have been the size of Dawn's head. She pressed back against the solid rock of her cell, terror filling her heart. She was helpless. She could hear her father and Cain shouting, trying to get the beast's attention, but it grabbed another bar, snapping it like a dried out twig.

The beast tried to ram its way into the prison cell, but its head didn't fit yet. A piece of a metal bar splintered free and flew back towards Dawn, who quickly picked it up and slammed it down against the creature's head.

It paused hardly for a moment, a deep growl rattling Dawn's bones, before grasping another prison bar in its mouth. One after another it snapped them between its teeth as Dawn whacked her metal pole into its head.

Finally, the creature snapped the final bar and stepped slowly into the cell with Dawn, staring at her with its hateful eyes.

XX

The Red Moon

T he world was on fire.

Kaela had seen a red moon before, but this time was different. She wasn't sure if the red moon had come from something spiritual, or from the fire that engulfed the city of Barlo.

Screams overwhelmed the city as creatures like which Kaela had never seen flooded the streets. She stepped over the body of a father who seemed to be guarding the rest of his family. He had failed. They lay in the corner of that street in a crimson pool, illuminated by the flickering light of the flames around them.

Bile bit at Kaela's throat. She fell to her knees, cursing the world around her. Cursing Fos. The God who allowed this to happen. The God who was supposed to be watching over them, but still let Ephras die. Still let men like Moldolor run rampant, killing families like this in the streets. Letting terror rule the world.

She knew he was real. Her magic was proof of that. It was a faith in something that was more than just what she could see. Belief that there was more. Ephras had taught her that. He taught her about believing in something greater than herself. But where was Fos now?

She stood as a winged humanoid beast burst through a window, a severed arm resting in its beaked mouth. It dropped the arm and flew at Kaela with a terrible screech, but a bolt of lightning crashed into the beast, slamming it into a nearby wall.

Dulin rushed into Kaela's sight with two swords gripped tight in his hands as three more harpies soared over the rooftop. One flew at him with a cry, but he sliced through it swiftly, turning toward the other two creatures. "Lady Kaela!" He shouted. "It's time to go!"

Kaela's mind hazed. The world around her seemed to spin and blur as Dulin slashed wildly at the flying creatures. He was able to clip one on the wing, sending it tumbling to the ground, but the other flew up high and swooped down toward Kaela. Her mind snapped back to reality and she jumped out of the way, jabbing her spear into the beast's side. It crumbled to the pavement next to the dead family.

"We have to get back to the Citadel!" Dulin said. "Warn them of the coming assault!"

"Fos isn't going to help us," Kaela mumbled. "Dulin, we are..."

She looked just in time to see a massive greatsword shear through Dulin's arm and continue to wedge itself into the city boy's ribs. Dulin grunted, thrown to the side as the demon released the sword from him and slammed it down in a two handed blow.

Kaela screamed, wind whipping up uncontrollably around her. The large, humanoid creature flew backwards as Kaela charged at it, ramming her spear through the demon's chest. She turned to Dulin, but couldn't bear to look at his body.

Gotta keep going, Kaela thought. *If Fos won't do something about it, then I have to. We just have to regroup.*

She didn't utter a prayer as she rushed through the streets. Silently, she ran back to the Citadel, the city burning behind her.

Chaos followed. Citizens flooded the streets as their homes were immersed in flame. Creatures chased them back into the fires, a seemingly better death than what these beasts offered.

People scrambled up the stairwell to the Upper District, clogging the passage between the two halves of the city. Kaela pushed through the people like a fish swimming upstream. Ash swirled around their heads as they watched bodies being thrown from the top of the bridge. Harpies screeched overhead, snatching citizens in their disgusting claws and dragging them across the Barlo city skyline.

Whatever weapons the citizens could scrounge up seemed to have no effect on the creatures that swarmed the streets. Barlo may have been one of the most fortified cities in the world, but the enemies were already within the walls.

I just need to get to the Citadel. Kaela thought. *Rendezvous with the fliers and the soldiers.*

As the thoughts filled her mind, a pegasus crashed into the ascending wall, covered with demons like ants swarming a picnic. The animal fell to the street with a *THUMP* that echoed louder than the screams it encouraged.

The beasts swarmed the bottom of the staircase, ripping through the people who stood in their way. Some people on the steps grabbed some stones and hurled them down towards the monsters, but that hardly did anything to slow them.

When Kaela finally squeezed her way through the crowd, she wasn't prepared for the carnage that awaited her on the bridge. People threw themselves from the ledge in an attempt to escape from the slaughter. Kaela just ran. Her vows rang in her head. To protect the city. To protect the people. She couldn't do that if she was dead as well, and stopping to help one person could easily end in her demise. She was only one person. Just a girl with a spear in the middle of Hell.

* * *

Dawn tightened her grip on the metal bar. The scaly creature tapped its claw against the pavement. A call to others? Dawn couldn't be sure. Right now wasn't the time to ruminate on it.

The beast charged forward, opening wide its enormous maw. Dawn screamed and jumped to the side, whacking the monster on the top of its head as its mouth snapped shut. She bolted to the prison door as the creature flipped around, its thorny tail crashing into the rock wall separating Dawn and her father's cells. It thrashed forward again, Dawn hardly moving out of the way back into her cell.

Once more the creature turned. Its tail was a battering

ram, slamming into the prison's foundation. Rubble fell from the ceiling between them. It opened its mouth again, lunging forward towards Dawn. This time, she stood her ground, reaching the metal bar forward to shove into the monster's mouth, jamming it open. The beast roared, throwing itself against the walls in pain, more rock and debris falling onto their tiny battlefield.

It slowed down, digging its massive heels into the ground. Suddenly, with a huge exertion of force, the monster bit down against the bar. The steel punctured through the roof of its mouth. Dawn backed up against the wall inside her cell. She hadn't even realized that Cain and her father had been shouting the entire time. Her mind had tuned out everything. It was just her and the devil.

Like lightning, the beast charged her again, but as she leapt out of the way it slammed its tail into her gut, smashing her into the wall of the cell. She could hear the sound of her ribs crunching beneath the enormous meaty club. Blood sprayed from her mouth as she coughed up the fluid filling her lungs.

Once again, I'm not enough.

The creature turned as Dawn knelt, gasping for whatever breath she could. Hardly anything came. She just wheezed under the shadow of death as the demon stepped up to her, its own blood dripping from its mouth.

The world spun around Dawn. Her entire body felt cold. She could hear her mother's voice echo in her mind. "The Wastes are dangerously cold at night." How much colder would she feel once she drew her final breath? Would she feel anything at all?

A stone thumped against the creature's scaly head. "You will not touch her again," Drake demanded, pressing through the newly made hole between the cells. He placed himself between Dawn and the monster.

It snarled, tapping its claws against the rubble that now lay before them. Dawn pushed herself away from the creature, her back quickly finding the wall. *Curses,* everything within her hurt.

The beast swung its tail at Drake, who moved swiftly underneath it, grasping another metal bar from the pile of rocks on the floor. He bolted out into the hallway, slamming the pole against the other prison bars. The sound of metal on metal rang loud throughout the corridor, echoing with each hit. The creature screamed, lowering its head and charging out into the hallway. Drake leapt out of the way again and the beast slammed into the bars across from Dawn's cell. The force was so great the beast almost crashed all the way through in one hit.

Dawn watched her father duck and dodge the infuriated creature while banging the steel bar against as much metal as he could. The monster was only getting more angry, growing even more reckless in its hasty attacks. It roared in frustration, swinging its tail into all the walls nearby.

Drake halted in the hallway as the beast dug its heels into the ground. Dawn could see his face through a hole in the stone walls of the prison. "I love you, Dawn," he said. He looked to Cain, who was working on pushing out rocks to escape from his own cell. "I will only be able to get you a few minutes. Get my daughter to safety."

What?

"Dad, no!"

"No father should outlive his daughter," Drake met Dawn's watering eyes. His voice was steady, his lips drawn to a line. "I am so proud of you, hon. You never heard that enough from me. I love you, kid."

"No," Dawn whimpered.

The beast roared and Drake flipped down the dark corridor, slamming his metal against the cell bars as he ran. After just a few seconds, they were both out of sight, the echo of the bars ringing in Dawn's ears.

Then the ringing stopped.

* * *

"How did we get here?" Kaela muttered to herself as she slammed her spear through the chest of a larger, humanoid demon. She wasn't sure if she was talking aloud or in her head. She didn't care. She slipped on blood as she stepped through Barlo's streets.

Men cried out. Women screamed. Children ran. It was like something Kaela had never seen. Horror attacked the unarmed people. Bodies lay in heaps in the middle of the road, blocking certain ways out of the city.

Kaela halted at a courtyard, watching as more and more demons poured in from the surrounding streets. So many different kinds, each one just as terrible as the last. They swept through the city like a tide of fire and steel, their eyes piercing through the smoke like daggers.

The guards and Barlo army was in just as much disarray as the rest of the city. Single squadrons of five or six soldiers at a time would rush headstrong into the awful enemy, all of them meeting a quick fate.

Kaela ducked into an alleyway, pushing through to another nearby street. Her mind was as numb as her feet. All this death, all this blood. It had an effect on a person. She was useless. She would try to save a person's life, only for them to be killed by another creature a moment later. There was nothing she could do.

As she exited the alleyway, another humanoid demon locked eyes with her and charged at her with a sword and spear. As it raced toward her, a pegasus swooped in and slammed the beast into a nearby wall. Silas landed next to her on his mount, offering a hand.

Kaela swung up onto the pegasus. "We've lost the city," she said.

The pegasus flapped its wings and flew into the air, ascending over Barlo's massive walls where an army of pegasus were soaring over the city with survivors cowering on their backs. Just over a small grouping of trees, Kaela saw the Citadel. Flames engulfed the great city. From the Gate District to the Temples, it was all on fire. Kaela had failed.

"Where do we go?" Silas asked.

"South," Kaela said. "To the coast. To Korio."

* * *

Dawn pushed herself to her feet, every bone in her body ached. More than an ache. Dawn was broken.

She grasped one of the stones laying on the floor of the

prison and hobbled to Cain's cell. The bars were bent, but still intact. In the cell next to his, however, the creature had destroyed the metal with its aggressive thrashing. Cain had been working at pushing through the gaps in the stone to make a way out.

As hard as she possibly could, Dawn slammed the stone against the rock wall still holding Cain in. It hardly did anything. Still not enough. Dawn slumped back to the floor and pressed her eyes shut. Defeated.

"Dawn..."

It wasn't Cain's voice. It wasn't even coming from the direction of Cain's cell. Dawn inched her eyes open to find a hooded warrior standing in the breezeway with a spear in his hands. His eyes were glazed over, like all the color had been taken from them.

And standing next to him was Krom.

Dawn jumped to her feet, completely ignoring the pain she felt in her body. She ran into Krom's arms with tears flowing from her eyes like a dam had been broken. Krom just held her as she cried, not saying a word as she stained his already dirty overcoat. She pushed away from him, finally noticing his missing hands.

"Krom, what happened?" She whimpered.

"I..."

The hooded soldier laid his hand against the stone wall of Cain's cell, whispering a prayer under his breath. In a sudden magnificence the rocks disintegrated, vanishing into dust and mist. "We have to go," he said, his voice stern. "We will have time for reunions later."

Krom nodded. "Fen is right. The Citadel is under siege by demons."

"The Fallen," Cain corrected as he exited the prison cell.

"We need to get out before it's too late," Krom continued.

Fen pulled out a sword and handed it over to Cain who nodded in appreciation, then pulled a blessed bow off his back and gave it to Dawn, along with gloves to match.

"It's yours," Krom smiled. "We raided the evidence chamber on the way in."

"There is someone I need to check on," Dawn said as they rushed through the corridor. Bodies of guards littered the prison halls, the stone coated in a deep maroon. Fen whispered another prayer and light exuded throughout the prison, fending off the encroaching darkness. Alongside the guard's bodies were more of the otherworldly creatures lying lifeless on the stone.

"Our worst fears have been realized," Cain said as they stepped over the corpses. "This is the unhinged power of Seor."

They passed a familiar stretch of the prison as Dawn rushed to find Maron's cell in as much shambles as the rest of them. She cried out, seeing the cell door still intact. A young man cowered in the corner of his room, hiding in the shadows.

"Maron," Dawn whispered. "We're getting you out of here."

XXI

Running Blind

Dawn followed Fen as he led the company up into the Temple District. The light was just as low outside as it was within the prison halls. The sky burned a deep red, the moon and stars all covered by the thick haze of fog and ash. Flames erupted from cracks in the city streets. The earth shook and shards of rock from both temples crumbled down their faces.

Fen held out his arm, halting the group at the prison entrance. Dawn glanced up to see a silhouette at the top of the stairs leading to the Temple of Fos. Her fingers winced, warmth beginning to fill her body.

"This is your destiny," Dawn's Reflection boomed in her head. "Death follows you."

Her Reflection flashed into an image of her father before disappearing into a soft vapor. Dawn collapsed, tears flowing from her eyes. Each hysterical gasp stung at her broken ribs.

He really was gone this time. She had a second chance to have a life with her father, and she ruined it by cursing him. She wasted their final moments together.

"We have to go," Fen said, scanning the streets for signs of enemies. "The city is no longer safe."

Cain leaned down, placing his arm around Dawn's shoulder. "There is nothing I can say right now, D. Nothing I can do to take away your pain. But your father made a choice. He chose for you to live. Let us honor that decision and get you out of here so you can grieve for him properly." Dawn gazed up at her mentor, wiping tears from her cheek. She nodded and grabbed his hand as he lifted her to her feet.

Fen led them up the stairs and into the Temple of Fos. It was a disaster. The marble fixtures and chandelier lamps had come crashing down, laying in pieces on the floor. Bodies of priests and soldiers alike littered the hallways. There were even some Obsidian Guards collapsed in their path, their unique plate armor mangled and bent beneath the trauma of the Fallen attackers.

As they continued through the halls of the first floor and down into the dungeons, Dawn heard a crash from the entrance, followed by a blood-curdling roar and tapping on the marble floors. Fen picked up his pace as they made it to the Old City entrance. He yanked open the cellar door, a single ladder descending down into the caverns beneath the Citadel. Tapping echoed in the dungeon as the creatures sniffed out the party. Fen pushed Maron to go first, instructing him to help Krom as he climbed without hands. It was difficult and time consuming, but he made it nonetheless.

The tapping grew louder. Dawn swore she could hear the

monster breathing, sniffing down the halls. "Cain," Fen said. "You go next. If there is danger down there, I would like an experienced reaver present to help."

Cain glanced at Dawn, then nodded, racing down the ladder at lightning speed. As he called up to Dawn to begin her descent, the creature rounded the corner. Dawn wasn't sure if it was the same one that she had encountered before, but it was just as monstrous.

Fen stepped in front of her, holding his spear in front of him. "Your turn, hon. It's time to go."

The creature rushed forward, snapping its mouth at the blind spearman. He sidestepped the attack, whispering a prayer and launching the beast into the wall.

"Now, please."

Dawn snapped back to reality, limping to the ladder. The creature jumped back to its feet and locked its eyes on her. It charged. Dawn tried to climb faster, but the monster's speed was unnatural.

Suddenly, Fen blasted it with a gust of wind, then hosed it with water. As the creature hit the wall, the water froze, locking it into place. It tried to writhe and kick, but the layer of ice was too thick. Fen readied his spear and rammed it through the creature's eye socket.

"Please," Fen said, wiping the blade of his spear with a cloth from his belt. "Move a little quicker, would you?"

Dawn nodded, descending the rest of the way down the ladder. Fen followed behind, snapping his fingers once at the bottom to reveal the city below. What had already been ruins was now even more destroyed. The Fallen knew no bounds. They had only one purpose; to destroy the world of men.

Fen led them on silent feet. The Old City was big, but wasn't nearly to the scale of the Citadel itself. They could hear creatures maneuvering through the city, leaving wreckage in their wake.

Laying in one of the shattered city courtyards was the Council's guardian. Its four lifeless red eyes gazed at them from within its broken skull. Dawn hadn't noticed its silver fur before, but now it was covered in blood. She couldn't decipher if it was its own or the blood of the Fallen. At length they stirred and looked around, searching for anything that would give them a hint of the battle that sealed the guardian's fate.

"This isn't good," Cain said. "This was one of the most dangerous beasts in the White Islands."

"Easy prey for these creatures," Fen said. "You know the danger of Seor's army, Cain. Your duty as a reaver just got a lot more complicated."

They heard chattering behind them, followed by a rolling boom that rattled the very ground where they stood. Scurrying feet echoed through the cavern.

"They're coming!" Maron whimpered. "If they can kill this thing, how do we stand a chance?"

"Silence!" Fen said. "Continue onwards. Quick!"

The company pushed forward past the felled beast. They were now further into the Old City than Dawn had ever been.

The walls shook as another *BOOM* crashed behind them. The chattering of the creatures was getting closer. There was a rush of hoarse laughter like stones sliding into a pit, followed by a deep, otherworldly roar. The words they spoke were dark. Vile even by nature.

The company came to a long bridge that crossed over a rushing underground river. The earth shook again and a chunk of stone fell from above, crashing through the bridge and washing away the rubble in the roaring waters. The chasm that now stretched between them was far too expansive. "We can't jump that!" Maron cried out. They halted, glancing back and seeing beady red eyes swarming through the darkness.

Cain groaned. "Even though I do feel my magic coming back, I'm not sure if I have enough energy within me to leap this gap."

Dawn pulled the blessed bow from her back and pulled back on the space between the shaft. An arrow of light materialized on the bow and she released it between one of the pairs of eyes. The creature screamed before its eyes faded. She pulled back again, the rest of the creatures racing toward them.

"I had hoped we could outrun them, but we must stand our ground," Fen said, readying his spear. "Our only chance for survival is together."

"What?" Krom shouted. "Your plan is to fight?"

Fen nodded. "Stay back with Dawn and the boy. We won't let these creatures take you. Fos has given us victory today."

As he spoke, the beasts emerged into the clearing, screeching at the company. Cain had taught Dawn about these creatures. The charun. Pawns of the underworld. Their small, grimy bodies were covered in steel armor, their hands replaced by two short blades. Their stubby faces wore no helmet, but spikes crowned their heads.

The creatures rushed forward, crashing into Fen who met them like a dam stopping a river. Long, sweeping blows from his spear slowed the demons' approach. Cain joined him, parrying the charun with quick, precise strikes.

Dawn pulled back on her bow, her arm aching. This wasn't a normal bow. The light that materialized created no real tension, so her still healing hand could handle the weight of the illusionary bowstring.

She carefully chose her targets, finding the creatures who had the best chance of closing in on Cain and Fen. She fired in rapid succession, one arrow after another finding its target.

The earth shook again under the weight of monstrous footsteps. Rocks fell from the city's ceiling, crashing around the company. Dawn hobbled out of the way as one came pummeling straight toward her.

As the new creature approached with its massive footsteps, the city continued to shake. The battlefield soon became a ruin of shattered rock and rubble. They completely blocked Dawn's vision of the fight, rendering her bow useless.

***

Krom watched the chaos unfold in front of him. He was helpless. There was nothing he could do for his friends. The thought passed through his head of watching them die while he stood back and did nothing.

He jumped out of the way of falling rocks, trying to keep his eyes on the battlefield as well as the chunks of stone overhead that threatened him. He couldn't even see Fen and Cain anymore. The debris had blocked his vision.

He watched Dawn climb atop one of the pieces of fallen stone. Even with a broken arm and shattered ribs, she had found a way to help. She continued to fire upon the approaching menace from her vantage point.

As he watched, he saw more demons scuttering along a balcony to the right, making their way behind them. Krom shouted, but no one heard him under the sound of the crashing footsteps and falling slabs. They leapt down and charged at the rock where Dawn stood.

Krom cried out. In an act of complete foolishness, he bolted toward the rock, ramming his shoulder into one of the smaller creatures. Another swiped at him with one of its blade-hands, but he jumped backwards just out of range of the short sword. More of them approached, probably two dozen demons all snarling and barking in their fowl tongue. Krom screamed, charging at them with reckless abandon. If this was his end, so be it. He wouldn't sit back and watch his friends die.

He wouldn't watch Dawn die.

One monster slashed at him, but he sidestepped it, kicking at its grimy head. Another lunged behind him, slicing his leg before he could get out of the way again. The pain hardly phased him as he rammed his shoulder into the closest demon. As he charged, his feet slipped underneath him. One of the little beasts jumped onto his chest. Krom pressed his eyes shut as it raised its blade into the air.

Just then, the creature's disgusting head fell from its shoulders. When Krom opened his eyes, its body fell away from him. He pushed himself back to his feet to see Maron hacking at the monsters as best he could. This was no warrior, but instead a survivor. Krom laid his foot into the back of one of the beasts as it readied to attack the Quarrinian boy. Krom may not be able to kill them, but he could help to slow them.

He ducked and dodged again as more rocks fell from the ceiling, this time larger than before. He jumped out of the way as one crushed a demon ready to lunge at him.

As the rocks fell, he heard a splash. He flipped to see a giant slab of stone set in the river, not washing away. Instead, it slowed the flow of water around it.

And an idea burst into his mind.

* * *

Dawn released another arrow past Fen and into an approaching charun. Their numbers were endless. They just kept swarming in from the shadows. Hearing shouts from behind her, she spun to see the creatures surrounding her new vantage point. Maron and Krom brawled below, hardly putting up enough of a fight to stay alive. She drew back on her bow again, thinning the crowds that surged around them.

A terrible roar emerged from the depths of the city. Dawn turned back to see two smoldering red eyes flickering in the darkness. A colossal hand crashed through the nearest stone house, flames bursting through cracks in its stoney-skin. It was a walking mountain. When it opened its gaping maw, sparks flew out from an inferno burning within. It slammed its massive stone hands into the ground, sending shockwaves throughout Dawn's entire body.

"You cannot defeat this creature alone," her Reflection boomed in her mind.

Cain and Fen continued to cut down the charun as the mountainous creature further wrecked the battlefield. They rolled out of the way of its earth-shattering attacks, coming mere inches of being crushed under its terrible weight. Dawn tried to fire at it with her bow, but the light arrows did nothing. Fire and ice erupted from Cain and Fen's hands, chipping little pieces of rock away from the creature.

It thrashed around in fury. With each slam of its hands, more rocks flooded the battlefield. They were nearly buried in the sheer volume of rubble and debris that covered the underground city.

Dawn placed her bow on her back and whispered a prayer under her breath. A storm rose up within her. The energy that had left her filled her to the brim. "That's the thing," she said to her Reflection. "I'm not alone."

She expelled a gust of wind beneath her, launching herself into the fray. She landed beneath the creature in an explosion of rock, shooting a blast of lightning into what looked like the creature's hand.

Fen raced around the monster, dousing it with water that froze as it made contact. The walking mountain slowed its rampage, breaking through the ice to search for Dawn as she scrambled between its hulking legs, holding her throbbing arm close to her body.

Cain joined the battle, blasting the monster with explosions of fire. Piece by piece, the mountain creature's stone-shell dwindled away. As the mages bombarded it with their magic, it only grew more furious, stomping and thrashing around whenever it could get itself free, which wasn't often. Fen was relentless.

Finally, Dawn saw a glowing red jewel within the monster's chest. She turned to fire lightning at it, but a charun leapt into her vision, slicing toward her body. She jumped backwards, her bolt of lightning flying into the ceiling, more rocks crashing to the battlefield. The charun attacked again, but she rolled off the boulder onto another, pointed stones slicing into her leg. Pulling the bow off her back, she readied a shot for the attacking charun.

As she pulled back on the illusionary bowstring, a chunk of rock exploded from nearby and flew toward her as the mountain creature crashed through the debris. She expelled a forceful gust of air beneath her to throw her backwards as the stone slammed into the boulder where she previously lay. She flipped through the air uncontrollably and landed on her back against more jagged rock, gasping for air and grasping her still aching arm.

The world spun as she attempted to climb back to her feet, to no success. There was a ringing in her ears that almost blocked out the chattering of the swarming charun.

In a flash of fire and ice, Cain leapt between her and her attackers. He breathed heavy and limped when he stepped, but he still had some power left. Dawn finally found her way to her feet and readied her bow, firing into the crowd of demons one at a time.

The world shook again. Dawn drew her lips to a line and scrambled to the highest rock overlooking the battlefield. Fen continued to unleash a barrage against the mountain creature as it spun about, trying to squash him under its massive hands. Dawn pulled back on her bow, readying an arrow of light. The creature's chest was open. Its glowing heart was exposed.

Dawn fired, and the arrow found its mark.

The creature screamed, thrashing around the battlefield in an uncontrollable rage. The glowing heart flared, burning as bright as the sun on a summer day. Suddenly, the red jewel exploded and the creature's entire body fell apart. Stones crumbled to the ground, lifeless and harmless.

"Let's go!" Krom shouted. Dawn turned to see him standing atop rocks that had fallen in the riverbed, stopping the flow of the river. "Let's get out of here!"

The mages jumped from rock to rock, racing toward Maron and Krom on the other side of the river. Charun swarmed close behind. Fen pressed his way to the front of the company, leading them down seemingly random alleyways toward the edge of the city. Eventually Dawn saw a glimmer of light at the end of a corridor, a promise of the outside world.

"Follow the light!" Fen shouted, turning toward the approaching enemy. "I'll meet you in the wilderness." He pulled a sack from his belt. It was labeled by a single circle, a line striking through the center. A fine green dust seeped from the opening as he gripped it in his hand.

Cain took the lead as the company rushed wildly up the narrowing path. Dawn drew her sleeve across her face, wiping away the grime and sweat. Soon, the tunnel didn't seem so dark. Rather, it seemed like they stepped out from a heavy fog and into a thin mist. Her weariness grew, but her will hardened all the more. The world outside was within grasp. They were so close.

An explosion resounded from behind them, bright green flames filling the tunnel. It reached its claws toward the company, but they were just out of reach.

"Fen!" Krom shouted, turning to rush back down the passage. Dawn grabbed him and wrestled him to the ground. Rocks fell behind them, collapsing the tunnel so that nothing could follow them out.

XXII

The Night is Darkest

Kaela dozed in and out of consciousness on the back of Silas' pegasus. It probably wasn't safe to close your eyes while up so high, but the day had finally caught up with her. The sun peeked over the horizon, lighting up the landscape with its rays. There was no color, though. What was once vibrant green rolling hills and fields of radiant flowers was now gray. Lifeless. Drained.

The squadron of pegasus fliers flocked together to the south, carrying survivors of the Citadel assault on their backs. The whole army, at least the ones who lived, had shifted to become transports. Normally, a pegasus could only carry two people at the very most. Desperate times called for even the animals to go above and beyond the usual call of duty.

"Hey!" Silas nudged Kaela as her eyes inched shut again. "Try to stay awake. We are almost there."

Kaela rubbed away the sleep from her eyes, peeking over

Silas' shoulder. She could see it. Her family's home. She had promised Alyina that she would be home for the anniversary of Ephras' death. At least she would be holding to her word.

Silas started the descent and the pegasus army soon landed on the gray hillside, racing down the hill toward the city. Horns blared, warning of the arrival of the fliers. Silas pulled back on his reins and held up a fist, commanding the rest of the fliers to stop as well. Archers readied their bows on the approaching army from outposts outside the city.

"I don't blame them for being skeptical," Kaela whispered. "An army pulls up to your doorstep, I'd get my weapons ready too."

Silas grunted. A squad of soldiers, at least what Korio qualified as soldiers, approached them. Rusted swords and splintered shields hardly made an intimidating impression on soldiers from the Citadel.

"Go back the way you came!" The lead soldier shouted. "We have no room for military occupation."

"It's not occupation we seek," Silas called out. "But sanctuary."

"No room!" The man shouted back. "Go fight your own battle, and leave Korio out of it!"

Kaela climbed from the back of the pegasus, making her way to the front of the pack. She recognized, if only hardly, each of the men that came out to meet them. They were older than she had last seen them, but still bore many of their same characteristics from when she used to play with them as children around the well.

"Please," she said. "We are in need of Korio's hospitality. We wouldn't be here if it wasn't necessary."

The men whispered about themselves. Kaela heard her name in their whispers, but not much else.

"Lady Kaela," the lead man said. "You vouch for these soldiers?"

"They aren't just soldiers," she responded. "We are refugees. There are families, women and children, who need shelter. They have experienced so much evil. So much pain."

The man turned to his subordinates, then back to Kaela. "You can camp in the field east of the city. We don't have room inside Korio for this many people, but we will do what we can to provide shelter from the elements while you stay. The first sign of trouble, and you're gone."

Kaela nodded, pointing Silas to the eastern side of the village. As the army of pegasus trotted along the outskirts of town, she found her way into the city, darting straight for her family's home.

Her mother and sister sat on the porch, watching the army maneuver to the field. Kaela could see the terror in their eyes. A foreign army at your city's border will do that to a person.

Kaela stood just out of sight. She tried to force herself to take a step, but she couldn't. Maybe it was embarrassment, or maybe it was fear. She just stood, frozen in place.

"Kaela!" Alyina shouted as she finally looked in her direction. She bolted out of Tess' grasp and threw her arms around Kaela, her tiny body nearly throwing her off balance. "I knew you would come back. Krom promised."

Kaela knelt down to her sister's level and wrapped her arms around her small frame, squeezing tight. She couldn't help the tears that flowed from her eyes as she buried her face into Alyina's shoulder.

***

Ash fell from the sky, the rising sun glistening through the slow, gray condensation. It probably would have stained Dawn's grimy prison clothes, if there was any space left on the discolored tunic for stains.

She could still hear screams from the Citadel as they ducked into a clearing of trees on the other side of the Old City passage. Krom slumped against the trunk of a tree, closing his eyes and slamming the back of his head against the bark. Dawn followed suit, holding her face in her hands. The voices of the dying citizens bit at her ears like a cruel winter wind.

"We still aren't safe," Cain said, grabbing Krom by the shoulder and lifting him up. "Those creatures will be swarming this countryside within the hour. Your friend may have slowed them down, but he didn't stop them."

"He was my only hope," Krom whispered. "He said he could help me with my hands. Help me to thrive. But now... How can I live like this?"

"He said he would meet us," Dawn said, climbing back to her feet. "Why would he say that if he was just going to give up?"

"He didn't give up," Krom said. "He gave us a shot."

Tears welled up in Dawn's eyes. "A lot of that today."

A branch crunched behind them. The company snapped to see Fen stumbling through the woods, his robes and hair singed by the horrible fire. "That stuff is nasty," he groaned. "Fos told me it was bad, but I didn't expect so little to do so much!"

Krom gasped, rushing to the blind man and throwing his arms around him. Fen winced under the weight of the Quarrinian's arms.

"If you could, my dear reaver. I don't know if I am in any condition to lead our company effectively. We will be safe at the Central Mountain Outpost, if you know the way."

Cain nodded, leading them across the Cirranian landscape. Dawn had seen the wilderness that neighbored the Citadel many times when she would go out for reaver business, but it was never like this. Even with the sun shining on the normally lush hillsides, the grass was colorless. The leaves on the trees wilted like fire had touched their bodies.

Eventually they came to an outpost made up of stone. The rock had withered underneath the sun over many years, but it still seemed to work as it should. "Here we are," Cain said, gathering some firewood and igniting it at the top level of the sanctuary. "You think we will be safe here?"

"Fos has spoken to me," Fen said, finding a seat on the rock. "We will be safe here until nighttime."

"Then let's get some rest," Cain said. "I will take the first watch. We will travel at night, or if danger gets too close."

Dawn watched and listened while Krom told Maron and Cain the story of his abduction. He was lucky to be alive, though lucky didn't quite seem to be the right word. Cain even called him blessed. Wouldn't blessed have been not being taken in the first place?

Dawn stared into the fire, rolling the cloth of her sleeve between her fingers over and over again.

Cain gathered some plants from nearby from the little that still held life, rummaging just enough together to cook up a pot of hot tea. It wasn't exactly sustenance, but some flavor in their mouths would be nice. He tried to explain to Maron the science of flavor in cooking, but Maron's eyes just glazed over. It wasn't that he wasn't interested. It was just hard to keep up with Cain once he got going.

Dawn closed her eyes as the four men chatted, trying to keep their spirits up. "You can see through this ruse just as well as I can," her Reflection whispered in her ear. "Their light-hearted brevity. It's all just a facade. A mask for the pain in the world. Joy is a lie, and time will always reveal the truth of human nature. We were created to suffer."

The outpost had probably grown silent long before Dawn realized it. Maron slept on the hard stone, snoring under the sun. Even these conditions were preferable to what his life had been for the last few years.

Dawn opened her eyes to find the fire dying. She thought about throwing more wood on the flames. She didn't. Krom maneuvered a log onto his arms and dropped it on the firepit, kicking the wood to stir the new embers. He exhaled a sigh of exhaustion, then looked to Dawn. She waited for his words.

None came.

Instead, he lowered himself next to her, resting his severed arm around her shoulder. There they remained, not speaking a word. The fire felt cold to Dawn. The grayscale landscape around them was dead, but Krom's touch was warm.

Finally, Dawn turned and lay her head on his shoulder and wept.

End of Part 2

Praise for the Author

Hargraves writing shows much promise and this book kept me interested the whole way.

~Brian Mitchell reviewing Reflection

Great mix of fantasy and real life situations. It kept me wanting to read more. can't wait for the next book!

~Amazon Customer reviewing Reflection.

The White Council

REFLECTION

After witnessing the tragic death of her closest friends and family, Dawn travels across the country with a weathered vagabond in search of her aunt. On the way, she discovers that the world is a much scarier place than she had initially imagined, and that she might have some darkness lingering within herself as well.

INSURRECTION

A year has passed from the fateful night in the Old City Prison, and Dawn, thanks to the intense training of her mentor, Cain, has honed her skills. But when political insurgency threatens violence in the Citadel, Dawn must decide which side of the divide she stands on. Walking a tightrope between her duty to the White Council and her sanctity for all life, she quickly realizes that sometimes the troubles of this world are too much for one person to handle on their own.

www.ingramcontent.com/pod-product-compliance
Lightning Source LLC
LaVergne TN
LVHW010310070526
838199LV00065B/5510